NOBLE TRAITOR

A Historical Novel of Scotland

J R TOMLIN

Albannach Publishing

Map of Scotland

Chapter 1

INVERKIP CASTLE, SCOTLAND

February 11, 1306

The clang of steel rang when their swords met.

"That's it," Thomas Randolph said. "Now roll your blade up to hit mine with the flat. Use plenty of force."

But then William de Gordon broke off and lifted his visor. "Look at that, Thomas. Is my father sending the bairns for training now?"

Thomas turned. A page stood next to the quintain, his hands tucked in his armpits from the cold. He scuffed his feet in the light covering of snow on the ground and said to no one in particular, "Lord Gordon... he told me I was to... to tell Squire Thomas to come to him."

"Where is he?" Thomas pushed sweaty strands of straw-colored hair out of his eyes.

"He's in the hall. There's someone with him, a man who just came with some men-at-arms."

Two other squires stopped whacking with their swords at the pell to listen.

"Run back and tell him I am on my way." Thomas shrugged at William and walked to the armory and hung up his sword. He shivered in the cold as he stripped off his battered mail and sweat-soaked linen gambeson, wondering why Lord Gordon had sent for him. Perhaps he needed an errand run or a message carried. Like any squire, Lord Gordon set Thomas to a variety of tasks, and carrying messages was one he relished as a break in the castle's routine. It didn't happen often, and most days after the morning's practice with sword and lance, he spent the rest of the day cleaning and oiling armor, sharpening swords and axes, and serving at the table.

He donned his blue wool tunic and chausses and pulled on his surcoat embroidered with Lord Gordon's boar's head armorial. He hurried through drifting snow flurries in the cobbled bailey yard of Inverkip Castle and sniffed the scent of coming snow before he bounded up the stairs and through a short passage into the hall.

A peat fire burned high in the old-fashioned central hearth, sending up earthysmelling tendrils of smoke. The hart's-horn chandelier was blazing with tallow candles. Four men-at-arms in steel-studded brigandine, strangers, sat at one of the long trestle tables.

Standing on the dais before the high table was Sir Adam, Lord Gordon, tall and upright, in his late thirties. He wore a fine wool tunic belted low around his hips with a long dirk hanging in the front. With him was another man who turned, threw his arms wide with a smile, and exclaimed, "Thomas!"

Thomas laughed at the sight of Alexander de Bruce, tall, auburn-haired, and his uncle though they were both in their twenty-first year.

"What are you doing here?" He sprang onto the dais and clapped his uncle on the shoulder. "I thought you were still studying at Cambridge."

"Nae, I am Dean of Glasgow now. But I am here

because Robert wants to meet with the whole family. I need you to come away with me."

"Come where?"

"To Lochmaben Castle."

"I can spare you for a sennight," Lord Gordon said. "And the earl has the right to ask for you to come to him."

"But…" Thomas's mind raced, and he paused, looking in askance at Lord Gordon. "Why does he need me there?" The five de Bruce brothers were his uncles on his mother's side. He'd visited them as a lad at their mother's Turnberry Castle, and they'd been raucous and fun., The de Bruce sisters were as wild as their brothers. Later, he'd been too busy serving the Lord of Gordon as a squire and learning the business of being a knight to visit, and the Bruces had been busy fighting the English until only a few years ago.

Alex paused a little too long, and now, Gordon was giving him a look with narrowed eyes. He shrugged. "King Edward is angry with Robert again. I think Robert wants us all to attend court in London to sweeten his mood, but he didnae tell me what he was planning."

"I assumed the Bruce must be out of favor when I heard that the King made him name a governor for Kildrummy Castle. It seems the King nae longer trusts him." Lord Gordon scrunched his forehead. "I shall need to consider whether it is wise for Thomas to be involved in the earl's political maneuverings though."

Giving a sweet-natured smile, Alex said, "Oh, aye. Robert will speak to you about it if that is what he has in mind. I cannae speak for him."

Thomas chewed his lip, remembering that cozening smile from Alex talking his way out of trouble with his mother. But Lord Gordon seemed satisfied and said, "He's always welcome at Inverkip. And all your other brothers."

Alex grasped Thomas's shoulder and gave a friendly squeeze. "Go. Gather your things."

"You want to leave now?"

Lord Gordon said, "You must sup with us and spend the night. Leave on the morrow."

Alex spread his hands. "I would that I could, but I also have business in Glasgow that will take most of the morrow before we depart for Lochmaben. If we make good time, we can reach the burgh tonight."

Lord Gordon raised his brows. "After having traveled here so far today, it will be a weary ride."

"We will rest at the Bishop's Castle. Bishop Wishart expects us."

"William and I were working in the practice yard just now," Thomas told Lord Gordon, in no hurry to leave. "You can hardly tell that his arm was injured, My Lord." William had been a squire to one of the Comyns until they sent him home after breaking his arm.

"Aye, I've seen that," Gordon said. "And he will miss you while you are gone."

Thomas turned to go. "I'll return as soon as I can."

Gordon smiled. "Good lad. God go with you."

Thomas took the stairs at the rear of the dais up to the top story of the keep where the squires shared a long chamber. He took his spare chausses and tunic from a peg to stuff into a bag. Kneeling at the small kist at the foot of his bed, he opened it and took out his sword and belt. His hand paused over his father's gold spurs, wrapped in a linen cloth. He pulled back the cloth and ran a finger over the surface. One day as a knight, he would honor his father's memory by wearing his spurs. Soon, he hoped. He closed the kist and stood.

He sat on the edge of his narrow bed, rubbing his lips with his fingertips. The more he thought on it, the more it convinced him that Alex was lying. Whatever it was, Thomas was sure it was something more serious than merely a trip to London.

* * *

AS THEY LEFT behind the high, snow-dusted mound on which rose Inverkip Castle, Thomas tried to ask why Lord Robert needed his presence. Alex shook his head, glanced back at his following men-at-arms, and said that this was no place to discuss it. Thomas gave an impatient huff but held his peace.

The cold wind from the south-west whipped their hair and cloaks. The last hour of the ride was beneath stars scattered like diamonds across a black silk sky, but at last they clattered across the bridge of the Clyde. A few words and an exchange of coins allowed them through Briggate into Glasgow.

Curfew had not yet rung, and merchants crowded the cobbled street as they closed their shops. Laborers made their way into taverns where an ale pole hung beside the doorways. Alex led them as they wended their way past the bustle onto the breadth of High Street.

They passed the massive tolbooth, and Thomas remembered having gone there with his father. Well ahead of them, Saint Mungo's Cathedral was a towering black shape that cut off the stars. "Bishop Wishart will have a chamber for us at the castle for the night," Alex said.

Before they reached the cathedral, they turned to climb the castle mound earthworks. A guard opened the gate for them to ride through the pele wall into a small bailey reeking of horse shit. Dozens of horses were tied and, munching piles of hay, crowded the bailey, too many for the stable. "He may not have room for us,"

Thomas said as he dismounted. "A large force has preceded us."

"Something has happened. Robert was meeting with John Comyn, Lord of Badenoch." Alex clicked his tongue against his teeth. "We'd better see what the to-do is."

Thomas followed on Alexander's heels as he hurried up the stairs to the doorway on the second story with their men-at-arms close behind into the great hall. Men-at-arms wearing the Bruce colors filled every space on the long benches, bent over bowls of steaming pottage, all talking in low voices that fill the air with a hum. On the dais, Nigel de Bruce and another knight, a gruff looking man with a bald head and shaggy graying beard, had their heads close together as they talked.

"Find yourself places at the table and eat," Alex said to his men. He strode up the narrow aisle between the long tables and onto the dais. "What has happened?"

Nigel turned and ran his striking blue gaze over Thomas. After a moment, he motioned them closer. "John Comyn is dead."

Thomas jerked his head back. "How?"

His mouth twisted into a snarl, the bald knight said, "Comyn, the damned traitor, tried to throttle the Bruce again. The earl drew his dirk and stabbed him."

"Again?" Thomas asked.

"Aye. The Comyn tried to strangle him once before when they were both Guardians of the Realm. If Bishop de Lamberton hadnae separated them, the earl would have killed him then."

Thomas realized his mouth was open and closed it with a snap. "But..." He blinked. "I'm sorry, sir. I dinnae ken your name."

"Kirkpatrick. Roger Kirkpatrick of Cill Osbairn."

"Why would the Comyn attack the earl? You cannae mean it."

"I mean precisely that, lad. The Bruce discovered that the Comyn had betrayed us to King Edward, revealed our plans to raise the standard for Scotland after the old tyrant dies. They met to talk at Greyfriars Kirk, and the earl taxed him with his treachery. Then it happened, as I said. They came out of the kirk. The Bruce said he thought the Comyn was dead. I said I would mak sikkar. And I did." The man's deep-set eyes blazed with fury.

Alex scrubbed his hand over his forehead and down his face. "This is too soon. We were to wait for the old King to die."

Nigel de Bruce frowned, his handsome features grave. "Even if King Edward were dead, England has other war leaders as good, mayhap better. And the new King might be as good as his father for all we ken of him. They still would outnumber us ten to one. But events have left us no choice. We must act now."

"Act?" The word came out in a squeak, and Thomas blushed.

Nigel gave him a quelling look. "Bishop Wishart has already heard Robert's confession and granted him absolution for the sacrilege of killing in a kirk. We will gather our forces and crown him at Scone. Robert will be King of Scots and hell mend England's King Edward."

The door at the rear of the dais opened, and Robert de Bruce strode in. His grim look softened into a smile when he saw Thomas. "Thomas, I am glad you are here." He looked at his brother. "And you too. I need you both."

Thomas could not help his smile at his uncle's warm greeting. Robert de Bruce was a big man in every sense. He had a big face, blond hair, well combed, a crooked nose, and a square chin. Half a head taller than Thomas's medium height and bulky with muscle, he moved and spoke with such purpose that it drew Thomas to him.

Alex snorted. "Aye, I suppose that you do. Could you nae rein in that temper of yours?"

The smile drained from the earl's face. "If I could undo it, I would. But what was I to do when he laid hands on me? After betraying me to the English? It was too late anyroad. I stopped the messenger to Edward from delivering the bond between Comyn and me, but Comyn had already told him of it and of my bond with Bishop de Lamberton. And it confirmed what was in the letters that Wallace carried when he was captured. We were out of time."

"What did you do then?" Thomas asked.

"We seized Dumfries Castle before they could learn of Comyn's death. And I sent word to Bishop de Lamberton in Berwick to tell him to meet us at Scone. He will put the crown on my head. Then we prepare for a fight for our lives."

Almost without a sound, Bishop Wishart came into the room, a man in his sixties, short and spare, in an uncreased black velvet cassock, quiet shoes, and an aura of gentle, self-possessed determination. A servant in the bishop's livery followed behind him.

"Put it there." The bishop pointed to the high table. Wishart lifted the lid. "I hid it for this day." He lifted out a circlet of gold and solemnly placed it on the table. A mantle of vivid crimson lined with miniver followed. Last he removed a yellow banner with the royal lion rampant of Scotland.

The earl's hand was shaking as he reached out and touched the coronet. "It was King Alexander's?"

"Not the crown of state. There was no saving that from the greed of King Edward, but this is the crown the King wore over his helm. I saw it on his head many times. And here, the mantle he wore for his coronation."

Thomas could only stare, eyes wide. The crown and mantle of Scotland's last true King and his banner.

Robert de Bruce laid his hands flat on the table on each side of the crown. He bowed his head and took a deep, shuddering breath. When he straightened, he shook his body like a hound shaking off water. "We have no time to waste. The first thing on the morrow messages must go out by our fastest riders to the Earls of Atholl, Menteith, and Lennox. I'll myself write a letter to Bishop de Moray. Nigel, I want you to leave at first light with your men to take Loch Doon. And I shall lead my men to Ayr Castle. If we can reach them before the news does, they will fall into our hands like an apple ripe from a tree. Then we shall sweep through Carrick, and I'll raise my men on our way to Scone."

"What about Lord Gordon?" Thomas asked.

The Bruce shook his head. "He is too loyal to the English for now, lad."

"But I'm his squire..." His mind raced. "I told him I would be back as soon as I could. It is my duty to return."

"I plan on knighting you after I am crowned, Thomas. Then you will no longer be his squire." He stood, looking at Thomas intently. He slapped a parchment down on the table marked with the Bruce's own seal and that of the Bishop of Saint Andrew's. "This I seized from one of Comyn's own men. He was sending it to Edward, betraying me. That for all my lands and titles, he would give up his claim to the crown and back me against the invaders. It was my death warrant and Lamberton's. He meant to see us dead.

"So we fought and I killed him. In a church. A deadly sin. There is no turning back. But I still have a purpose.

The one I have always had. That Scotland shall have her king. We must have our own king, a Scottish king, that the English would deny us. And there is no longer any other but me. You understand?"

Bishop Wishart looked up from gazing at the treasure he had kept hidden for ten long years. He turned to Thomas, and his gentle face took on stern lines. "It is our duty. This fight is as much a crusade fighting the cruel English invaders as if you were fighting the Saracen in the Holy Land. And remember that a crusader has all his sins forgiven. Including yours for leaving your lord."

"I will fight for Scotland. Of course, I will." Thomas's heart raced. "But I owe Lord Gordon some loyalty. I should go to him and tell him I'll fight for you."

The Bruce patted Thomas's shoulder. "You're a good lad, and I need you to stay with me. Go find the bishop's armorer. No doubt there is armor in the stores. Tell him you are to have the best that he can find for you."

As the royal vestments were once more being put away, Nigel de Bruce shouted for messengers to give them their orders.

Thomas watched like a branch swept up in a flood.

Chapter 2

AYR, SCOTLAND

Robert de Bruce had left most of their force camping an hour's ride behind, and only twenty-five men-at-arms rode in the earl's tail. Thomas rode behind him with Alex, Seton, and Kirkpatrick, tired, and his mind spinning with thoughts. He wondered if he might have a chance to get drunk tonight.

Overlooking the road that ran alongside the River Ayr atop a castle mound rose Ayr Castle, a square stone keep surrounded by a high curtain wall with round towers flanking the closed gate. There beneath a leaden sky flew the Saint George's Cross banner of England. A man-at-arms walked along the parapet.

The day's march had been hard and fast. In the gray light of the winter mid-afternoon, the icy wind cut at Thomas's face and made the earl's banner crack like a whip over their heads.

"Who comes?" the guard shouted down from the wall.

"The Earl of Carrick. We seek food and shelter for the night."

Chains creaked as the iron portcullis rose. There was a

screech of bars being lifted. On one side of the wide gate, a door opened, barely big enough for a mounted horseman to ride through. After a glance over his shoulder and a nod, his uncle led the way through.

Christopher Seton, the Bruce's goodbrother who was always at the earl's side, followed. By the time Thomas clattered inside, Boyd's sword came ringing from his scabbard. He brought it down on the head of the guard standing beside the door. The guard dropped to his knees, his helm sheared in half, his face covered in blood. He toppled face down.

Thomas's eyes popped wide, and he stared. "You didn't—"

"Kirkpatrick, Seton, see to any other guards," Robert barked. He put his heels into his warhorse, and with a lunge, it surged up the wooden ramp to the second story door of the keep. "The rest of you with me. Into the keep before they have time to bar the door."

Halfway up the ramp, Thomas jumped from his horse and ran, drawing his sword as he went. He was sure too many horses trying to pass through the door would slow them down. Around him the earl's men-at-arms must have decided the same as they ran along with him.

The earl bent, threw open the door, and rode in. Inside there were shouts of alarm.

Thomas plunged through the doorway. The Bruce pulled his charger around in a half-circle, its iron-shod hooves cutting through the rushes and scoring the stone floor.

The Bruce cursed as hands grabbed at his bridle and slashed with his sword. "Surrender!" he bellowed. "The castle is taken!"

Thomas ran to him, using his sword two-handed he made a vicious side swing at a man who grabbed the

Bruce's reins. The blow hit the man's neck with a sickening splatter. Blood flew from the blade. Alex shouted, "A Bruce! A Bruce!"

The great hall was a chaos of shouts and screams as the Bruce's men flooded in. One of them caught a guard full in the chest with a battleax as the man came at him at a run, the ax shearing through leather and muscle and bone. On the dais, a knight knocked the high table over with a crash. He pulled his dirk. Beside him, a lady screeched in terror.

"Throw down your weapons!" The Bruce's horse reared, and another man reeled away, his shoulder a bloody mess. With his good hand, the man threw his sword onto the ground at the feet of the earl's mount.

Alex shouted, "You'll come to nae harm if you surrender."

As a man-at-arms jumped onto the dais, the knight threw down his dirk and raised his hands palms outward.

Thomas lowered his sword. The smell of blood mixed with that of smoke from the hearth made his stomach roil. Burning bile washed up his throat into his mouth. He swallowed hard.

His uncle climbed from the saddle. Handing the reins to one of his men to lead out, he looked around the hall. His men were scooping up weapons and shoving the English garrison to one end of the hall. He motioned the grizzled serjeant to him. "Escort them to the gate. Allow them to leave unmolested."

"Mounts, My Lord?" the serjeant asked.

"They can walk to the village or wherever they like." When the serjeant walked away to carry out his orders, the Bruce turned and patted Thomas's shoulder. "Well done, lad. I always saw the makings of a braw knight in you." The Bruce turned to lead his steed out the door, calling out to Alex, "Select twenty-five good men to hold the castle. On the morrow, we leave for Lochmaben."

Thomas frowned after his uncle, his jaw clenched. They had to talk.

* * *

THOMAS STARED about him as he rode with the hundreds of Robert de Bruce's followers up the promontory toward Lochmaben Castle, surrounded by water. The hulking fortress stood even higher on a mound that rose on the top. The Bruce's red saltire banner fluttered in the breeze above the towers flanking the outer gatehouse. Past the drawbridge and through the gate, his eyes widened at the size of the place.

The men-at-arms spread out across the outer bailey, dismounting, talking and laughing with relief at a respite from the saddle. Thomas followed the earl and his small band of companions clattering across the bridge over the inner moat and through the inner gate. He craned his neck, gawking at the defenses. Unimaginable trying to take this castle, but he had been told that Robert the Bruce had done so when the English had held it.

He shook his head. He had to talk to his uncle again, to convince him he needed to do what was honorable, to go talk to Lord Gordon. But every time he tried, Robert was busy with something else.

Once they were inside the inner walls, there was a squeal of laughter. Marjorie de Bruce, twelve years old, came running across the cobblestone bailey, skirts swirling around her long legs and auburn hair streaming behind her. She came to an abrupt halt when almost to her father's horse, smoothed her skirts, and walked toward him, face beaming. But Robert leapt from the saddle and lifted her to spin her around as though she were still a bairn. She laughed, shouting, "Father! I'm too old." The earl put his daughter's feet back on the ground.

A woman caught up to them, shaking her head. "What have you done now? Who would be so foolish as to marry one of the wild de Bruces?" she asked.

He gave her a kiss on the mouth. "A wild Irish woman, mayhap?"

She slapped his arm before she gave him a fierce-looking hug. Most definitely Elizabeth de Burgh, the earl's second wife, though Thomas had never seen her before. He had to smile, watching their reunion. She wore a rose-colored tabard over a green kirtle. Beneath her barbet and fillet, a lot of brown hair flowed down her back. She had large brown eyes, a narrow nose, and a determined mouth. A fair woman in a well-cared-for way.

Behind them streaming out to greet them, was a river of mostly women but also a few men. As Thomas slid from the saddle and tossed his reins to a groom, he strained to pick out familiar faces. Mary de Bruce bustled through the crowd to greet her brother. She was never one to stay behind. She had more than once thumped her brother for trying to leave her with Thomas, Alex, and Nigel running behind to catch up.

When Mary saw him, she bustled over, smiling. "Thomas Randolph, it has been too long since I have seen you."

Thomas held her back by her shoulders to look at her. His elder by four years, she was tall and handsome, but he thought she had changed little in the years since he had last seen her, though she now wore fine silk instead of the dust-smeared kirtles of her youth.

"Do you still box your brothers' ears if they displease you?" he asked with a grin.

She laughed. "Nae so much the now though they do tempt me." She linked her arm through his. "Come, I must present you to Lady Elizabeth. It is hard to believe we shall soon call her 'Your Grace,' nae to mention that wayward eldest brother of mine."

They wended their way through the noisy crowd. Mary waved to Lady Elizabeth to catch her attention. She gave Thomas her hand to bow over, and he murmured the expected courtesies. She turned and shook her head at her stepdaughter, who was pulling on her father's arm for his attention. "Margery, that is enough."

Margery's mouth pursed into a pout until her father tugged on a strand of her hair. "No pouting, lass. Give your cousin Thomas a proper greeting and show him about the castle."

Thomas grinned when she cocked her head and looked him over, much like a buyer examining a suspect nag.

She tilted her chin up and held out her hand. "Cousin."

He bowed over it and then tucked it under his arm. "What is the most interesting part of the castle? Let us skip all the dull bits."

"Oh, the stables! I'll show you my palfrey." She tugged on his arm, guiding him in that direction through the press. "He is swift, but Lady Elizabeth tells me nae to make him gallop." She glanced over her shoulder for listeners. "I do anyroad."

He laughed. "Certes, you do, My Lady." She was much like her father. He could not bear to be short with her, but he kept looking over his shoulder, wondering where Robert was when they stood in the crowded stable. The smell of hay and horses with an undertone of manure made him miss tending the lord's tack at Inverkip. He fed Marjorie's bay a withered apple and promised to have her show him the eyrie soon.

By the time he returned to the bailey, much of the chaos had calmed, and Robert was talking to Christopher Seton. Sir Simon Fraser, burly with brown hair streaked with gray, joined them. They turned and walked toward the steps to the keep. The earl said, "We will give a week for more to arrive before we start for Scone. That will give time to prepare."

"Robert!" Thomas called. "Wait. I need a word with you."

The earl waved the other men on and stood to wait for Thomas. "What is it, lad?"

"Robert. My Lord. Just… just let me go to Lord Gordon." His breath was fast as though he had been running. "This cannae be the right way to do things. Sneaking away. Lying to him. He trusts me."

"As do I, Thomas. There is nae choice left. We must fight or die."

"Damn it! I will fight for you. I mean to." Thomas squeezed the bridge of his nose hard. "But Lord Gordon has been good to me. He will think I betrayed him. I need to explain it to him."

"He will come to understand, Thomas, even though he is on the wrong side for now." Robert de Bruce patted him on the shoulder, turned, and strode into the keep.

Chapter 3

The assembly that set out from Lochmaben a fortnight later under a clear distant blue sky, the air moist and warm with the coming of spring, was a changed one. The soon-to-be King and his lady both clad in their finest colorful silks led the way. Behind them rode minstrels playing flutes, harps, and gitterns. Scores of banners fluttered above the over five hundred riders, almost half women, all clad. More hundreds rode, men-at-arms, guarding their flank against attack from the English, or from the Comyns who would soon seek revenge.

But the gayer the music and the laughter, the more Thomas wanted to rail against his uncle's stern warning and being torn away from the knight whom he served.

But Robert de Bruce was descended from kings, rightful King of Scots. Bishop Wishart said it was as good as a crusade to fight to throw the English out of Scotland. Thomas wanted to argue and to shout at them that he had a duty to Lord Gordon. But who was he to argue with the Bishop of Glasgow? All he could do was scowl across at the distant hills as they rode. The more the minstrels played, and the hundreds of men and women chattered, the more his mood darkened.

It started when a huge, gnarled yew tree came into sight. Thomas was sure it was the tree he had passed many times riding with his father. The Giant, he had called it as a child. The massive trunk rose from the ground like a monster rising from the earth, blending into the bracken from which it arose. Its twisted, bare limbs reached out like a skeleton's hands. The Giant was so misshapen that when Thomas was a wee lad and of an imaginative mind, he was sure when they rode by that it would grab with creaks and groans and drag them under the earth to never escape from the dark. He fought not to show his terror, forcing himself to sit erect on his rouncy while sweating with fear. When his father noticed, he smiled and told Thomas that the old tree would not harm them. He said that it was the place where King Arthur's treasure had been hidden, and it crouched to protect the treasure until the King returned. Its twisted limbs waited only for any thief that came in the night. He said the poor Giant must be lonely waiting for the King, so Thomas should wave to him, and the Giant would wave back with branches that moved in the breeze.

Even years later, when he was far too old to believe in childhood tales, he would wave to the tree that was really a giant, always renewing its loyalty to its king, smiling when the branches waved back. And in the bright early spring sunlight, his heart lifted as he waved. So throughout the journey across Scotland, the day spent riding through braes newly carpeted with the spring-green heather and spotted with gorse, its yellow flowers sending up their spicy scent, something changed inside him.

By the time they rode up the heathery braeside to Arickstone, he was riding erect in the saddle, and grinning as Roger Kirkpatrick told a tale of the time he and William

Wallace dressed as plain laborers, met up with some of King Edward's men in a tavern and drank them under the table, helped themselves to the coins in their scrips, and slipped away as they snored on the floor. Thomas stood in his stirrups to look at the vast checkered carpet of flowers, and bracken spread all around them.

"Glad to see you've cheered up, lad," Kirkpatrick said. He, too, sat tall to look around, taking a deep breath of the spring air, but then pointed ahead, frowning. "Rider heading this way."

A sole rider rode down the braeside on a gray, high-stepping palfrey. The earl held up his hand for a halt as the rider hopped from the saddle and led his horse to face them. The music waned and stopped as they all came to a stop. Curious, Thomas nudged his horse through the crowd until he was behind the earl.

The rider stood, his legs slightly spread, facing Robert de Bruce—but no, Thomas thought, it was not a man but a youth, no more than eighteen years old at the most. He was long-legged and broad-shouldered, and black hair hung to his shoulders. Overall, he wore a disconcerting air of maturity, and the fierce set of his mouth would have done credit to a wolf.

The youth said, "I come from Bishop de Lamberton, My Lord. He sends word that he will meet you at Scone."

The Bruce leaned forward in his saddle, looking down at the newcomer. "I mind you it seems to me."

"Aye, My Lord. My name is James of Douglas. You kent my father well." He dropped to one knee. "And if you will have me, I offer you my sword and my service."

"Ha! William le Hardi's son. To be sure, I mind you, and any son of that gallant fighter is most welcome." The Bruce leapt from the saddle. He held out his hands. "I most gladly accept your service."

Douglas put his hands between those of the Bruce. "By the Lord God and all the holy saints, I become your liege man from this day forward of life and limb, bearing to you against all men that live, move or die, so help me God and the Blessed Mother."

"I accept you as my man and swear before God and man that I will hold you against harm from all men."

Douglas bounced to his feet with a laugh. "I have waited much of my life for this day!"

Elizabeth de Burgh leaned down, smiling, and offered her hand. "Welcome."

Douglas bent over it, "Thank you, My Lady. I am the earl's and yours to command. To the death."

The minstrels resumed imparting their music. Larks soared high in the sky. The Bruce swung back into the saddle. Douglas whirled and dashed to his horse, leaped into the saddle, and set it to a fast amble to join the crowd. Thomas nodded to him, wondering where a youth had gained such confidence.

Chapter 4

SCONE, SCOTLAND

The Abbey of Scone, a few miles north of Perth, above the grassy meadows of the River Tay, was a lovely place. In the middle of the acres of abbey buildings, square spires rose like massive pillars above the church building. Thomas walked past the south side, where an elaborate, covered cloister ran next to a garden with trees and bushes covered in green buds and new flowers. The abbey grounds were vast, and he was seeking the West Range of the abbey where the monks lodged the Bruce, his other uncles, his aunts, and the earls. Below, their armor and weapons were stored.

At last, he opened a heavy wooden door and a monk in a black cassock greeted him. "How can I help you, my son?" the man asked.

"I am a mite lost. Would you tell me where to find my armor?"

"Aye, I can help you. Come." The monk led through a side door and down a winding stair into a long chamber where armor and weapons were stacked in bins, and tables were stacked. It took several minutes of searching until he located his own harness.

"Thomas."

He turned his helm in his hand, at hearing Robert de Bruce's deep voice. "My Lord."

Robert shook his head. "It is still Robert to you in private, lad."

"It hasn't seemed so these past weeks. I mean…" His face heated. He had no right to reproach the man who would soon be the king. "Everything is changing. And it is happening so fast. I hardly ken what is happening."

"That has nae changed. You are my nephew, my sister's son, and you always will be. But with so much to do, we've nae had time to talk. The changes are as great for me as for you, lad, and if I have handled it poorly with you, I ask you to forgive me." He picked up Thomas's sword, turning it in his hands. "Longshanks deceived us, brutalized us, and forced our oaths at sword point. And every day since then, I have meant to see it put right. And the now, it has all come to the point. I am afeart it leaves little time for explanations."

Thomas held Robert's gaze, his heart speeding up. "Bishop Wishart said it is as good as a crusade to fight the invaders. I understand that. I do, Robert. And I willnae fail you."

"I always saw the makings of a braw knight in you." With a broad smile, his uncle put down the sword. "Now you want your armor for the jousting, aye? Go, and I shall have it sent to the arming tent."

Thomas broke into a grin and gave a quick bow. He bounded up the stairs, out of the abbey, and down the slope toward the meadow beside the River Tay. The tents of hundreds of knights and the larger pavilions of the lords and ladies were spread out before him. Every manner of banner and pennant snapped and waved in the sharp late March wind. It was nearly a city.

Past the tents and pavilions were two lines of booths for merchants who had come from Perth, trestle tables beneath striped awnings held up by four poles. He meandered that way where business was in full swing. An excited buzz of chatter and gossip, shouts of haggling over prices, and a few stumbling from an excess of ale, though the Bruce had men-at-arms patrolling between the booths. He caught the oniony, meaty scent of sausages being cooked from further down the row.

At one point, everyone stood aside to shout and clap as a cart with a sword swallower and some jugglers trundled past toward a clearing where acrobats and jugglers were attracting a crowd. As Thomas watched, the crowd cheered, and a few threw coins onto the cart. When it had passed, he followed some urchins and dogs that ran behind it until it reached the edge of the fairground where a miracle play was being put on.

A priest was shouting the story of John the Baptist. A man with a copious black beard was standing in the River Jordon formed by two horse troughs laid end to end, dumping pitchers of water over three shivering young apprentices who were no doubt not acting in the sharp wind. Pacing up and down behind them was another apprentice in a woman's kirtle with a generously padded bosom and a black wig. She held a tray aloft on which rested a realistic severed head in a puddle of 'blood.'

Thomas watched, fascinated. He'd never seen the like before, but after a few minutes, he let out a sigh, realizing he needed to hurry if he was to be on time at the jousting field.

He loped to an acre where a rope marked a rectangle a

hundred yards long, all spread with straw. At one side were crude wooden stands, three levels of planks nailed to stout posts, where fifty or so onlookers sat, brightly clad, many of them women. At each end were two small tents to serve as a shelter for the contestants. Flags flying from poles and multicolored pennants rippling in the wind above the tents brightened the whole affair.

He shoved his way into one of the arming tents hoping he would find the armor that Robert had said he would send. He understood that Bishop de Lamberton had done the same for James Douglas. Robert had forbidden forfeiting armor, saying they would need it for battle and had put up purses as prizes instead.

Kirkpatrick grinned as he ducked his head on his way in. Thomas beamed. As Kirkpatrick sorted the armor, they could hear the increasing hubbub of the crowd.

"Sounds as though your meeting with the Douglas will be almost as popular as when the knights joust this afternoon," Kirkpatrick said as he helped Thomas pull his gambeson over his head.

Thomas snorted through his nose. "Neither of us is well-kent, so I doubt it. But I am looking forward to the match. There is something about him..."

"He has the build of a good jouster, though light still."

Frowning, Thomas paused with his hauberk in his hand. "You dinnae think I am wrong to joust someone younger?"

Kirkpatrick took the heavy hauberk. "You are nae that much older, and you're both well fit for a match." He helped Thomas to put on the awkward armor with its hundreds of chain-links woven into the canvas and long arms down to the wrist. "Do you want to wear your greaves?"

Thomas shook his head. "My mount will do better

without the extra weight. And I have a feeling that Douglas is too proud to target my legs." He pulled on his mail coif, and Kirkpatrick helped him into the pixane that added protection to his neck and upper chest. He grimaced as he added his great helm that narrowed his vision with its slit to a sliver of what was in front of him.

"And this." Kirkpatrick held up a linen surcoat with the red three cushion-shaped symbols of the Randolphs.

Thomas ran his hand over the familiar symbols he'd seen his father wear so often. "Where did that come from?" He slid it over his head.

"They had stored it at Lochmaben and planned to surprise you with it for when the King dubs you a knight. But I said you should have it for jousting." Kirkpatrick helped him put on spurred leather boots and his gauntlets. He stood back and looked Thomas up and down. "Done except for your sword." He belted the leather belt around his hips.

Thomas shifted his body. Everything felt right.

He nodded to Kirkpatrick and strode out of the tent where his charger was watching people with interest and flicking its ears as they strolled past. The talk and shouts and laughter combined into a hum of noise as Thomas gripped the saddle and flung himself into it. The charger had only leather armor to protect its head and neck and a leather croupier to protect its hindquarters from flying shards or accidental strikes.

Christopher Seton, acting as judge, came up and asked, "All set, Thomas?"

When Thomas nodded, he vanished around the corner. Kirkpatrick handed up the blunted lance and shield. Thomas walked his horse to the front of the benches. He scanned the audience, and his eyebrows went up at the number of spectators. There was no more room left. On the second row of planks in bright finery sat Robert Boyd, Edward de Bruce, and Alex between them. Simon Fraser and Mary de Bruce and Mary's husband Sir Niall Campbell laughed about something. Several priests were yon in spite of the church taking a dim view of jousting. Burgesses and their wives in simpler garb filled the rest of the benches. Standing along the ropes setting off the jousting area were more spectators, gamblers accepting wagers.

Thomas's heart pounded. He had never expected so many to be watching.

Christopher Seton gave a signal, and the trumpeter blared with his horn.

James Douglas cantered out of the recet on the opposite side. To shouts and some cheers, Thomas met him at the center where Seton was standing. Seton nodded amiably to them both and called to the herald, "Announce that Squire Thomas Randolph and Squire James of Douglas will contest the first trial."

In a resounding voice, the herald announced them to the crowd. The crowd cheered. Alex shouted, "You can do it, Thomas!"

Seton waved them away. Thomas wheeled about and trotted to the far end of the field. He eyed Douglas, erect, hauberk glinting in the sun, as they waited at opposite ends of the field. Seton raised his hand again, the trumpet sounded. There was a flutter of white, and Seton dropped the flag.

The crowd grew quiet.

Thomas dropped his lance into position and kicked his horse hard. It lunged, straining to reach a gallop. He pulled his shield hard against his chest as he focused his sight on that shield with its three stars on a blue band. He must hit it there. In the center.

The shield got larger. And larger. At the last second, Douglas shifted to the left, angling his shield. With an ear-splitting crash, Douglas's lance hit his shield. Chips of wood flew as Douglas's lance shattered. Thomas rocked from a blow like being hit by a boulder. His back whacked painfully against the high cantle of his saddle. Thomas muttered a curse that his lance had only scraped a deep gouge in his opponent's.

A cheer went up from the stands

Already Thomas had thundered past his opponent. At the end of the field, he wheeled his horse in a tight circle. Someone had already handed Douglas a fresh lance.

Again, they galloped toward each other. Douglas shifted in the saddle again. This time Thomas followed. He realized his mistake. It was a feint. He fought to straighten his lance. Too late. His lance missed. Douglas's smashed into his shield with a force that tore him out of the saddle. His lance sailed out of his hand.

He slammed onto the ground, his body giving a painful bounce. Sparks danced before his eyes. His horse galloped on.

Thomas lay prostrate for a moment, the breath knocked out of him, ears ringing. He pushed himself up on one knee in the dirt. Douglas slid from his horse. As the crowd cheered, Douglas offered a hand. Face hot, Thomas accepted it and let Douglas pull him to his feet. He swayed a bit, but then gave Douglas a bow.

As they turned and walked back to opposite recets, the trumpet sounded, and the herald called out, "Squire James of Douglas wins the match!"

Kirkpatrick met Thomas at the edge of the field and

helped him off with his helm. "That Douglas lad is braw. There is no shame to lose to someone who fights well."

Thomas stripped off his gauntlets and wiped the sweat from his face. "Aye. You're right. He is." He turned to look toward the other recet. "But I will ride against him again. And I will defeat him next time."

Chapter 5

March 25, 1306

Thomas emerged from his small tent dressed in borrowed finery suitable for this sunny, dry, March morning. He joined the crowd of knights, lords, ladies, and burgesses in every color of silk and wool, as he made his way across the trampled grass toward Scone Abbey past the high bell towers until Moot Hill rose above them. Bells tolled a joyous clamor. Today he would become a knight, and everything around him was so bright it made his eyes burn.

Men-at-arms in polished brigandines topped with surcoats embroidered with the lion rampant formed a crescent halfway up the grassy hill as a barrier, pikes held erect. A massive gilt throne topped the hill's green crest. When Thomas neared the men-at-arms, he pushed through the vast crowd. Alex de Bruce nodded to Thomas through the press of bodies. Kirkpatrick was at the front watching intently next to Christopher Seton and Mary de Bruce. Robert Boyd poked Thomas and pointed to a good place to watch next to Simon Fraser.

They elbowed their way through, gaining quite a few glares. The crowd gave a steady buzz of excited comment.

Fraser gave them a nod. "I have fought long for this day."

From beyond the hilltop, a trumpet fanfare resounded. It rang out again. Men-at-arms cleared a pathway through the midst of the crowd. Robert de Bruce strode up the hill to stand before the throne. Behind him, a double row of boys in white robes followed singing *Gloria in Excelsis Deo*.

A deep hush fell over the onlookers. Thomas sucked in his breath, and his heart sped up.

The trumpets called out again. Stern-faced, the Earl of Atholl carried the two-handed sword of state, knelt, and the Bruce touched it. To Thomas's surprise, he recognized the man who strode up carrying the royal lion rampant banner, Alexander Scrymgeour, Lord Gordon's good-brother who had frequently visited them at Inverkip. He stood behind the King, holding the banner aloft.

Three bishops strode up from the side, crimson vestments glittering with gold thread and jewels. The one in the lead must be Bishop de Lamberton, thought Thomas. Primate of Scotland, dark-haired, carrying the small crown Thomas had seen at Glasgow. Bishop Wishart carried the royal mantle draped over his arms. The third, burly Bishop David de Moray, held a massive, leather-bound Bible.

Wishart draped the crimson mantle about the new King's shoulders and fastened it with a gold pin.

The trumpets blasted again, and Robert de Bruce seated himself on the throne.

Bishop de Lamberton stopped before the throne and intoned, "Sir, are you willing to take the oath?"

Robert the Bruce said, "I am willing."

"Will you solemnly promise and swear to govern the

People of Scotland according to their ancient laws and customs?"

"I swear I will do so."

"Will you use your power to execute Law and Justice, in Mercy, in all of your judgments?"

"I will."

"Will you defend your realm and its people against all foreign enemies and invaders?"

"I swear by Almighty God, I will."

The King rose from the throne and knelt. Bishop de Moray carried the Bible and held it out for the King.

The Bruce laid his hand on it and said in a booming voice, "The things which I have here before promised, I will perform and keep. So help me God." He kissed the Bible, rose, and once more sat on the throne.

The trumpets cried out.

Bishop de Lamberton went to stand behind the King. The bells of the abbey rang out, and the choir intoned *Te Deum Laudamus*. He raised the simple gold crown high and solemnly lowered it onto the King's head.

"God save the King!" burst out all around Thomas. Robert Boyd bellowed it out. Thomas joined in the shouting. "God save the King! God save the King!"

"Go on. It's time for the oath-taking." Robert Boyd nudged Thomas with an elbow. "And for you to be dubbed a knight."

He could not seem to catch his breath, and his heart was pounding. This day had been his whole lifetime coming.

The Queen was kneeling before the King, her hands between his, giving her oath. Behind her, forming a ragged line, were the Earl of Atholl, the Earl of Lennox and the Earl of Monteith, and after them the King's four brothers. With Boyd urging him on, Thomas took a place in the queue that soon snaked all the way down the hill.

"Are you all right, lad?" Boyd asked, frowning.

"Aye. I am fine." He faked a smile and tried to take a few breaths. His head was spinning. His heart hammered so hard his blood pounded in his ears.

Suddenly, he was at the head of the line with the Bruce looking at him. The surprise made him forget about whether he could breathe. He dropped to his knees. His throat was closing up, so he burst out with his oath of fealty as fast as he could. "By the Lord God and all the holy saints, I become your liege man from this day forward of life and limb and truth and earthly honors, bearing to you and your heirs against all men that live, move or die, in good faith and without deceit, on condition that you will hold to me as I shall deserve it, so help me God and the Blessed Mother." He gasped, out of breath.

With an understanding look, the King said, "I accept you as my man and swear before God and all here who witness that I will hold you against harm from all men." He rose, accepted the sword of state from Atholl, and clouted Thomas on first one shoulder and then the other. "Arise, Sir Knight, in the name of God. Be you ever loyal, brave, and bold."

Thomas felt someone fastening on his spurs. Roger Kirkpatrick knelt behind him. Those were not his father's spurs. That made his heart hurt. He stood, and Scrymgeour buckled a sword around his waist. The crowd cheered.

Kirkpatrick slapped his arm. "Congratulations, Sir Thomas."

A laugh surged up from his chest. That was the first time anyone had called him a knight. No. That was not true. The first had been King Robert de Bruce.

* * *

THOMAS PATTED the neck of the courser that the Bruce had gifted him with. It tossed its head and stamped. He laughed. He shared its impatience to leave.

Roger Kirkpatrick, preparing to mount his own bay, said, "It is a pity that Isabela MacDuff didnae arrive sooner, but it was a braw ride. A brave lass she is. We should go watch."

"Aye." Thomas mounted. It was the right of the MacDuffs to crown the King of Scots, but Thomas had to wonder if a second coronation would matter. He thought she must not much like her husband, for she was married to a Comyn, the Earl of Buchan, cousin of the man that the King and Kirkpatrick had killed.

The stables and courtyard of Scone Abbey were all noise and motion. Loaded wagons were rattling onto the road. Men were mounting their horses. Serjeants were shouting at men-at-arms. A brisk wind scuttled thin clouds across a pale morning sky, and everyone was anxious to be off. Thomas followed Kirkpatrick, wending their way through the confusion, and rode the short distance to the foot of Moot Hill.

But at the crest, standing behind the King were the three bishops. Before him, with a face of alabaster and back as straight as a spear, stood Isabela MacDuff. She held his crown in her hands. He dropped to one knee before her. She held it aloft and then placed it on his head.

Trumpets blared and blared again. There was a cheer and shouts of God save the King from onlookers, then preparations to leave resumed.

"She is a brave woman," said Kirkpatrick, "to defy the Comyn and all his Ilk."

"Mmm…" Thomas had no doubt in his mind that she

was a brave woman, but word had arrived at the same time that she did that, Aymer de Valence, Earl of Pembroke, was already leading an army toward Scotland. He chewed his nether lip, wondering, fearing that Lord Gordon would join Pembroke. He felt a chill at the idea of meeting him in battle.

Thomas dismounted to wait, for it might be some time before the Bruce led his troops away. All around him, the bustle grew into chaos. Wishart and de Lamberton led men-at-arms to the south, Bishop de Moray to the north where he would raise more men, Edward and Alex back to the King's own lands in Carrick and Annandale to rouse the country. The royal company rode to the north.

Chapter 6

KILDRUMMY CASTLE, SCOTLAND

At each town and abbey, the King had called a halt to accept fealty and let his people see him and the Queen, bestowing such largesse as he could. It would have been days of boredom if at every moment they hadn't been watching for an attack by allies of the Comyns and waiting for news of where Pembroke's army was. Thomas grew more irritable by the day, snapping at Robert Boyd's frequent jests. The older knight shrugged and gave him a knowing look.

They had reached the enormous northern fortress of Kildrummy Castle when the King called for a halt to give their horses a few days' rest. The castle fascinated Thomas with its shape like a shield, the wide part overlooking a high cliff. He spent the day exploring it until the late summer nightfall sent him inside, his stomach grumbling for food.

He walked into the great hall to a buzz of excitement from the hundreds of men sitting at the long trestle tables. The Bruce, his brothers, Christopher Seton, and Robert Boyd were nowhere in sight. Thomas took a seat next to Roger Kirkpatrick. "What's the to-do?"

Kirkpatrick picked up his cup of ale, swished it around for a moment, and said, "A messenger arrived from Bishop de Lamberton. Pembroke is moving faster than expected and will soon cross the border."

"So soon? How is that possible?"

"He's marching with a smaller force than usual. Only three thousand men they say, so they are wasting little time with foraging." Kirkpatrick drained his cup. "And they have raised the dragon banner."

"But..." A chill went through Thomas. "That means no quarter given."

Kirkpatrick's mouth pressed into a thin, grim line. "Any captured will be executed." He shrugged. "Except priests, of course."

Thomas stared past the wall and shuddered. "Robert... I mean the King, he willnae do that though, will he? In retaliation?"

"Nae. It is a heathen thing to do. Forbye why would you kill hostages you can trade for ransom or for your own who are captives?" Kirkpatrick grimaced. "If King Edward leaves any alive to trade for."

"So, what do we do now?"

"That I am nae sure. I am better at fighting than planning, so I have nae part in the council." He thrust his chin at a door at the back of the dais. "They will be making plans. I can tell you that we dinnae have enough men to fight Pembroke. The King will have to summon his brothers and all the followers they can gather. Then I suppose it depends on where Pembroke goes next. And it depends on what the Comyn does."

The next day they rode out from Kildrummy Castle, leaving behind the Queen and the other women and Nigel de Bruce in command of its defense. They traveled north, riding over roads dusty in the summer sun. The braes were still covered in swathes of heather starred with yarrow and gorse., the fields golden with grain awaiting harvest, and in the pastures, shearers bent over sheep bleating and cut off the blanket-like fleece. With only brief stops, they hurried through the King's lordship of Garioch. Crowds cheered at Inverurie, where another two hundred spears joined them.

They rode to the Earl of Atholl's ancient Strathbogie Castle, and the earl sent out commands for his levies to join them. Alex and Edward de Bruce arrived with a thousand troops from south of the Forth and brought with them more bad news. Pembroke had taken Bishop Wishart prisoner, captured Cupar Castle, and come gone north. They believed he intended to take the walled city of Perth. Moreover, the Prince of Wales was leading a much larger army advancing from London.

In the vaulted great hall, Thomas listened, biting his nails, to a long and noisy debate between the King and his closest advisors. Grimly, the Bruce announced that there was no choice but to turn south and bring Pembroke to battle before he had a chance to take even more castles and before the prince's army joined him. Such a huge force might be undefeatable. The next day they turned toward Perth.

Chapter 7
PERTH, SCOTLAND

June 19, 1306

A hot June afternoon sun battered down, the air muggy, and sweat rolled down Thomas's face. The fields outside the walls of Perth were empty. Golden plants, ready for the harvest, waved in the wind, but no laborers were in sight. Christopher Seton's scouts had reported seeing men with scythes while sheep were being driven to graze in the Lower Inch. By the time they reached the burgh, all had long since fled.

The gates were closed, and archers paced atop the thick high walls. Thomas licked his lips and tried to slow the rush of his heartbeat.

The King, astride his massive stallion, commanded the four thousand men to spread out with the blue of the River Tay on their left and the marshes of the River Almond on their right. He sat with the other hundred knights at the front of their force, the closed gate before them. Thomas shifted in his saddle. He wanted to ask if Kirkpatrick what Scots he thought had joined de Valence, but he feared the answer.

"Sound a salute," the King commanded the trumpeters. They gave a brazen blare.

As they waited for a response from the burgh, Thomas eyed the banners flowing above the walls, the three leopards of England, the blue and white stripes of Aymer de Valence's banner, and England's banner of Saint George as well.

"Do you think he will come out to fight?" Edward de Bruce asked the King.

"He is a proud man. Proud of his honor and his prowess in battle, especially. I have never heard of his holding back in the face of an enemy. And we dinnae have the siege machines to bring down the walls. Challenging him is our best chance."

"Could we starve them out?" asked James of Douglas.

"Nae, lad," Robert Boyd said. "They would just bring food in on the River Tay. And Prince Edward's army would attack to relieve them and crush us in the doing."

Thomas was glad that Douglas had asked, so he didn't embarrass himself with the question. But there had few sieges in Scotland since he was grown, none he had witnessed. He had much to learn.

There was a bustle of movement at the gate. King Robert waved forward his herald under the royal banner. When the herald was close to the gates, he shouted, "Robert, King of Scots, makes you challenge. Come out and put your right to the test. King Robert will meet the Earl of Pembroke in single combat or meet him and his men in battle. Fight or surrender his royal burgh."

There was a long pause. Thomas's heart hammered so hard he wondered if the others could hear it.

Finally, a loud voice called down, "The day is too far spent to enter battle. Return on the morrow, and I shall meet you at the head of my men."

The King exchanged a look with Christopher Seton, eyebrows raised, and ordered the serjeants to send patrols on all the roads into Perth. As afternoon shadows lengthened, he led them west to a wooded ridge above the banks of the River Almond. The light of the afternoon was fading as they rode under the elegant, upright ash trees. The crowns of the trees thick with leaves grew together overhead, shutting out most of the red sunset.

The shade gave welcome relief from the summer heat. He pulled up his courser and dismounted. He listened as Christopher Seton called out names of men to act as sentries, but he was not one of them. A fallen tree trunk was overgrown with brambles surrounded by tufts of dried grass. He tied the reins to a branch and breathed in the earthy scent of damp earth and old fallen leaves.

In between the trees, men and horses passed by. Fires sputtered into life, and sparks drifted on the breeze. Hundreds of voices murmured as men stripped off their armor, amid the creak of horses' harness, the whicker of horses. Someone laughed. Men grumbled. Someone sang a bawdy tavern song. His horse was dining on the meager patches of grass, and Thomas could hear the scrunch and then the faint clink of the bridle as it ate. Past some trees, King dismounted as Scrymgeour planted the Lion Rampant on its tall pole.

With a deep sigh, Thomas pulled off his helm, an evening breeze ruffling his sweaty hair.

"Och, feels good," a gruff voice said behind him.

Thomas flinched, hand dropping to his hilt. Then he grimaced, hoping that in the dim light that Roger Kirkpatrick had not seen his start. He turned. "Aye." He squatted and set his helm on the ground. "Do you think it is all right if we take off our armor while we rest?"

Kirkpatrick had his helm tucked under his arm and

removed his gauntlets. "I'll tell you, lad, I dinnae like to do so, but we need to rest to be fit for a fight on the morrow."

Speaking of the coming fight made his pulse race, but Thomas took a deep breath. "I can break some branches from that downed tree. Will you share a fire with me?"

"That I will, lad." Kirkpatrick unbuckled his sword belt and hunkered down to drag a piece of wood over to use as a seat. "A pity we didnae have time to do a little hunting with our supplies running low. These woods must be full of small game. But I have some dried meat in my saddlebags."

As Thomas piled some brown bracken and used his flint and steel to set it alight, he asked, "Did you ride with the King?" He frowned at the little flame that was sending up a tendril of smoke. "I mean before. Did you ride with him when he fought with Wallace?"

"I did. The King is a braw fighter, the best with a sword or an ax I have ever seen. There is no man better to lead us. I promise you that." He dragged his chain-mail hauberk over his head and laid it across a small bush beside his gauntlets and sword belt. "Your first battle." His voice sounded considering. "All the practice in the world does nae prepare you for it."

Thomas pushed a few branches into the flames. "I killed a man in a fight when we took Ayr Castle." He was ashamed to tell the older knight that afterward, he had feared he might throw up. "I had better unsaddle my horse. He needs rest for the morrow too. And I have a couple of apples in my bag."

The night was rapidly falling, but Thomas could see the gleam of the fire reflected in Kirkpatrick's eyes. "Go ahead. I'll build up the fire, and we'll share what we have."

Thomas unloosed a canvas bag from the front of his saddle. He pulled out two withered apples and turned to toss one to Kirkpatrick. He froze at the sound of a trumpet.

"Enemies! To arms!" a sentry cried out somewhere in the darkness. "They're upon us!"

Shouts wrapped through the trees. Someone yelled, "Where? Where are they?"

Thomas dropped the bag and jerked his reins free. He spun toward the fire, trying desperately to recall where he had laid his helm.

Trumpets shrilled and shrilled again. He heard crashing of men through the underbrush and thousands of hoofbeats, so many the ground trembled beneath his feet. Kirkpatrick was struggling into his hauberk, cursing.

Christopher Seton shouted, "To arms! To arms!"

Edward de Bruce's loud voice bellowed a wordless war cry and then, "Form up!" The air filled with yelling and screams. In the darkness, men were closing in from all sides. There was no time for his helm; he must fight without it. He swung into the saddle, drew his sword, and wheeled his horse around.

All around in the murk was the sound of crashing steel, shattering lances, and snorting, galloping horses. "I have him!" a voice shouted but was cut off by a scream of pain.

A horse trumpeted in rage.

The King yelled, "To me! To me!" In the confusion, Thomas turned in every direction. On his left, his uncle stood beside his downed horse and swung his blade in tremendous sweeps to keep back an English knight circling him like a hawk after a hare. Seton came from the darkness. His courser reared, lashing out with iron-shod hooves that slashed the King's attacker.

Then a man ran at Thomas, hands grabbing at his reins, and he was too busy to look. He rode the man down, cutting at another who leapt out of the way. Roger Kirkpatrick bellowed a wordless shout as he hacked at men who surrounded him. Thomas rode to him, bringing his sword down on one attacker's helm with a blow that jolted him to the shoulder. Kirkpatrick cut down another, giving himself a little space, but a knight rode at him, lance couched. Kirkpatrick tried to dodge, but the knight followed his movement. The lance took him in the belly. It went clear through him.

"No!" Thomas shouted.

The knight jerked on his lance, but it stuck in Kirkpatrick's fallen body. He tossed it down and grabbed for his sword.

Thomas put his heels to his horse's flanks, urged it to a gallop, and rode at him. His opponent, tall and square, caught the blow on his shield and aimed a swipe at Thomas's head. He knocked it aside and circled around him, looking for an opening.

In the dark, his horse's leg tangled in the fallen branches. It crashed forward onto its knees, its head almost to the ground. The stumble threw Thomas forward, and he flew out of the saddle like a catapult shot, hitting the ground flat on his back with a crash. He lay, limp and numb, the trees wavering as though they were under water. He blinked, and his sight cleared to see the dark shape of the knight bending over in his saddle.

Thomas groaned, shoving with his elbows to rise, but they were too limp to work.

Someone kicked his head and said, "He's only stunned. Should I finish him?"

Sparks flew in the blackness that crept around the edge of his vision like an engulfing fog.

"No, the earl will send him to hang with the rest of the prisoners, but that horse of his and his armor are fine prizes. Hand me the reins."

The man-at-arms kicked his head again. Thomas's vision grew darker as the foot drew back again. In his muzzy brain, it took a long time as it came toward him until it was all he could see. The foot slammed into Thomas's face, and darkness swallowed him.

Chapter 8
NEAR PERTH, SCOTLAND

Hearing came back first. One moment strange, distorted dreams filled his head. The next, he lay in still darkness with every sound clear and distinct.

A man said, "Strip his armor. It is mine for his capture." The voice left, but other sounds went on, the clank of armor, the murmur of distant voices, someone groaning, the whicker of horses. He listened without caring what the sounds were.

After a while, he knew he lay on his back on the ground, sharp rocks digging into his back. Sick. Stiff, aching. He wondered where he was. He wondered how he got there. Why was he on the ground? He could feel his linen gambeson against his skin. But no armor. He drifted into darkness again.

The next time he awoke, he opened his eyes. The heaviness had gone though they were swollen half shut. He was on the ground with morning sunlight beaming down, and Lord Gordon hunkered at his side. "...beg you, My Lord. He is only a lad." His words seemed strange until Thomas realized he spoke French. Of course. The English knights and nobles all spoke French, and Gordon was talking to one of them.

He struggled to sit up and realized his hands and feet were bound.

"My command from the King is that I am to send all rebels for execution."

"His uncle lied to us both about why they wanted him. In God's mercy, I beg that you not execute him for his uncle's crime."

Above them towered a tall man with fair hair to his shoulders. He had thin features, a smooth-shaven chin, and wore gleaming armor and a tabard with the easily recognized arms of Aymer de Valence, Earl of Pembroke. He glowered down so hard that Thomas felt himself color. "I like executing youths no more than you do." Pembroke sighed. "If you swear to me it was not of his will, that they forced him to ride with the Bruce, I shall spare him. Because he served unwillingly... I must do my best to justify sparing him to the King."

"I swear it, My Lord!"

"Then I give him to you to keep in close ward at Inverkip Castle. He is not under any conditions to be released." Pembroke thrust a forefinger at Lord Gordon. "Under no circumstances."

"Thank you. We will keep him in close ward as you command." Gordon put a hand on Thomas's shoulder. "Before, he served me well as a squire. If they gave him a chance to redeem himself in King Edward's service—"

"I am interpreting the King's command... generously. Because you gave me your oath. Beyond that, we must wait to hear if the King agrees with my decision." De Valence turned his back and strode away.

Because he served unwillingly... Then who would they execute? He managed to raise himself onto an elbow before he spewed up burning bile. He brought his tied hands up to wipe his mouth.

Beyond Lord Gordon, guards jerked Simon Fraser, his hair blood-caked and stripped of his armor, to his feet. He was tied next in line with scores of other prisoners to be led away. Alexander Scrymgeour was being held upright by another prisoner. Thomas shook his head slowly back and forth in denial. He wanted to look away, but he couldn't.

At last, he croaked out, "Did any escape?"

"Aye. The Bruce managed to escape. He was unhorsed three times and still fought his way free. Few can ever best him in a hand-to-hand fight, hell mend the man!"

"The others? How many…?"

"He led an escape with his brothers and a few hundred of his followers." Gordon gripped Thomas's shoulder hard, and his voice was bitter. "They are taking the captured to Newcastle to hang. Including my own good-brother. I telt the earl that Alex lied to us to convince you to go with him. You heard him agree that if you had nae joined willingly that he would let you live. He does so at some risk interpreting the King's command thus. So, lad, say nothing—Nothing!—that would put that to the lie. For the sake of all our lives."

Thomas leaned on his elbow, head hanging limp. "I swear before God… I will nae do anything to cause you harm. On my honor."

There came a new sound—of shovels scraping in the earth. Past Lord Gordon bodies were piled and men labored at digging a long hole.

Chapter 9

INVERKIP CASTLE, SCOTLAND

Thomas stumbled a step when the guard gave him a shove in the middle of his back and muttered, "Daftie."

The door slammed shut, and a bar thumped into place. He propped his back against the door and leaned his head against it. The ride back to Inverkip Castle had seemed to last forever, his hands tied, the ropes rubbing his wrists raw, and his head hammering with every beat of the horse's hooves. He told himself it could have been worse. The four guards, all men he had known long at Inverkip, had done nothing worse than give him hard looks and refuse to speak to him.

Lord Gordon had used the room when he held a felon for trial at the castle, secure at the top of a corner tower. There was a pile of straw and a rough blanket in one corner and a bucket in the opposite. An arrow slit in the rounded outer wall let in a narrow beam of light. He straightened and went to stick his head as far into the opening as he could. It was too narrow to push his head through, but he could see the sky and below the sharp cliff.

In the distance, a gannet with its white body and black-tipped wings soared in freedom.

He pushed away from the arrow slit and sank down onto the blanket. He tried for a while with japes like "All this luxury, by the saints," and "King Edward would envy this bed" and "When does the serving wench arrive?" to lighten the situation. They did not help.

He considered as calmly as he could the possibility that they would leave him here to starve, but he discarded the idea. Lord Gordon had not saved him just to kill him. So they would hold him for King Edward's will, and he could only hope that he was not forgotten here. With one hand on the wall, he limped to the arrow slot. The setting sun spread the western sky with waves of crimson. His stomach rumbled because, during the two-day ride from Methven, they had given him only a few pieces of oat bannock and water when they had stopped to rest the horses. He wondered if they would think to bring him food. He thought about juicy roast capon and crusty fresh baked bread and a rich cup of ale.

At about the time he had begun to wonder if they had indeed forgotten about feeding him, the hatch in the door slid open. William was there, his broad face drawn up into a morose frown. "Thomas." He shook his head. "Why did you do it?"

Thomas propped his shoulder against the door and leaned his head. "There I was, and everyone said it was the right thing to do. Bishop Wishart said so and Bishop de Lamberton. To have a new king—a Scottish one. Who was I to say nae? But I wanted to come back. To tell your father. I couldnae, but I wanted to."

"It is horrible. My uncle was there. He was captured, and they are going to hang him and mother... I can see that she cries at night. I dinnae think she sleeps, and she worries all the time, as well. What if King Edward blames us?"

"Your uncle carried my uncle's royal banner." He thumped his head against the door. "I'm sorry, William. I am... just sorry." After a wrought pause, Thomas asked, "Have you heard any word—" He swallowed, his throat tight. "—about my uncles? The others? I ken they escaped the day. Have they been captured?"

"Nae. I've heard nae more." William's rubbed his hand down his face, his lips pressed tight. "But the English are hanging hundreds. Simon Fraser has been hanged, drawn, and quartered. They plan even to hang the Earl of Atholl!"

"I dinnae..." There was nothing he could think of to say to such dire news, but then his stomach grumbled, and he rubbed it. "I dinnae suppose you have something to eat?"

"Och, aye. I forgot." Will stepped back and pushed a bowl and a wooden spoon through the opening. A big cup of water followed. "The guard was going to bring it, but I asked mother to let me come. She said aye, but I had to swear not to open the door."

Thomas grabbed them, the scent of mutton and beans and rosemary made his mouth water, but first, he took a deep drink of the sweet, fresh well water. He smiled in gratitude. "I ken that you cannae. Your father gave his oath, and your lives depend on it. I'm glad to see your face."

"I had better go. If I can, I'll come back tomorrow." He looked sorry as he drew the slide closed.

Thomas carefully carried the bowl back to the straw bed and sank down. The pottage was warm and delicious too. He ate it all and used his finger to wipe out every drop. He drank the water and reluctantly relieved himself in the bucket, because who knew how soon they would empty it. It would quickly stink in the summer heat.

In time, he gave up wondering how long they would keep him imprisoned. He gave up his apprehension that King Edward would decide that they should execute him like so many others. He tried not to picture Kirkpatrick being cut down and the piles of bodies he had passed as they had ridden away. He gave up wondering if his uncles had been captured or killed. He gave up feeling stiff and miserable, his head thudding with pain from the kicking and body aching in every muscle made even worse by the long ride. He wrapped the blanket around his shoulders and stretched out on the hay.

Chapter 10

A cold wind whistled through the arrow slit carrying splatters of rain with it. Thomas pretended that he was holding a sword and went through every possible move. Stroke, block, and parry. Again and again. He worked until sweat dripped down his face in spite of the autumn chill.

Fergus, the guard who brought his meal most days, slid open the hatch and held through a steaming bowl of beans and kale with a hunk of bread and the usual cup of water. Unlike Alex, he only grunted and slammed the hatch closed.

Thomas did not blame William for the days he did not come. He was busy with chores and practice. Besides, he sometimes wondered how William could stand to come near him from his stink. Thomas was past being able to smell it, but he'd not even been able to wash his face much less his body in the four months he'd been locked in here. He suspected he must smell worse than a leper.

The food warmed him from within for a while. He wrapped himself in his blanket and listened to the drip of the rain on the stones, unable to stand the pretense that he held a sword in his hand anymore. The noise was a comfort. The thick stone and the height cut off all sound from outside. Even the arrow slit opened over a cliff, so no noise drifted in except the occasional call of a bird. Even the dripping of the rain was better than no noise at all.

He reminded himself that he was lucky. Lucky that he had not died in battle or been hanged like so many others. He was lucky not to be in chains. Not to be in a cell in the dank undercroft. He was lucky to be in Lord Gordon's hands, given food from the family's table. He still did not feel lucky.

It had been four months, hadn't it? An existence in limbo. Limbo was the next thing to Hell. How long did it take for a man's mind to shatter, alone with the uncertainty in the silence, the isolation? It would take a long time, he swore to himself. He would not be reduced to a howling madman.

Tough thoughts… As long as William occasionally came to tell him what was happening. As long as there was hope that someday he would be released.

What word he had received was grim. Nigel de Bruce captured, hanged, and beheaded. Christopher Seton hanged and beheaded. Dozens captured at Methven hanged. Lady Elizabeth de Burgh, Mary, Christina, and young Margery de Bruce all captured and imprisoned. But since then, no word. Not for months, except that King Edward had decided to winter at Carlisle. Lord Gordon had gone with the English, William said, anxious to show his loyalty to the English King.

There had been one skirmish in the Highlands with followers of the Comyn, and then the Bruce and his remaining men had simply fled. No one knew where. To Ireland? To Norway where his sister was queen?

Fled from the battlefield and now fled from Scotland.

When Thomas closed his eyes, Robert's words in his coronation that day on Moot Hill echoed in the room.

"Will you defend your realm and its people against all foreign enemies and invaders?"

"I swear by Almighty God, I will."

Then he fled from the battle, leaving friends to die an ignoble death. Or be imprisoned. He ran!

Thomas pounded his fist on the cold stone until blood smeared the wall, and he sank down to crouch, hands plunged into his hair.

That night he lay on the straw and tried to imagine himself back as a squire doing tedious chores around the castle. His hands twitched at the memory of sharping swords. He let his mind drift. He lay awake for hours and hours, wondering if he could keep himself from going mad in the blankness. He drifted into sleep and dreamt of riding across heather-covered braes with his father.

Chapter 11

Thomas's teeth chattered, although William had brought him a second blanket when the weather changed. He tented them over his head, knees up to his chest, pulling them even more tightly around himself. The wind whistled through the arrow slit carrying a few flurries of snow with it to drift in the air before they settled onto the cold floor.

He rested his forehead on his knees with a shuddery sigh. At least the beard from months of not shaving helped keep his face from the chill. He should move about, use his practice moves to warm himself up, but it was so damnably cold. The thought of unwrapping from the blanket—

A door banged, and a loud voice carried up the stairs, too faint through the thick door to make out the words, but definitely not William. Thomas raised his head and let the blanket fall back, listening intently. Yes, there were loud footfalls on the stone stairs, more than one person.

The bar grated, and then the door made a rusty squeal as it opened. Lord Gordon stood in the doorway. Thomas blinked for a second, wondering if he was imagining it. Perhaps, after all, he had gone mad.

But Gordon motioned. "Come with me, Thomas. There's news."

Thomas scrambled to his feet, dropping the blankets. "My lord…" He shook his head. "I cannae believe that you're here."

"Come on." He grimaced. "By the saints, but you stink. First, you bathe, and then we talk."

Rubbing his hands to warm them, Thomas hurried past him out the door where William was waiting along with Fergus, the guard. "May I shave?" he asked eagerly. "This beard itches like the gey devil."

"Aye, and my chamberlain is finding you some clean clothes. Come."

Thomas threw William a hopeful look but received only a faint smile in return. He followed Lord Gordon, his mind working furiously. Was there bad news that Gordon delayed telling him? Was he not to be released? Surely, Lord Gordon would not have Thomas bathing and donning clean clothes to throw him back in a dungeon. He wanted to beg Gordon to tell him what was happening, but as soon he started, he was impatiently waved off, so he hurried after, glad for the warmth. He tromped down the four flights of stairs, out of the great hall, and dashed through the cold bailey yard into the kitchen.

A fire was blazing on the vast hearth, and a spit-boy was turning a haunch of venison. The scent of roasting made his stomach growl, but a boy pouring steaming water into a barrel was an even more welcome sight. "Go on," Sir Adam told him. There was a sliver of soft soap and a cloth on a stool too. He shed his filthy clothes, grabbed the soap, and climbed in. He sank down as the boy poured deliciously warm water over his head. He thought that perhaps he did not even care if the news was dire. Anything was worth soaking the dirt and sweat from his body. He leaned back his head and closed his eyes.

After a bit, William poked his shoulder to wake him and handed him scissors. He snipped and hacked until at least most of the softened beard was gone but had to wonder if he looked like a mangy dog, but it did not matter. Fergus thumped a stack of clothes and a big linen cloth on the stool, grumbling under his breath, which Thomas took as a strong hint that he had taken long enough. He soaped all over with the bit of soap, rinsed, and climbed out. A quick rub down, and he was ready for the unimaginable luxury of clean chausses and tunic and shoes.

"The master is waiting in the hall," Fergus grumbled.

When he went into the yard, the snow had stopped but blew from the ground in eddies under a leaden sky. William, at the door of the keep, waved to him, so he hurried across, scraping his wet hair out of his face and tugging at the tangles with his fingers as he went.

"I wish I could have had you out sooner." He pulled the door open. "You ken that?"

"Aye, certes I do." He dashed inside. "Where is your father?"

"In here, Thomas," Gordon called from the dais. "Come. I must speak with you."

Two score of men-at-arms were eating at the long tables, a few wearing the boar's head device of Gordon but most with that of a purple lion rampant. Thomas strode across the great hall, breaking his pace for a second when he came to the central hearth. How often he had thought of standing next to it and warming his hands. But he walked on and stepped onto the dais as Gordon sat in the high-back chair at the center of the high table. He took a seat on the next place on the bench when the Lord of Gordon motioned to it. William had followed and sat beside him, giving him an encouraging nod.

Gordon rested his clasped hands on the table and gazed at them somberly.

Thomas's breath caught. *Had the King decided to execute him after all?* he thought wildly. "What is it?" he blurted.

"Dinnae fash yourself. It is nae bad… It is nae exactly bad news." He shook his head. "William telt you that the Bruce disappeared. None kent where he was. We thought he had fled to his sister in Norway to take refuge in her royal court. But King Edward just received news that the Bruce carried out an attack on the Isle of Arran. He escaped after with much loot."

Staring into the dancing flames in the hearth, Thomas sat silent for a minute and said, "Not on the mainland then."

"Nae, but Arran is close. And it changes things for you and for me as well."

"How so?" Here we come to it, he thought, bracing himself.

"You are to be given over to Henry de Lacy, Earl of Lincoln." Gordon shrugged. "I have made nae secret of my fondness for you and that I wanted you released, so they fear I might let you go. They want you under safer eyes than mine and further from where he might be. To be sure you do nae manage to him."

"I wouldnae do that to you!" Thomas exclaimed. "To put you and your family at such a risk."

Gordon leaned and patted his shoulder. "I believe you. The truth is that they dinnae trust me either."

"Because of me." Thomas shook his head. "My fault."

"Nae, the fault of my goodbrother. They hanged him after..." He scrubbed his hand across his mouth. "Anyroad, this can be a good thing for you. Lincoln is nae ordered to keep you in ward, and he is a good man."

Thomas felt his face flush, the hope seeming like too much to take in. "Does that mean nae locked away?"

"You'll be with him under close guard. But you will have a chance to convince him to speak to the King for you. To be taken into the King's peace. Mayhap even fight for him."

"Where is Lincoln?" He laughed, not able to contain the burst of hope... relief... joy that flooded through him.

"He is with King Edward at Carlisle. Tomorrow we prepare and the day after we depart. It is a full two days' ride and that if we make good time and have no delays."

"I am going as well as his squire," William said, his eyes gleaming. "My arm is long since healed."

Two days' ride. Nothing had ever sounded quite so wonderful, even if it blew and snowed. He did not care. To be in the open air with a horse between his legs. He let another laugh escape that made Gordon's lip quirked in a smile.

"You will need a cloak and such. I have ample clothes stored in kists. My chamberlain is going through them now. He will find what you need."

"Even taking charity, penniless and landless, I dinnae care. I have a chance to earn my freedom."

Gordon raised his eyebrows. "Thomas. Nithsdale is still yours. I thought you kent that. But friendship is enough to see you clothed."

Thomas stared at him. "I thought... I was sure they would seize my lands."

William jumped up. "Let us go to the stables. Father brought a good, solid palfrey for you."

Thomas stood and said to Gordon, "I cannae give you thanks enough. You saved my life after the battle. Dinnae think I dinnae ken that or shall ever forget it." Then he followed William through the doors, not caring in the least how chill it was outside.

Chapter 12

CARLISLE CASTLE, ENGLAND

Under a cold, cloudless blue sky, they rode across the draw-bridge of Carlisle Castle. Thomas, sore, tired, and hungry, stared up at the fortress, one that might have been made by giants playing with massive sandstone blocks. Atop its towers flew the leopard banner of England. He sat erect in the saddle and lifted his chin, wiping the sweat from his hand on his thigh.

The castle chamberlain met them in the inner bailey to tell Lord Gordon that the lord earl was in the keep and required Gordon's and Thomas's attendance. The rest of the troop of guards was riding in behind them.

"Very well," Lord Gordon said. A look of irritation passed over his face, quickly suppressed. He dismounted and ripped the riding gloves from his hands.

Thomas slid from the saddle, and Gordon nodded for the chamberlain to lead the way. And so he followed Lord Gordon striding into the first-floor hall, sweaty and dressed in clothes covered in the dust of the road.

The hall was plainly furnished. A modest fire burned in the side hearth. Faded tapestry with figures of knights and their ladies covered the walls. They found the de Lacy, Earl of Lincoln, standing before the fireplace in the side wall, eyes intently focused on a parchment. With smoothly combed gray hair, red cloak trimmed with vair, green tunic and chausses, and black, pointed shoes, he looked up, spreading his air of his noble confidence across the room.

Gordon removed his helmet and bowed. "Your Lordship,"

"Gordon." Pembroke looked Thomas up and down. Speaking in French, he said, "So this is the nephew of King Hob."

Thomas darted a glance at Lord Gordon and bowed to the earl. He responded in the same language, "Thomas Randolph, Your Lordship."

Lincoln raised his eyebrows and gave a stare as cool as a winter's day. "Lord Gordon convinced Pembroke on your behalf. I am not so easily persuaded. You will be under close guard and under my own eye."

"I..." What was he to say to that? "I am at your command, Your Lordship."

With a curt nod, the Earl of Lincoln said, "So you are. You may have the freedom of the castle. If you make any attempt to leave without permission, which you will not receive, I shall have you thrown back into a dungeon."

Lord Gordon cleared his throat. "Am I to join Pembroke? Is he still in Carlisle?"

"He is leaving for Scotland shortly, and I believe you are to join him hunting down King Hob. This young knight will remain in Carlisle with me."

"Is it permitted that I train in the practice yard?" Thomas asked.

The earl looked Thomas up and down. "I am curious to see if you have any of King Hob's admitted ability with the sword. So yes, you may. The practice weapons can do no harm."

Gordon said, "Mayhap I could—"

"Lincoln," Aymer de Valence said in the doorway, cutting Lord Gordon off. "There is someone in the bailey yard you had best see. The King is on his way from the great hall and wants you there."

The Earl of Lincoln strode out of the room on Pembroke's heels. Thomas threw a puzzled glance at Gordon, and they both followed.

The large inner bailey yard had filled with men-at-arms, and most of the voices raised in a cacophony were Scottish. Three men were on their knees, hair blood-matted, faces bruised, ripped clothing filthy. The first man Thomas recalled from the coronation but did not know his name. Thomas's heart began to race when he recognized one of the men as Thom de Bruce, his face blood-caked, was hardly recognizable with all the injuries. He held his shoulder as though it was broken. Thomas did not recognize the second. The third raised his face, misshapen with swelling, hunching his shoulder as though it were broken. Thomas gasped. Alex de Bruce!

Gordon gave Thomas a gentle push and urged him away from the door and against the wall. In Scots, he muttered, "Wheesht, lad. Dinnae say a word, or you risk all. My life and yours both."

Thomas grasped his hands into fists, his chest tightening so that he could barely breathe. He realized that Alex was looking at him, and he stared at his uncle's battered face. Dear God, have mercy…

The keep door was thrown open with a bang.

A man stepped onto the top of the stairs. He was tall, thin, had a strong nose, and iron-gray hair still vigorous and well-shaped on which rested a gold coronet. A beautifully made belted silk tunic encased his body below which showed dark chausses. Under his wrinkles, and the folds of his eyelids, one of which sagged half-closed, his features were elegant and refined. He had the basic equipment of a handsome man, and one might have thought he had mellowed to a genial grandfather had it not been for the ill will that glared out of his eyes, his dour trap of a mouth, and deep lines running from the corners of his nose to his chin that gave him a look of cold determination.

One of the Scots stepped forward, his face thin and hard, eyes unsmiling. He dropped to one knee. "Your Grace, I, Dugald Macdowall, have the honor to bring you the traitors Alex de Bruce, Thom de Bruce, and Reginald Crawford. Two days ago, we defeated their force in our lands of Galloway." He motioned to one of his men who emptied out a bag. Two severed heads thudded on the ground. "The leaders of the Irish gallowglasses we beheaded on the spot."

"Well done." King Edward gave a haughty nod. "We shall reward you for your loyalty."

Thomas tore his gaze from the king, and Alex was still staring at him, his lips moving slightly as though in prayer.

The King turned his intense gaze on the three men on their knees. "It was my decree that any who have aided the traitor Robert de Bruce are to be executed. Have these felons dragged through the streets of Carlisle so all may see them in their shame, hang them from the gallows at the market until they are dead, and behead them. We command their heads be displayed on spikes above the gate of the city."

Gordon put his hand on Thomas's shoulder and squeezed hard.

Thomas raised his eyes to watch feathery clouds racing before the wind. He wondered what prayer Alex was saying. Was it for himself or for Thomas? He closed his eyes. Mother of God, aid them in their hour of need. And he gave thanks to God Almighty that he was forbidden to leave the castle.

Alex, he was jerked to his feet and his hands roped to a horse's tail. Thomas and Crawford were already being dragged out. Alex straightened, raising his head to a proud angle as he trudged behind the horse. The rider sped up, and Alex was nearly jerked off his feet. Macdowell and his men whistled, shouted jeers, and followed along after. The castle gate slammed shut behind them.

The King stalked back into the keep, followed by the two earls.

Still grasping Thomas's shoulder, Gordon turned to face him. In a low voice, he said, "You listen to me, lad. We lost years ago. Wallace is dead, his head rotted on a pike. We are ruled by the English King. The Bruce was a fool to start the whole thing again. We cannae win. My own good-brother—my friend, too, he was—they hanged for the Bruce's mad idea. Simon Fraser is hanged, drawn, and quartered." He dug his fingers deep into Thomas's shoulders. "His people's homes burnt and driven from the land. We cannae let our families and our people die for a kingdom whose time is done and gone."

Thomas's heart stuttered in his chest. He was too numb to reply.

* * *

IN THE SMALL HALL, Thomas splashed cold water from the basin on this face. He wet the cloth and used it to wipe the back of his neck and scrubbed the soil from his hands. Lincoln's men-at-arms were noisily tromping up the stairs to the great hall above for dinner. One paused behind him and Thomas stiffened. During the past two weeks, most had learned to leave him be, but occasionally he found himself on the receiving end of a shove or outthrust foot. He laid the cloth on the table. Whoever had paused apparently thought better of it and stomped away, following his fellows.

He stripped off his tunic that was sweat-soaked from hours spent swinging a weighted sword in the practice yard. Months locked in a cell had sapped his strength, but he had no doubt that work would restore it. He pulled his second tunic over his head, buckled his belt around his hips, and went to join in the meal.

He settled in his place at the end of the bench at the far end of the hall from the dais. Lord Gordon had been right that some things about being sent to the Earl of Lincoln were not entirely bad. He filled his cup from a pitcher of ale and thought that being able to freely eat and drink was one of them. The fresh, fruity taste of the ale filled his mouth and made him smile.

The second level hall of Carlisle Castle was heavy with the smell of wood smoke from the hearth and the earthy smell of a hundred men. Its brown sandstone walls were covered with banners. Red and gold: the three leopards of King Edward, Pembroke's blue and white with a circle of red starlings and Lincoln's purple lion rampant. Up in the minstrel's gallery, a minstrel was playing the vielle, but at Thomas's end of the table, the music was only a faint tinkle mixed in with the crackling of the fire, servants rattling the cups and serving trays, and the gossip and jokes of the men-at-arms.

"Be upstanding for His Grace the King," the chamberlain intoned, and they all scrambled to their feet.

King Edward came in, tight faced, escorting the Queen, Margaret of France. She was almost as fair as people said, young enough to be the King's granddaughter. She wore a linen barbet but a jeweled coronet served as her fillet, its sapphires exactly matching the gleaming silk of her kirtle. The King helped her up the steps of the dais. She smiled up at him when he escorted her to her place beside his high-backed chair, and they both sat.

Next came Edward, Prince of Wales; tall, hair as bright as beaten gold, with intensely blue eyes in a youthful, tanned face, and an unconsciously roguish smile. Thomas raised an eyebrow at how short the prince's green tunic was, embroidered with gold thread and its edges elegantly scalloped.

Thomas watched him, fascinated. He did look like a young king, however short his tunic was.

Half-hidden by the prince's great height, Bishop Langton shuffled along, garbed in a rich velvet cassock, a gold chain about his neck from which hung a large crucifix. He was about fifty, sharp-featured, and earnest with church-colored skin.

The last of the lords to enter was the Earl of Lincoln and his goodson, Thomas, Earl of Lancaster, a lean man in his early twenties.

Thomas filled his cup again and loaded his trencher with a slice of roast pork and piled fried onion from a platter a serving boy held before him.

"Geoffrey, tell one of your japes!" one of the young knights said.

The one he'd called Geoffrey rapped on the table. "Have you heard this one? In London, a young wench, somewhat of a simple mind, was on the point of delivering a babe. It had taken so long that the midwife took a candle in hand to inspect her secret part to see if the child was finally coming. 'Look on the nether side, too,' said the poor wench, 'my husband sometimes takes that road.'"

Even Thomas had to chuckle. Everyone was cackling and slapping their thighs when a gaunt messenger in dirt-covered livery and a livid red mark on one cheek sidled up.

"Shove over." He sat on the bench, hunched over, and grabbed a cup, filled it with ale, and drained it. "If I have any luck at all, I'll never have to carry such a message again."

"What message?"

The messenger looked around to see if anyone of importance was listening. "A week since, King Hob landed with his men near Turnberry Castle and attacked troops garrisoned in the town while they slept. Killed many." The messenger twisted his mouth as though he wanted to spit. "Henry Percy was too afraid to venture out of the castle and sat on his arse while they looted the town. Then King Hob and his men slipped away into the mountains of Carrick. Pembroke is searching for him, but so far no sign." He upended his tankard to drain it. "I had the joy of giving the King the news." He pointed to what would soon be a bruise on his cheek.

Thomas leaned forward to look at the dais at the other end of the hall. The King was observing all the courtesies to his young wife, but his face was flushed. He looked out over the hall with cold, hooded eyes. Beside him, the Queen was touching his arm and murmuring something to him. Two seats away, the Earl of Lincoln's face was tight. He said little as he took precise bits of the food before him.

Lincoln looks upset as well, Thomas thought but kept the thought to himself. Nor was he going to mention that Carrick was the Bruce's own country, his mother's country, where he had grown up. Thomas had chased with him over those hills. If he did not want to be found, Pembroke would be hard-pressed to do so.

The conversation continued around the table, speculating in quiet voices whether he would be angry at Percy for not facing King Hob at Turnberry and whether the King would send more troops north to Scotland. The messenger said in a low voice, "Mayhap he will send Prince Edward."

One of the guardsmen disagreed. He leaned forward across the table. "When I was on guard at Bishop Langton's door, I heard him say that they are expecting an envoy from France regarding the prince's marriage. Surely, the King will want him here for that."

Servants carried in platters of next course, herring and capon with bowls of cabbage and parsnips. Others topped up their tankards with ale. The food was good and generous, although no doubt the high table ate even better. Thomas refilled his trencher and swallowed the rest of his ale.

Chapter 13

A towheaded page found him in mid-afternoon as Thomas worked in the stable, carrying sacks of oats into storage. Even as a noble prisoner, he was not set to do such work, but it was an excellent way to regain his strength, so he willingly volunteered for it. The boy panted as though he'd been running.

"You, Lord Lincoln sent me to give you a message," he said. He looked about ten years old and seemed wary of stepping too near Thomas. "He says for you to attend him directly at the King's palace."

He started to leave, but Thomas yelled, "Stop." His shout made the boy jump. "You had better lead me to wherever he is, lad. He will not be happy if I must waste time searching for him."

He brushed the dust off his tunic as he followed the nervous page across the bailey yard to the building that was the royal residence and through a long corridor busy with nobles and clerics coming and going, through waves of the smell of stale furs, lavender, and musk. They climbed the stairs to the upper floor.

Thomas let out his breath when the earl dismissed the page and gave him an easy smile.

"There has been news from Scotland, Randolph, and it has decided me to give you a chance to redeem yourself."

"I… I am most grateful, My Lord."

"I have had no reproach for your actions the short time you've been here. Pembroke assured me that you had no part in the murder of John Comyn, and he values Lord Gordon's word that you were an unwilling participant in de Bruce's later treachery."

"It's true that my uncle…" He licked his lips. "He sent for me after John Comyn's murder and lied to Lord Gordon about why I was wanted." He studied the rushes. He could not put Gordon to the lie. Could not. But no one had forced him to swear fealty. No sword had been held at his throat. He smoothed his expression. "I was surrounded by his followers and did not see what else I could do." It was close to a lie, but the best he could do.

"You were young and were not yet a knight, so I have convinced the King to forgive and take you into his peace. You are to go to him, fall onto your knees, and humbly beg his forgiveness. You will swear your fealty to him, and, boy, if you give me any reason to doubt you, I will see your head over my gate."

If that was what they required, he would do it. "I swear by the Blessed Virgin and all the saints, My Lord. I shall give you nae reason to regret this."

The earl gave a brisk nod and motioned for Thomas to follow him. Courtiers crowded the inmost chamber. Spanish carpets covered the floor instead of rushes. Tapestries depicting feasting and crusaders on horseback covered the walls. Near the hearth where a small fire burned, the King and Queen sat with goblets of wine at a table covered with a silk tapestry, a chessboard set up on it.

Thomas rubbed his palms on his thighs and swallowed hard. Holding himself rigidly erect, Thomas walked to face the King and dropped to both knees. The floor beneath the rug was no harder than the gazes from the onlookers. Intensely aware of the King's cold stare down his nose, he bowed his head in the required attitude of humility.

"Your Grace," he said, "I plead for your forgiveness for my transgressions in Scotland and beg to be allowed into the King's peace."

A tense silence stretched out, but Thomas dared not raise his eyes.

"Sire," the Queen said, her French slightly different from that of the English nobles, "he is still little more than a boy. Surely in your kindness, you can forgive him."

"We forgave his uncle and look what that came to."

"Please, my lord husband, there is so much bloodshed. Show him your mercy."

"Very well, my dear." He reached out for Thomas's hands and gave them a bone-crushing squeeze. "You are pardoned and come into our peace solely on the intercession of our dearest consort. Now give us your oath."

Thomas took a deep breath. He had given this oath his uncle, and he had meant it. But now he must give his oath again, mean it, and keep it this time. God forgive him! Too many lives depended on him. Lord Gordon's, Gordon's lady wife, and Williams's, not merely his own. The lands of Bruce's followers had been harried, the people killed or left homeless. He could not bring that down on Inverkip or his own Nithsdale. He must keep this oath—to the death. He raised his gaze to King Edward's cold and calculating eyes. "By the Lord God and all the holy saints, I become your liege man from this day forward of life and limb and truth and earthly honors, bearing to you and your heirs against all men that live, move or die, in good faith and without deceit, so help me God and the Blessed Mother."

The King abruptly released his hands. "You shall serve in the Earl of Lincoln's retinue until I say otherwise."

Thomas rose, bowed deeply, and took a couple of steps backward and turned to go.

The earl stopped him with a gesture and said, "I have commands for you. Wait until I am through here." and turned to approach the King. Bishop Langton reached the monarch first.

Langton bowed and said, "Sire, Prince Edward came to me and entreated me to bring you a most important request."

The King's nostrils flared. "What business is it of yours to carry requests for my son? He is a man and must speak for himself."

Langton stepped back, eyes widening in alarm. "Your Grace, forgive me. I merely thought to fulfill his request."

Thrusting his finger toward one of the courtiers, he barked, "Tell my son I command him to attend me. Forthwith."

Lincoln's eyebrow twitched. He bowed to King Edward. "Your Grace, excuse me for a short time while I give this young knight his orders. His time is better used elsewhere." He caught Thomas's eye and nodded toward the door.

Thomas quietly blew out a breath, walked carefully through the door, and stepped to the far side of the outer chamber out of sight of the King.

The earl stepped close and said, "That was very properly done, Randolph. Now you may——"

He stopped when the prince strode through the room and into the inner chamber. His loud voice carried, "Sire?"

King Edward demanded, "On what business did you send Bishop Langton?"

"That I might with your permission give the county of Ponthieu that I inherited to my dear brother Piers Gaveston."

There was a crash as though a chair had been knocked over. "You bastard son of a bitch!" the King screamed. "You want to give away lands—you who never gained any? Almighty God as my witness, were it not for fear of breaking up the kingdom, I would cast you out and disown you, and you would never be king!"

There was the smack of a blow and sounds like a struggle.

"Sire! Please!"

The prince was thrown through the doorway onto the floor. He slid on his back, mouth open, eyes wide. His hair was disheveled, sticking up as though it had been ripped at.

King Edward rushed after him and kicked him in the ribs. He kicked the prince again. "Get out of my sight." The prince scrambled to his feet and, mouth still agape, rushed from the room.

Thomas's heart was hammering like a galloping horse. The King scowled at him.

Calmly, the Earl of Lincoln said, "Go. I shall speak to you later."

Thomas bowed to both men and, repressing the impulse to run, walked slowly back to the bailey yard.

Near dusk as Thomas swung a weighted wooden practice sword at the pell, the Earl of Lincoln said, "You are skilled with that."

Thomas started and nearly dropped the sword. He turned and wiped his sweaty forehead with his forearm. "My Lord, I can thank Lord Gordon for that." He opened his mouth to ask what the earl wanted but clamped it shut.

This day had been strange enough that he would not chance affronting the earl by questioning him.

The earl held his hand out for the wooden sword, and Thomas reversed it to hand it to him hilt first. Lincoln weighed it in his hand. He nodded and tossed it onto the ground. "Come with me."

He started across the bailey yard but paused after a few steps. "What you heard today in the King's palace…"

Thomas shrugged. "Only the King accept me into his peace."

"If you're wise, that is all you will remember about the day. Not that there will not be gossip." He started walking again, and Thomas realized they were heading towards the long wooden building that was the armory. "The King is not pleased with the lack of progress in locating King Hob, so I am joining Pembroke and Gloucester. The King is sending with me what I am sure is a strongly worded letter expressing his displeasure."

"Mmm…" Thomas mumbled a response. He was not going to comment on the greatest men in England being taken to task by the enraged king.

"You are part of my retinue, so you will go with me." He stopped in the doorway. "You have a chance to prove that loyalty you swore to. I expect you to do so." He stepped through the door of the armory and called, "Armorer!"

The man who tromped toward them in response had a neck and shoulders as thick as a bull's. His brows were coarse and black, and his head so bald it was shiny. But he had a pleasant smile. "Aye, My Lord. Here I am."

"We are leaving in two days, so there is little time, and this knight needs armor. See to it. And convey for me to the blacksmith that he needs a good sword and dirk as well."

The man gave a clumsy bow. "As you say, My Lord."

A corner of the gray-haired earl's mouth twitched. "Randolph, the cost will come out of the income of your lands." He turned and left Thomas watching after him in astonishment.

The armorer was shaking his head. "They always think I am a miracle worker. I cannot make a good harness in two days, but I shall do the best I can. I have some good pieces that can be reworked to fit you."

"I thank you."

The man tilted his large head. "A Scot, are you? A pity to waste good armor on you, but if the earl wants you to have it, so be it." Muttering, he went to a shelf and searched through the pieces there until he found a gambeson. He tossed it to Thomas. "Try that. Let me see." He moved to another shelf. "This hauberk might fit you with a little work."

Thomas watched the disgruntled armorer in bemusement until he was sharply told, "Put on that gambeson so I can see if it will do. Don't waste my time dawdling."

After an hour of the armorer making him try on hauberk, chausses, poleyns, gauntlets, coif, and helmet, muttering under his breath, Thomas was told to return on the morrow. With a sigh of relief, he went to the great hall for supper.

He took his usual place at the end of the great hall. There were no loud jests as he poured his ale and slid some fried fish onto his trencher. But there was a constant murmur of gossip. The earls and bishop took their places at the high table with no sign of the King, Queen, or the prince.

"I never did like that Piers Gaveston, so good riddance," one of the younger knights grumbled. "He always swaggered prouder than a peacock and bragged that he was the best man in England with a lance."

"Aye, surely it cannot be true that the King tossed the prince out on his arse," the messenger with the bruised face said. "It is one thing to knock about one of us messengers. But the prince?"

Thomas took a drink of his ale to hide a wry smile.

The first man shrugged. "All I know is that I saw Gaveston ride out of the castle with guards. And everyone says he is banished from the kingdom for life."

Away from Carlisle might be a good place to be for a time, Thomas mused, though he would miss the ale. He drained his tankard and refilled it.

Chapter 14

SOMEWHERE IN SCOTLAND

It was a cold and gusty winter day. The column kept pace north into Scotland toward Lochmaben Castle. As they neared, clouds covered the sky and the light turned as gray as smoke. They passed the hill where the massive hoary old yew tree rose, and Thomas turned his horse's head. He stared up into the Giant's bare branches, dusted with snow. Placing his hand on its trunk, he whispered, "It's been a cold winter, old friend." Cold indeed. Thomas's stomach twisted, picturing Alex's face.

"Randolph, what by God's nails are you doing?" a voice yelled.

He turned to see a thin, hawk-featured knight, Hugh of Newent, his blue eyes glittering with intelligence, staring up at him.

"Nothing. I am coming."

"You had better. You heard the earl's orders. No straying from the column. Hurry, or he'll have your testicles."

By midafternoon they rode through a burned village, winding their way between the charred remains of cottages poking through a thin coat of snow and past the bones of a half a dozen men hanging from a stand of pine. Hugh crossed himself, but the earl made a broad sweep of his arm. "The village served one of Simon Fraser's castles. His people paid for his treachery." He gave Thomas a pointed glance and rode on. Thomas looked over his shoulder at the unshriven dead, men and women who had only followed their lord, in their rotted shreds of clothing and said a prayer for their souls.

Before nightfall they reached the loch, its waters shining like polished silver. On a cliff above the waters rose the walls of Lochmaben.

At the foot of the promontory, the earl told his serjeants, "The castle will not have room to accommodate five hundred additional men. Make camp here. I want the perimeters well-guarded. Double the number of sentries."

Lincoln said he did not expect trouble this close to the castle, but Percy had thought his men safe at Turnberry. It was best not to take a chance, an opinion that Thomas could not argue.

When the earl was ready to ride up to the castle, he took Thomas with him, along with the dozen other knights and the squires in his company, the earl's yellow and purple banner flying over their heads. The scouts had reported that the gates of the castle were shut, chains and pulleys squealed as the drawbridge lowered, and the portcullis rose. Crossbowmen paced the parapet walk. Thomas glanced up at the murder holes as they passed through the gatehouse.

The scars of its capture by the English were already repaired. The outer gates were new, thick oaken planks reinforced with iron bands. New stables in the outer bailey stood next to blackened scars where the old one had stood. How fierce had been the battle to take this strong fortress?

But when they rode into the inner bailey yard, nothing had changed from the last time Thomas was here except everything. No dark-haired lass ran to greet her father. No Irish woman met her husband with a laugh and a kiss. No crowd of smiling women came out to greet them. All gone and not to return. Something twisted in his gut.

A steward emerged from the keep to meet them. "Lord Lincoln, forgive our lack of a proper greeting. We did not expect you so soon." Thomas frowned and wondered what had happened to the old man who had been the steward for the Bruce.

Dismounting, Lincoln tossed his reins to a groom. "Where is Pembroke?" As governor of Scotland, even the Earl of Lincoln would answer to him.

Thomas followed suit, full of curiosity at how Pembroke would take a rebuke carried from the King.

"The earl is within the keep, My Lord."

Lochmaben's great hall was worthy of the name, wide and vaulted. Even so, trestle tables crowded it from wall to wall, empty at the moment except for a manservant scrubbing up spills. Thomas was pondering Pembroke's banner hanging above the dais when the man emerged from a rear door. "Lincoln!" he said. His muscular figure, even taller than he had seemed that day at Methven, was now clothed in a red silk tunic instead of armor, but still a man of power whose very presence filled the chamber. "Should I assume that you bring me the news that our dread lord is not pleased with me?"

Thomas hung back, not particularly eager to renew his acquaintance, if it could be called that, with the man. His voice brought back the sounds of horses thundering through the bracken and moans of the dying.

Lincoln barked a laugh. "Yes, I am now playing at

being his messenger. But why have you not yet managed to hunt down King Hob?"

"Easier said than done, my friend. He is as slippery as a fox with hounds on its tail. But we have him boxed in, so if the King will be just a little patient, we shall have him."

Lincoln laid a letter on the high table. "Nonetheless, you had better have this."

"I shall save the joy of it until later. But why do you not have refreshments after your ride?" He tucked the letter away, looked around, and spotted the servant. "You! Tell the bottler to bring wine for the earl and his men." As the servant dropped his scrubbing cloth and scurried away, Pembroke's gaze fixed on Thomas.

"I remember you," Pembroke said. "Your station has changed, I see. And your allegiance."

Thomas squared his shoulders, took a deep breath, and bowed. "My Lord, it has. I owe you gratitude for my life."

"You do, for had I been more punctilious in following my orders, you..." He shrugged. Pembroke had no need to repeat that the King had commanded all rebels to be executed. "You are King Hob's nephew I recall."

Thomas nodded. "His half-sister was my mother."

"And you know him well, then?"

"Passing well, My Lord. I visited his mother's Turnberry Castle often when I was a lad. His brothers were my playmates, but he was the eldest. We followed him about like pups begging for his attention." Thomas couldn't help a wry smile. "When we were a little older, we hunted—and just rode the hills."

"So, you know the lands and the man. Know the routes and passages that he could travel."

Thomas rubbed the back of his neck. "I know many of them, My Lord. I have hunted yon with Lord Gordon as well, so I suppose I know them as well as most."

Several servants scurried in with trays with wine flagons and goblets. Pembroke told one, "Put that here." He picked up a cup and thumped it down on the table. "Look. Here in the west, Henry de Percy, strengthened with your friend Lord Gordon, guards the approach to the sea at Turnberry Castle." He placed another wine cup. "To the south, Sir Dugald MacDowell and his men guard the way." He thumped down another cup. "Here on the east, Robert de Clifford and a good-sized force guard the fords across the River Cree." One more cup forcibly slapped down completed a circle. "And to the north, John of Lorn with his savage Highlanders cuts off King Hob's escape.

"We have him cornered like a rat, but he is deep in a hole, and I must dig him out. But he is a dangerous rat. Two days ago, he attacked a camp of Clifford's scouts here —" He slammed down another cup. "—at a place called Clatteringshaws Loch and disappeared again into those hills. So tell me the best places to find him."

"But you must know the land. You've fought for it. Turnberry Castle. Douglas Castle. Ayr Castle."

"And those are the places that King Hob is not to be found."

Thomas rubbed his chin. He pointed to near one of the cups. "There spreads the vast Forest of Galloway as you must know. If he is in there, even Macdowell might take a very long time to find him, though the Bruce could not stay there forever, nor would it gain him followers. More likely, it seems to me is the Range of the Awful Hand, about there." He pointed to where he thought it would be in the circle. "The highest is Meurag, where he can have a lookout to see a large part of Carrick and Galloway all the way to the sea if the weather is fine and spot any force hunting him. Loch Enoch is there. Meurag is not far from Glen Trool—there—and much of it is steep and narrow. Loch Trool fills most of it." He shook his head. "I am sorry, My Lord. I don't know any way to make finding him easy except to take a force and look for him."

"Mmmm… If he has lookouts at… Meurag you called it?" Pembroke continued when Thomas nodded. "If he has lookouts there, then he would need to be near them to receive messages, to know our movements."

"I suppose. There are five hills in that range, like fingers of a hand with valleys twisting and turning between them. But they are bare of trees, have little cover. Loch Trool is another matter." Truthfully, nothing he'd told Pembroke was any secret. He could have learned it from any other local. Perhaps it was only a test, but Thomas could not bring himself to regret, whatever his oath to King Edward, that his knowledge was unlikely to be his uncle's final downfall.

"However hard they are to search, the King is quickly running out of patience," the Earl of Lincoln said. "I recall Andrew de Moray used hiding in the mountain fastness and moorlands as a strategy, the same as Wallace used Ettrick Forest as a haven. They withdrew into them when in danger of attack. The mountains are vast, and even a large force can lose itself."

"I may have been mistaken to concentrate my search near Turnberry Castle. Since that was where he was only a few days ago, I thought to find him still lurking, looking for the chance of another attack."

Lincoln puffed a soft snort through his nose. "You underestimate him. Calling him King Hob does not change that he is no tyro at this business. He knew both Moray and Wallace well and is using their methods."

"These hills… Awful Hand? And the glen sounds worth searching. If Meurag is a good place to use as a lookout, we should do so." Pembroke nodded briskly. "Lincoln, I shall borrow this young knight of yours. Since he knows the country, he may prove himself of value. We will march for Bothwell, but on our way, I shall send a goodly patrol to search that area and him with it. Tomorrow is Sunday. We shall remain for the holy observance and leave as soon as we prepare our forces."

Thomas picked up the cup that represented Henry de Percy and filled it to the brim. He drank almost half, strong and red. When it was empty, he filled it again.

* * *

A CLANGING CRASH made Thomas sit straight up. His head clanged like a blacksmith's anvil. "What the devil was that?" he said softly. Shouting felt like a terrible idea.

"What was what?" asked one of the knights. He put his mail chausses on the table with a loud clatter.

Thomas squinted at him. Hugh. Hugh something… What was the rest of his name? Using his hand to prop himself against the wall, he gained his feet. The blacksmith continued pounding in his head with rhythmic thuds.

Hugh pointed at a pitcher. "There's ale. A good drink of that may bring you back to life. I've seen livelier looking bodies dead on the battlefield."

The great hall where they'd slept on hay-filled pallets had thankfully emptied. Most of the trestle tables had been taken apart to make room. Hugh's noise from oiling his mail added to the thudding in Thomas's skull. Another knight across the hall began honing his sword with a head jarring *swish swish*.

"Where is everyone?"

"Most are out tending to tack and in the practice yard. I am about to go to the chapel." Hugh snorted. "Pembroke is still talking with the steward and marshal to arrange enough supplies and sumpter horses to carry them, so we don't have to depend solely on foraging for food. And I would wager that he is not pleased with the delay."

Pembroke stalked into the hall and slammed the door to the upper floor behind him. "Why are you lying about? If you do not have work, I shall find you some."

Tempted though Thomas was to hold his head, he thought better of it. "I must clean my armor, My Lord. I was about to start."

A guard opened the main door of the keep and hauled in a filthy, grizzled man with a face like a dried apple. "Where is the earl?" Then he bowed to Pembroke. "My Lord, this man claims he is a man-at-arms at Douglas Castle and says he has important news for you." The guard's mouth twisted into a sneer. "Will you hear him, or should I toss him out."

"Under the dirt, that is a good brigandine, My Lord," Thomas said.

Pembroke's face was sour, but he gave a curt nod. "Spit it out, man. What are you doing here?"

"My name is Iain of Alway. As I told the guard, I serve... served at Douglas Castle. They attacked us yester-day. I had been patrolling our perimeter and returned in time to attend the mass. So I tied my horse behind the church and went in with the rest. As soon as we were inside, they attacked. All screaming, "A Douglas! A Douglas!" He pushed back his hair to show a gash across his forehead and into his hair. "I was knocked out and bled like a stuck pig. Good fortune for me that they thought I was dead."

"And that they did not make sure of it." Pembroke crossed his arms and scowled at his feet. "Are you telling me that they slew the entire garrison?"

"I came to myself as they dragged some prisoners bound by hand and foot back to the castle. The whole garrison was in the church, so no one was in the castle to defend it." The man staggered and rubbed his head as though he was pained.

"Sit, sit," Pembroke said,

"Thank you, My Lord." The man-at-arms collapsed onto the bench. "My horse was behind the church. I knew they'd be back, so I managed to climb on. I got away into the woods." He propped his forehead on his hands, elbows on his knees. "Once there, I had to stop, I was that sick and weak from the blow, and after a time, there was a cloud of black smoke in a thick column. From the castle."

"Wait. You say they shouted 'Douglas'?" Thomas asked.

"Yes."

Thomas blew out a breath. "James of Douglas. He was with the Bruce at the coronation. Swore fealty to him. And he fought at Methven."

"What about King Hob?" Pembroke asked. "Did you see him?"

The man lifted his head and shook it no. "Most of the attackers I knew by sight. They were local men. There was the one knight, young and slender with black hair. Not at all what I have heard the Bruce looks like." He shrugged. "If I saw all of them, I cannot say. I rode all the day and night. Had to rest a few times, I was so dazed but managed to stay on my horse to reach here."

Thomas curled his lip. A sneak attack in a church. "That was James Douglas of a certainty. There is no mistaking the description."

"God damn!" Pembroke slammed his fist into his palm. He paced furiously back and forth several times. Finally, he stopped, legs spread. "Go to the kitchen for food. Go."

"Had it been the Bruce, there would have been more than local men," Thomas said. "It must have been Douglas on his own, raising men in his own country."

Pembroke pushed his hand through his hair. "But we will have to go to Douglas Castle to see if any survive. And to be sure this Douglas is no longer there. Then we will search these hills you spoke of."

If Douglas fired the castle, he would no longer be there, Thomas mused. But he was not going to argue with the earl. Instead, he went looking for a cloth and oil to clean his mail. It never took long in the damp Scottish winter for rust to start. It was well to care for your armor.

* * *

THOMAS WOULD BE glad to put Lochmaben behind him. He had no taste for the memories of Marjorie laughing and family now enemies. He sat amongst a dozen knights and as many squires next to the stables when Pembroke and Lincoln joined them. Hugh of Newent carried Pembroke's banner.

Thomas's palfrey was the sturdy bay palfrey given to him by Lord Gordon, no courser but well trained enough for battle. He had given up on growing fond of his horses; he had seen too many die or lost to him in the last year. He had no squire but did his own duties, familiar as coming home. He did not bother to mind. His cloak and surcoat were plain, with no embroidery of his standard. Would there ever be time for such niceties?

Thomas rode behind the earl, looking like the poor relation at a feast in his makeshift mail next to the earl's gilt plate armor. A castle hound followed them out until the kennel master called it back. The greater part of the earl's army awaited them beyond the castle walls, not a great host. Fifteen hundred mounted men-at-arms were already formed into columns along with the baggage train of food and supplies. In a sharp late winter wind, the banners of England, Pembroke, and Lincoln cracked and snapped above their heads.

This near to Lochmaben, the way was as safe as any in Scotland, but Pembroke still sent out scouts. Pembroke grunted. "I took him unawares at Methven. He owes me for that, but he will never catch me so."

The earl had given strict commands that no one was to wander from the column to forage or loot. Since word of a slaughter at Douglas Castle had spread like fleas on a dog, no one was eager to be caught riding alone by the savage Douglas.

Riding in the small army behind the two earls, Thomas felt almost happy. The sun was bright in spite of the chill, there were the first scents of coming spring in the air, he had a good horse between his legs, and he was home in Scotland once more. If there were other things he would have wished for, this day and this hour, it would do.

As the sun was halfway down the afternoon sky, they crossed Douglas Water. In the distance were the thatched roofs of Douglas town, and above them at the top of a steep slope rose the smoke-stained remains of Castle Douglas. Pembroke and Lincoln ordered their squires to set up their pavilions, and Pembroke summoned his serjeants. Soon a hundred tents sprang up like mushrooms along the bank of the river. He ordered the sentries doubled.

Thomas unsaddled his horse and tethered it in the horse line. Then he turned and hiked up the hill. He wrinkled his nose at the acrid smell but trudged through the opening where burnt boards were all that remained of the gate. He breathed through his mouth though that filled it with the bitter taste of ashes. The wind whistled through merlons in the curtain wall but did nothing to lessen the reek.

Strange. Where were the bodies?

All the wooden buildings were piles of charred rubble, stable, kitchen, armory. The ceiling of the keep had fallen in, the walls blackened but still whole. The well near the kitchen was intact, so Thomas walked to it, then a putrid reek hit him in the face like a blow. He bent to see over the edge. Jumbled shapes were piled in its depth. He gagged and whirled, stomach heaving.

He squatted, pressing his palm to his mouth.

"What did you find?" Pembroke said from the ruined gate, his nostrils flared, and eyes scrunched.

"They fouled the well—" He backed away from the opening and spat, trying to get the bitter taste from his mouth. "—with the bodies of horses and men."

"Mmmm…" Pembroke put his hands on his hips and looked all around what was left of the yard and the keep. "They cannot have thrown all the bodies into the well. At least thirty men were holding this place."

Thomas heaved a sigh as he stood and turned to the keep. Like many keeps, the door was on the second floor, and the wooden stairs to it were partly charred. The level above that appeared an empty hulk. "They must be in there."

"I shall have to send a messenger to Lord Clifford. This keep is his as were the men. I believe the King gifted him with it when the first Lord of Douglas died in the Tower of London."

Thomas nodded his understanding. They had neither the time nor the resources to deal with what was not even Pembroke's responsibility. "I'll look inside. Someone might still live."

"Those stairs would collapse under you, and no one could have survived such a fire."

"I think I can make it up them if I'm careful." He carefully picked out spots that had not burnt all the way through and grabbed the stone opening when he was close enough. The door was nothing but shards and blackened iron. He peered down past where the wooden floor had collapsed. He froze. In the undercroft, a pile of burnt boards, cinders, ash, and charred bones were all that was left of the inside of the castle. He backed his way down to the ground as fast as he could.

Thomas shook his head at the earl.

"Let's leave this stench." Pembroke turned and started down the slope to the camp. "A black deed."

Thomas followed. "Yet James Douglas is a young man, younger than I." He gritted his teeth. "The Black Douglas, I suppose we should call him. With his black deeds matching his black hair."

At the camp, the earl walked the perimeter of the camp, checking the sentries. A hundred cookfires gleamed in the lengthening shadows. Men crowded around them, sending uneasy looks up at the ruined castle.

Thomas went to sit by a fire near the earl's tent. A hare sizzled above the flames. The smell so like that at the castle it made Thomas curl his nostrils, but he still did not turn down a slice that Hugh offered on the tip of his knife.

The usually jocular Geoffrey of Abingdon thrust his chin toward the castle. "So... they're all dead."

He chewed and swallowed the stringy meat, sighed, and told them what he had found. "The Baron of Clifford will have to deal with that."

Hugh crossed himself. "*Requiem æternam dona eis, Domine.*"

Geoffrey made a disgusted sound. "Threw the bodies

down the well? Burnt the rest? Damn them. But we'll find King Hob and put an end to it."

Thomas clenched his fists in his lap and ground his teeth. How could any knight have committed an act so foul? He pulled his cloak tight around his body, loosened his dirk in its sheath, and stretched out in the dried grass. Against the black sky, the stars were like the whirls of a snowstorm, but Thomas began to count them.

"Not sleeping in the tent?" Hugh asked.

"No. It's cold but I want to be outside."

* * *

A BLUSTERY DAY FOLLOWED, but wind and rain made no difference. Their columns kept pace west until at the Dalwhat Waters. Pembroke called Thomas and one of his knight bannerets, Sir Walter of Colchester, to him. He thrust his chin toward Thomas. "He knows the land you'll be scouting, so take advantage of that. If you can catch King Hob, you'll be well rewarded."

A day later, they forded the Water of Minnoch into grass-covered slopes. Their horses sloshed and splashed in the narrow, waterlogged valley floors. An occasional cow plunged away at their approach. Scrubby, undergrown hawthorns and willows dotted the slopes.

Thomas pointed eastward. "Loch Enoch is only a little way. There should be moor grass and heather for the horses, good water. If I may…" He hesitated to give the knight advice.

"If you may what?" asked Sir Walter.

"A suggestion. Our main body could camp there, and we're large enough to be safe from a surprise attack. It's well placed to send out scouting parties to search the valleys."

"Size does not always protect from a surprise attack."
Sir Walter had a mean tight-lipped mouth, jabbing forefinger, and cold stare down the nose. "But you were sent to advise on the country, so I expect you to do so."

"As you say, Sir Walter. I have much to learn."

Sir Walter's mouth curved in a sneer, but he turned the column in the direction Thomas had pointed. They splashed along the pewter waters of Loch Enoch with the Earl of Pembroke's blue, white, and red banner and Sir Walter's green pennant streaming in the wind. The moor grass and heather had already started to put out green shoots surrounding the sandy beach on the shore. A few twisted oaks grew on the rise. To the east rose Corserine, Dungeon Hill, and Craignaw. To the west loomed Meurag, the highest in the region, and the four other hills that made up the Range of the Awful Hand.

On a low rise above the loch, Sir Walter pulled up and called his serjeants to him. He pointed. "Horse lines there. Baggage there. Have a latrine trench dug there. Sir Hugh, you see to the sentries." He dismounted and motioned to his squire. "Raise my pavilion at the highest place and plant the banners."

An *aahng-ung-ung* like the baying of hounds filled the air from a flock of mottled greylag geese as they flew in to land in the loch.

Geoffrey of Abingdon who had dismounted next to Thomas nudged him with his elbow. "If we can scrounge up some bows, those would make a good change from our supplies."

"They would," Thomas agreed, "if Sir Walter gives us enough time to do any shooting. Those are big, fat geese. They're returning early this year, lucky for us. They make good eating." He'd brought down more than one of the large birds, and his mouth watered at the thought of their skin crisping over a fire. But first, he trudged to set up his own tent. In fours and fives, the men were building small fires beside the tents. When he turned, their commander was standing in front of his tent, scowling.

"We need more wood for fires. Those few trees will barely do for one night." He looked at Thomas. "Take three men and five sumpter horses. We passed enough trees in that last valley to last for a day or two. Later we may have to go all the way to the forest, but for now, that will suffice."

Thomas sketched a bow and had one of the serjeants take axes from the stores and assign three men who grumbled the whole time that they were fighters, not woodcutters. Thomas barked at them that if they had a complaint, they could take it up with Sir Walter — after they chopped the wood. As the men chopped, Thomas wondered at the knight sending him on such a task, one that, if he wanted, allowed him to try to flee and find the Bruce. He clenched and unclenched his hand. His uncle had abandoned him and all the others at Methven. To follow the man who had allowed the savagery at Castle Douglas. No, he would not betray Lord Gordon's or even Pembroke's trust. He could not risk so many who depended upon his oath. He growled and grabbed a wood ax and hacked it into the trunk of a scrubby tree. Again and again and then chopped it into pieces until sweat ran down his face and his body.

One of the men-at-arms snorted and said, "There's a sight I never expected to see. A knight turning his hand to chopping wood."

Thomas plopped down on the stump and wiped the sweat from his face. With a bitter twist to his mouth, he said, "Well, do not expect to see it again. I shall stick to my sword from now on." He poked at a blister he'd raised on his palm. Losing control of himself did no good. "But at least we'll have wood for cook fires and that wind will be cold after dark."

They loaded the sumpter horses high with faggots and rode for camp as the western sky empurpled with the setting sun. When they rode past sentries into camp, dusk had settled. Thomas tied his mount at the horse line and unsaddled it while the men took the wood to unload. He passed a dozen cookfires as he walked toward Sir Walter's tent to report the errand done. Catching the smell of roasting goose made his empty stomach growl. In the distance, a voice raised in a tavern song. On the shore, two men-at-arms were practicing hacking and blocking with their swords.

Geoffrey of Abingdon chuckled as he passed the embers of a cookfire. Hugh waved the leg of a roast goose at him and said, "About time you returned. Have a seat. We have one of those geese roasted nice and juicy."

Thomas smiled. "So I see." The fat bird was on a stone by the cookfire, juices pooling around it. "I'll gladly take a piece, but I had best report to Sir Walter first. Save me at least a bite, will you? My stomach is as empty as your head."

Geoffrey picked up a stone and threw it at him. He dodged and hurried to stick his head through the opening of the pavilion. "Sir?"

The knight motioned Thomas in and to a camp stool. A brazier filled with glowing coals filled the tent with a cozy heat. "James, refill my cup." The squire, a skinny youth, served the wine in a pewter cup. "Now, I need to know more about those hills we are searching."

Thomas shrugged. "There is not a great deal to tell. Meurag has the best sight of the land as I explained to Lord Pembroke. There is nothing for it to but to check them. There seems little risk of being ambushed. Now further along Glen Trool toward Loch Trool, that is another matter."

Sir Walter sipped his wine, looking down his nose at Thomas. "How so? It is wooded?"

"The loch takes up most of the glen. The glen is narrow, very narrow in some places. There is a steep slope on one side, part of the way there is a precipice on the other. It is different from the hills."

The knight tapped his forefinger on the small trestle table, his gaze distant as though looking at the hills through the canvas and darkness. He nodded. "Then that will be all."

Thomas hurried out, hoping there was still at least some of the goose left. It had been a large bird, and he found enough meat left to fill his empty belly. He ate every bite and sucked the marrow for good measure.

* * *

ALONG WITH THE OTHER KNIGHTS, Thomas stood waiting for Sir Walter to emerge from his tent. It was a golden day, crisp and clear, the first scent of early spring in the air.

The earl stepped out and quickly gave his orders. He chose two knights to remain with the camp. The others he divided into twos with a score of men-at-arms, Thomas and Hugh were assigned to go up Meurag and take the ridge to the next hill. There were six parties each to go to the top of one of the hills to scout for signs of the Bruce's small force.

"All of you check everything as far as you can see. King Hob is said to have perhaps three hundred men with him when he attacked the scout camp. In this wilderness, they should be easy to spot. If any of you see any sign of an armed camp or movement of men, you hie back as fast as your mounts will carry you. Now go."

Thomas and Hugh mounted and gathered their party. Thomas led the way at a steady walk toward Meurag. Soon the way began to slope up until it was a sharp, bracken-covered rise scattered with broken rock. As they went higher, horses' hooves scraped and scrunched in the scree.

"You really think this will work?" Hugh asked.

Thomas shrugged. "I suppose it's this or wait to see where he makes a sneak attack next." Overhead a pere-grine soared, seeking its prey beneath the climbing sun. "Keep alert!" he called back to the men-at-arms that trailed behind them. The wind whistled as it whipped their cloaks.

The horses were sweat-covered by the time they heaved onto the summit. Thomas slid off and patted its neck. "Hard work, eh, lad?" He let the animal munch at some dry grass as the others dismounted. Shielding his eyes with his hand, he peered westward. "That is Glen Trool." He pointed to a deep green line surrounded by pines and a shimmering blue loch. "And Loch Trool." He watched for any sign of movement or a flash of reflection from armor or weapon.

"I just saw a flash of something black," one of the men-at-arms exclaimed. They waited, but it was merely a large bird blundering its way into the sky.

Crossing his arms, Thomas paced around the gently rounded summit, kicking at a stone here and there. He hunkered down over something white to pick it up. He held up a leg bone of a hare, picked clean.

Geoffrey shrugged. "A bone. Some fox's prey, probably."

Andrew snapped it in two. "Brittle. Have you ever known a fox to cook its dinner? And no tooth marks." He threw the pieces down and turned slowly in a full circle, scrutinizing every valley and crevice. "Any of you see anything that looks out of place?"

They all shook their heads.

"They've been here. I'd lay a good wager on it. And if that bone had been here long, something would have carried it off. There must have been a lookout here."

"We may as well move on. If they were here, they're not now," Hugh said.

Once more, Thomas paced around the rounded summit. The valleys around the hills had no cover, only an occasional bare tree being beaten by the wind.

"I am not sure it will impress Sir Walter that we found a bare bone," Hugh said.

Thomas laughed. "I would rather not tell him about that, but I think we must. Mayhap it is better than nothing."

"Look!" One of the men at arms shouted, pointing down toward the opening of Glen Trool.

Thomas spun. At the mouth of the glen, five horsemen were riding at a fast canter toward the loch.

"Now we have something to tell the earl," Hugh said. "Let's go."

Chapter 15

Early April 1307

They were the first of the scouting parties to ride into camp since Meurag was the closest of the hills. Unsaddling his mount would have to wait. He tied the reins and jerked his head toward Sir Walter's pavilion.

Before they reached it, the earl emerged. "Find anything?"

"Aye," Thomas said. "Five riders entering the glen."

"Five..." That gave the knight pause. He looked in the direction of the glen, thoughtfully rubbing his lips with his fingertips.

"At the summit of Meurag, we found a bone."

"A bone." One side of Sir Walter's mouth curled up. "You found a bone."

Thomas shrugged. "It was of a hare that had been cooked. It could not have possibly been there long, or it would have been carried off for the marrow. So someone had been there and recently. If not a lookout, then who?"

Sir Walter grunted but looked a little less scornful. "Anything else?"

Thomas thought that was rather a lot, but merely blew out a breath.

Hugh said, "Should we have followed the riders?"

"I said to return. That is what I expected you to do." He waved them away to pace in front of his pavilion, eyeing the way to Glen Trool.

During the afternoon, the other knights straggled two-by-two in from searching, shaking their heads at their lack of success. Rumor whispered around the camp that on the morrow, they would go after King Hob.

Thomas sat with Hugh, and Geoffrey relit the fire from the previous night. From the stores, Geoffrey fetched some dried meat, a double handful of grain, and a pot to make pottage. Once it was bubbling over the fire, they lounged on the grass, watching the flames.

"We should outnumber them and be better armed," Hugh said at last. "They have no chance."

"Mmm…" Thomas plucked a piece of dried moor grass and twirled it between his fingers. They had outnumbered the earl at Methven. It had done them no good.

"Well, of course, they have no chance."

"I saw King Hob joust once," Geoffrey said softly. "He was amazing. Defeated everyone he came against. Never saw anyone so good."

Hugh huffed. "Yes, but riding at the tilt and fighting a battle are not the same thing. I say they have no chance." He gave the bubbling pot a stir. "Almost done."

They spoke of it no more, but after everyone slept, amongst snores and sleepy mumbles, Thomas watched clouds racing across the stars and thought that his uncle did indeed have no chance. And in spite of the horror that had been committed at Castle Douglas, he prayed to the Virgin Mary that he would have no hand in his death.

* * *

THOMAS WAS PULLING his hauberk over his head when Sir Walter came out of his pavilion. His squire ran to and fro carrying orders, and then a trumpet blared. He hurriedly belted on his sword and strode along with the other knights to stand to wait for the knight banneret's orders. Behind them, the men-at-arms crowded, the muttering of speculation a low, steady rumble of hundreds of voices.

"Quiet!" Sir Walter let his gaze sweep over his men as silence settled. "If King Hob thinks I am going to lead my army through a narrow valley without scouting it first, he is wrong. But I must know where he is." He pointed to Hugh. "You will lead a patrol, but one strong enough not to be easy prey. But remember, your task is to find him, not to attack. Sir Thomas, Geoffrey, and Reginald will accompany you and a score of men-at-arms. The rest of the army will be ready to move once you report."

Thomas raised his eyebrows at Geoffrey. Hugh clapped each of them on the shoulder and gave them a shove. "If we capture King Hob, we will be well rewarded. Let us go!"

Like a beehive kicked over, the camp turned into a swarm of noise and movement. Spears were being handed out, serjeants were shouting, horses were being saddled and led from the horse lines. Sir Walter's banner hung limp in the still air. He was in the middle of the camp, calling out commands for the men-at-arms to form into a triple column.

Thomas grabbed his great helm with its pointed top where he had left it beside the fire and loped across the camp to saddle his mount. Soon they rode at a fast canter around the foot of Meureg and into the shaded depths of

Glen Trool. The track was wide enough to ride three abreast.

Muldonnoch towered dizzyingly above their heads, steep, stony, and bare. The hair on the back of Thomas's neck constantly prickled as though they were being watched. But look up and back over his shoulder as he might, there was no sign of watchers.

The path narrowed until they could only go two abreast. Their horses' hooves clattered on the stony ground. Riding beside Thomas, Geoffrey leaned to peer over the other side, down at the loch's edge, at least twenty feet below. He jerked back and turned to Thomas, his eyebrows high. A misstep would be deadly.

The track turned to the south, and Hugh called out, "Halt!" He pointed ahead.

On the west side of the loch beneath heavily wooded slopes was a camp. Campfires sent up tendrils of smoke. A banner flew over the tents, limp in the still air but yellow and red, but too far to make out the device. Thomas could see men moving about. He sucked in his breath. Did they not know after all that the English were nearby?

Hugh commanded two of the men-at-arms to return to Pembroke with all speed. Their quarry was within sight. Once the messengers had galloped away, he dismounted and walked to the edge of the precipice. Thomas joined him and shielded his eyes with his hand to try better to make out the camp. Hugh did the same, muttering under his breath.

"Can you make out how many?" Thomas asked.

"No. There are only fifty tents, but probably most of the Bruce's men have not had the chance to steal one." He pointed to the left of the camp to horse lines. "About fifty horses, which seems right. Most of their men will be afoot. It looks like their main camp true enough." They both remounted. Hugh wheeled his horse and signaled them to follow him back to meet Sir Walter with the main party.

Sir Walter met them, leading his men at the mouth of the glen. Thomas and the others squeezed past them to take a place behind him in the column.

"Is it this narrow all the way?" asked Sir Walter.

Hugh grimaced. "It worsens. But their camp is there on the far side of the lake. I couldn't count the men. Probably many were asleep or foraging, but they had fifty horses in the horse line. It is clear all through the glen, though. We saw no one."

Sir Walter snorted and ordered two men to scout ahead, one on the path and one on the flank. "Better to be safe." He raised his arm and signaled the column forward. Behind them, the double-column stretched for a quarter of a mile.

The air was still. There was no noise except the rattle of hooves on the stony ground, the clank of horse tack, and the cry of a gannet high overhead. Thomas craned his neck to stare up at the slope. He tried to shake off the feeling that they were being watched. They had seen no one.

"What are you looking at?" Geoffrey asked.

Thomas drew his brows together, his face tightening. "Nothing. But I keep feeling like there is something up there. Or maybe right behind my back."

"I have felt that way ever since we were at Castle Douglas. At this rate, the day will almost be spent before we reach their camp."

"And they are sure to see our approach."

Geoffrey shuddered and tilted his head toward the precipice. "True, but I wouldn't want to ride this in the dark."

Thomas glanced up at the sky. They were lucky it was

a beautiful spring day. Rain or worse, a spring snow, would have been as bad as riding it in the dark. Mayhap worse. They were halfway through the glen. He loosened his sword and shifted his hold on his lance.

From high on the slope and behind, there came a rumbling. Stones clattered, thudding, and smashing. Horses danced and neighed as they were rained with shards, and then a massive boulder crashed down. Panicked horses reared, riders shouting and fighting to gain control. Another boulder rolled down further back, gaining speed.

A small stone bounced off Thomas's shield. More small stones showered down, bouncing and skittering. Thomas's horse jumped to the side, snorting. Thomas patted its neck and dropped his voice, "Easy boy. Easy." Overhead, a crash made him jolt in his saddle and look up. His horse neighed. A boulder as big as a horse rolled, banging toward them. Sir Walter wheeled and it crashed into him. The horse screamed as they disappeared over the edge of the precipice. The boulder careened, smashing into two other riders.

Thomas circled his mount, heart thundering.

Hugh's horse reared, eyes rolling, as he fought for control. Another boulder smashed behind Thomas. Smaller rocks followed. He craned his neck. More stones and boulders were thundering down the steep incline. Another horse squealed in pain. Men were shouting. A fist-sized rock hit Geoffrey, denting his helm. He slumped forward, swaying in the saddle and clutching his high pommel.

Which way to go? Dear Mother of God, have mercy.

Thomas reached and grabbed Geoffrey's reins, looking desperately in every direction. The horse behind him was down, thrashing, its rider's leg trapped beneath it. In both directions, more rocks crashed around them. Behind most of the horses and riders were down, others galloping back the way they had come. An arrow thunked into the ground in front of Thomas's horse.

With most of their column behind in pandemonium and fleeing, going forward was no longer a choice.

"Geoffrey!" Thomas shouted. He gave the knight's horse a slap on the rump. It snorted and took off at a terrified gallop around the downed horses and men. "Where are our scouts?" Then he realized they must have been the first victims of the deadly rockfall.

Hugh jerked his horse under control and drew his sword. He circled his mount, looking no surer of what to do any more than Thomas. Then he bellowed, "Retire! Retire!" Behind them, the rockfall had missed only a handful. "Thomas! Go"

Another rider screamed as a boulder knocked him over the precipice, horse flailing, into the water below. A rock smashed into Thomas's left shoulder, nearly knocking him from the saddle. He groaned and gripped frantically with his legs. His horse reared, the sweat of terror flying, and he struggled to control it, hands too busy for drawing a weapon.

"Come," Hugh said, pointing. They both leaned forward and urged their horses to a fast canter, dodging the bodies that littered the narrow path. For a hundred horse-lengths, only a handful had survived though a few were crawling away from the mangled, bloody chaos. Thomas reached a hand down and boosted one kneeling, dazed man-at-arms up behind him.

Then Thomas realized that the deadly granite rain had stopped. Instead, there was a clatter of shod hooves on stone and, from behind, of shouts, "On them! On them!" Panting, he let go of the reins with one hand to grab his sword, cursing. He turned his horse to face the attackers as Hugh pulled up beside him.

Groaning, the man-at-arms slid from behind Thomas and fumbled for his sword.

"Go!" Thomas shouted.

It had been a well-laid trap. The attackers had only fifty yards to cover on fast-moving steeds, though they dared not risk their horses at a gallop down such a sharp slope. Brandishing swords and battleaxes, they shouted, "A Bruce! A Bruce!"

Hugh muttered, "Jesu God, help us." Their own forces were so decimated that they were now outnumbered and at a standstill against a well-armed charge. What was left of the column was in total disorder, terrified horses fighting, in no formation, some trying to retreat and others to rejoin Hugh and Thomas, so they were in a nearly impassable jumble.

Geoffrey and four others spurred forward around the chaos to reach them.

All around was madness, desperate fightin.

"Retire!" Hugh screamed to the men behind them. "Retire!"

Then there was no more time. The Bruce's men swept around them like a flood. Thomas's shoulder screamed every time he moved, but he looped his reins on the pummel and grasped his sword in a two-handed grip. Standing in his stirrups, he cut down his first assailant with a tremendous right-left hack, but the force made his shoulder burn. He lay about him, fending off another attacker until Hugh came to his aid.

Thomas slashed furiously as two more men-at-arms rode at him. There was only one end to this, and it would not be long coming. His horse reared and stove in one of their heads, saving him. He must act and had only seconds to do it.

"Form on me!" He wheeled and raked his horse's flanks with his spurs, plunging through a narrow opening in the surrounding Scots. "Form up! Into a wedge!"

Only a wedge gave them any chance of escape. He risked a glance to see Hugh riding tight to his right and half a length back and a man at arms to his left. He hacked one-handed as he urged his horse to a gallop. There ahead, where the press was thinnest—there was the chance to cut their way through. "Ride! Ride!" he shouted. Gathering momentum, they slashed their way, only seven of them. They plunged at a gallop past the opening of the glen.

Thomas's stomach curdled. Leading a flight from a field of battle and defeated by such means. As bitter as gall. When Geoffrey waved to him, he blew out a breath of relief and kept up his speed. Ahead in a ragtag line were the few who had fled ahead of them.

Panting, Hugh called a halt. Behind them, the enemy was forming for pursuit. "Eastward." He pointed. "It's the only way."

"No," Thomas said through his clenched jaws. "We must ride through our own camp. They'll stop to loot it." The sumpter horses and supplies would be a good prize for the Bruce's men.

"You're right." Hugh turned his horse's head in that direction and waved them forward.

Soon they caught up with the dozen or so other survivors who had been in the rear and fled first. The men-at-arms left to guard the camp were mounted and ready. They fled eastward through the barren valley.

They would lose horses if they continued at a gallop, so they slowed to a fast walk. Looking back, Thomas breathed a sigh of relief to see he was right. The attackers had lost interest in pursuing the survivors and were looting the camp.

His shoulder grumbled with pain. Most had wounds, but they dared not halt. The shame of having to recount the failure to Lincoln and Pembroke made him cringe inside.

"Two days' ride to Bothwell," Hugh muttered.

Thomas grunted. "Longer. Three days. We must stop as soon as we find a good place to camp and tend our wounded and let the horses rest. And no supplies. No food. We will have to forage." And a bitter draught to drink when they told the earl what had happened.

Chapter 16

BOTHWELL, SCOTLAND

Thomas would have gladly stopped for an ale beneath the spreading oak in front of the alehouse they passed, but the red mass of Bothwell castle loomed on a promontory ahead. He sighed. He was hungry, and his shoulder was stiffly sore, aching insistently. At least it was not broken, merely bruised. But then his entire body ached, so it all seemed a piece.

Geoffrey glanced at him and grimaced, eyes blackened from the blow to his head.

The foraging had been scanty, so there had been no reason to tarry, but it still had taken three long days to reach Bothwell. And two more men had died on the way, their bodies tied across their saddles. At least those two would have proper burials.

The rutted dirt road curved through the castle town, daub and wattle cottages that edged runrigs planted with oats and barley and some fenced to contain goats and chickens. Men and women working in the fields looked up to watch uneasily as they rode past.

At the foot of the promontory, they were met by a

patrol with the Baron of Clifford's blue and yellow checky banner fluttering over their heads. The serjeant recognized them and waved them on, so they clattered up the winding road past the tents for the soldiers, too many to be lodged within even so large a castle.

The drawbridge was lowered for them, and they rode into the vast fortress. The bailey was busy, men wielding sword and lance in the practice yard, the hammer of the smith from the smithy, the nicker of horses in the stables, boys sweeping the yard, chickens clucking near the cooking hut. The stablemaster was yelling for grooms to stable the horses.

Thomas slid stiffly from the saddle and rested his head against his horse's neck until a groom took the reins from him. He exchanged an unenthusiastic glance with Hugh, who shrugged. There were weary groans and creaking leather as the remains of their scouting party dismounted.

"Leave us have done with it." Hugh nodded toward the round keep that towered ninety feet above them.

Thomas gave a brusque nod and trudged up the stairs up to the door of the keep. As they reached it, it swung open to reveal a pudgy, round-faced man in a good woolen tunic. "Sirs." He looked flustered. "Who are you seeking?"

An upper servant of the castle, Thomas supposed. "Where is Lord Pembroke?"

"He is in his privy chamber with Lord Lincoln. Who is seeking him?"

"Tell him that Sir Hugh of Newent has returned to report," Hugh said.

Thomas followed Hugh through the entry hall into the vaulted great hall as the man hurried away. Hugh, as the eldest of the remaining knights, had taken command since Sir Walter's death, and Thomas was only relieved that he did so.

Let him have the joy of reporting to Pembroke their disastrous scouting foray. Looking at his feet and trying to find a way to stand that did not pain his shoulder, he muttered, "You may want to stand well back when you tell him this tale."

Geoffrey huffed a chuckle, but Hugh gave him a stern look. "Pembroke is not a man to lose his temper."

"If you say so."

Pembroke stroke furiously into the hall. "What the very devil? Where is Sir Walter?" Immediately behind him came Robert de Clifford, muscular, thirtyish, with uncompromising bones that gave his face a look of toughness and determination.

Hugh stepped forward. "Dead, My Lord. We were ambushed, and—" He cleared his throat. "—it was a rout."

Pembroke turned a narrow-eyed stare on Thomas. "How did you come to be ambushed?"

"It was not Sir Thomas's—"

"Leave him speak for himself."

Thomas licked his lips. Surely he could not be blamed for this debacle. "We camped, and Sir Walter sent out small search parties. We... Geoffrey and I, that is... we caught sight of riders entering Glen Trool. He had Hugh lead a scouting party through the glen." Hugh nodded, so Thomas continued. "There was no sign of the Bruce's men, but we spotted a camp past the loch. Sir Walter decided to lead us to attack it."

"Go on," prodded Pembroke.

"There is a high, steep hill on one side of the glen, Muldonnoch. When we were all strung out along the narrow path..." He raised his palms. "It was a well-laid trap. They rolled boulders down upon us. Those brought down showers of rocks with them, and our horses went mad with terror. Many plunged into the loch. And we had nowhere to go."

Hugh gulped and stepped forward. "My Lord, more than half our men were dead from the rockfall before King Hob's men attacked. I led the scouting of the glen myself. If there was any fault in that, it was mine."

Thomas made a slashing gesture. "No, Hugh was not at fault. Our orders from Sir Walter were to scout the glen, and that is what we did. We had an outrider partway up Muldonnoch, but we had no reason to scout all the way to the top. And no one ever even imagined any knight would make such an attack as the Bruce made on us. Mayhap Sir Walter should have thought of it, but it is such a steep defile and with a camp in sight..." He shrugged. "I am not sure anyone would have made another decision. I believe they must have planned it from the moment we camped to have so many boulders ready." His throat grew tight with fury, his voice rough. "There was no honor in it. It was no real battle, but an attack by savage brutes."

"It was by God's own grace that we were able to escape at all," Geoffrey said. "I would not have if not for Randolph."

Pembroke rubbed his forehead as though it ached. "I cannot fault you for following your orders." He waved a hand. "You must have food and rest." He looked around. "Chamberlain, have the kitchens bring them a meal." He turned and tilted his head toward the door. As he and Clifford walked out of the hall, he said in a grim tone, "I must prepare a message for the King."

"Since he has called for a new army to muster—" The door closed behind them.

Thomas flopped onto a bench and plunged his hands into his hair. Benches scraped and armor rattled as everyone took a place.

Geoffrey sank down beside him. "Did you hear what Clifford said?"

Servants were pouring tankards of ale, and Hugh grabbed one up. After a long drink, he said, "I expected it. It has been one disaster after another and no sign of cornering King Hob. The King was bound to call a new muster."

"We made it back alive. It could have been worse." Thomas wrapped his hands around a tankard, hoping the food would be served soon and that it was hearty. His stomach was as empty as a drum.

Hugh snorted. "That is the only thing that could have made it worse. And you know what Pembroke did not mention. What by God's nails will the King say?"

Thomas shook his head. "I am right glad not to be there when he receives the news." He took a deep drink to wash the taste of the dust and defeat from his mouth.

THE MASSIVE KEEP of Bothwell Castle cast a dense shadow across the bench where Thomas sat. He ceased running the whetstone down the blade of his sword. Through the door of the armory came clanging, hammering, and the whirr of a grinding stone. The familiar tang of oil and metal in the air comforted him as he tested the sharpness of the blade with his thumb.

"Thomas," Geoffrey called from across the bailey yard and strode towards him. "Be done with that. Let us find priesty-faced Hugh and go to the alehouse. I have a thirst."

Thomas held up his sword and squinted at it. He shrugged. It was as sharp as it could be. "Aye." A warm breeze rustled the earl's banner atop the keep. "His heat builds up a thirst, right enough." He stood and sheathed his sword. "Do you know where Hugh is?"

"At the stable, I think. He wanted to check his horse and tack."

A dozen men-at-arms crowded around the wooden stables against the curtain wall. There was a buzz of talk and the sound of a farrier shoeing a mount. Hugh waved to them when they were halfway across the bailey. "What's the to-do?" he asked when he joined them.

"Ale and no more work for the evening." Geoffrey winked.

Hugh looked across at the chapel. "I thought I might make my confession. And I do not want to ride out tomorrow with a pounding head."

Thomas sputtered a laugh. "When did you ever do anything to confess? Forbye, you don't have to drink yourself dizzy. One ale isn't going to hurt you. Come with us. Hugh and I are going to the alehouse."

Giving a put-upon sigh, Hugh agreed to join them. A guard opened the side door in the gate for them, and they tromped in the mid-summer heat out of the castle. Bothwell stood high, on a steep bank above a bend in the River Clyde. Outside the thick curtain wall that surrounded the bailey and keep were tents and a few rough huts where most of the soldiers slept. As they trudged down the twisting road, they passed fields green with barley and oats where men and women bent weeding in the summer's heat. Sweat trickled down the back of Thomas's neck.

Not yet the end of the workday, only a few were in the street, a woman scolding a protesting boy beside a wattle and daub house and a man carrying a bleating lamb. But the doors and shutters of the long, low houses stood open to catch any stray breeze. Even the air smelled hot.

The road was like rock under their feet. Around a bend

in the way, the alehouse was much like its neighbors with a peaked thatched roof except with trestle tables in the yard under a big spreading oak. Beside the alehouse a girl stirring a cauldron over a fire flashed him a grin. He grinned back. Next to her in a shed, three women were raking barley malt in a large pan that gave off a sweet, nutty smell. A soft *buk-buk-buk* came from chickens around the back.

The alehouse was a single crowded room. By the door in front of a barrel of ale on a trestle stood four men and a woman loudly discussing the day's happenings. Beyond them, at a table, two men sat eating. At the far end of the room, a peat fire burned in a brazier, and a boy stirred a cooking-pot that hung above it.

A woman's voice called, "Padraig, you have lords come a calling."

A huge man in a tavern keeper's apron turned and called out, "Have you a seat, and I'll bring your ale." He was a Highlander, ginger-haired with a mustache that drooped to his chin,

Thomas sprawled on a bench behind a table next to a window. Geoffrey and Hugh sat on stools. "I cannot imagine anyone deciding to make trouble here," Geoffrey said, tilting his head toward the impressively muscled tavern keeper.

Padraig thumped three wood tankards onto the table. "Just tapped today, and anyone who makes trouble drinks nae more of my wife's good ale."

Geoffrey hastily picked up his tankard. "And fine ale it is."

Thomas took a long drink, and it was as good as the man said; fresh with a hint of tartness like apples. "Aye, a braw brew." He leaned back against the wall and closed his eyes with a satisfied sigh.

The tavern keeper raised his eyebrows. "I heard you are leaving on the morrow. Are you going after the Black Douglas?"

Thomas cocked his head. "What makes you think that?"

"A merchant was in a while ago and said he ambushed some of Clifford's scouts out in Ettrick Forest. Surely Clifford will want to put a stop to that. After all the rest the Douglas has done."

With a wry smile, Thomas said, "The earl doesnae tell me his plans."

Geoffrey grimaced as Padraig walked away. "That damned Douglas is a thorn in our side."

"Aye," Hugh said. "When do you think Lincoln will have us return to Carlisle?"

"Who knows?" Thomas said. "But the muster is to be in the middle of July, so not for a while."

"Mayhap we will catch King Hob and all his followers, including this Black Douglas before then, especially since Clifford has joined us. If our scouts are right that he is near Galston, we could reach there in two days' riding."

Thomas grasped the tankard hard, and a bitter pang went through him. "I hope so. To fight by ambush and rolling down boulders like brute savages. There is no honor in it." He slammed the drink down. "The man who knighted me!"

"And damned little profit in it this fighting either." Hugh grimaced. "I was hoping for better looting so I could improve my lot, mayhap even buy a small manor. No chance with pickings so thin and disaster in every fight."

"We need something else to think on. Like women," Geoffrey said. "I did not come to the tavern to talk about the war."

Thomas motioned around the tavern. "But where are we to find these women?"

Geoffrey sighed and then brightened. "But I heard a good jest last night. Now listen—"

Hugh groaned and rolled his eyes.

"A young Londoner was going down to the Thames with a net to catch some fish and met a frolicsome boy who asked him what birds he was going to catch with that net of his. 'I am going to the brothel down the road to spread my net there and catch your mother.' The boy laughed and said, 'Mind you be careful where you place it. Otherwise, for you will be sure to catch your mother there too.'"

Thomas shook his head and laughed. They finished their ale and had refilled on new cups when the door opened, and a couple of women came inside. He eyed the first, pretty if a bit haggard and thin, and only about twenty. She stood out in her bright yellow kirtle that was low cut. The second strumpet was a decade older, but of a more generous build with a bosom that threatened to spill out the top of her green kirtle. Thomas grinned at Geoffrey.

Geoffrey immediately stood and pulled over two stools. He winked at the two women as he signaled to Padraig for more ale. Thomas dragged one of the seats closer to his spot on the bench and drained his tankard, ready for more.

When the generously bosomed woman sat next to him, Thomas smiled. "Let us become acquainted. They call me Thomas."

The woman's full mouth quirked. "They call me the best thing they ever had." She ran a hand up his arm. "But my name is Florie."

He patted the bench beside him. "Slide over here." He took another deep swallow of ale and put an arm around her shoulder. She cuddled against him, bosoms soft against his side. He nuzzled her ear. "Now, about that best thing…"

She gave his chest a playful shove. "My belly is empty. I am ever so much nicer to a man if he buys me some supper."

Thomas sniffed the air. A scent of mutton, beans, and onions came from the cauldron. Why not? He would have days of foraging or living off dried meat soon enough. He kicked Geoffrey under the table to get his attention from the young woman. "I think we all need some food."

Geoffrey's strumpet, who was sitting in his lap, gave a little bounce. "Aye. My stomach is growly too."

Hugh, looking on disapprovingly at their companions, shrugged.

Thomas shouted for the tavern keeper. He had the boy dip up bowls of the pottage and bring over a loaf of bread. When Thomas dug out a handful of quarter-pennies, he recalled that he needed to speak to Lord Gordon about receiving the midsummer rents from Nithsdale.

Florie took the piece of bread that Thomas cut off for her and dipped it into the pottage. "I didnae ken how hungry I was." She licked her lips.

Thomas watched fascinated by how full her mouth was and the tip of her tongue as she licked. He had an urge to kiss her right then, but she took a bite of the pottage and hummed her pleasure. Her hearty appetite made him eager to have her alone, but he made do with the mutton for now. When she wiped her bowl clean with the last bit of bread and sucked gravy off her fingers, it was as much as he could stand. Putting a hand on the side of her round cheek, he bent his face to hers. With a gasp, he pressed his mouth to hers and opened his lips when she touched them with her tongue.

It was late afternoon by the time they reached his tent

under the walls of Bothwell Castle. They ducked inside. Florie dodged Thomas's hands and reached to the hem of her kirtle. She pulled it up over her head to toss it aside. Beneath was only her soft roundness. Thomas bent to put his lips to one of her tawny nipples. Her hands were swift and sure as she found the lacing of his chausses.

Thomas awoke in the darkness, hearing the bells of the castle church tolling lauds and the mutter of men rousing from slumber. The tent was dark and muggy with the scent of sex and summer's heat. He sat up. The horns would blow assembly soon.

Florie rose to an elbow and touched his chest. The linen sheet fell away to reveal her breasts and shoulders, rosy, smooth, and wondrous. "Dinnae go yet."

A trumpet sounded a brazen blast. "I must. We will march soon."

"Fighting always comes first, does it nae?" She lay back with a hand under her head, displaying her temptations.

"Aye. Will you be in Bothwell when we return?"

Her lips twitched. "Mayhap."

He laid an extra half-penny on her belly and a kiss beside it. Next to the cot, his small kist was the only furniture. He unlocked it and jerked on his hauberk, chausses, and surcoat. As sunrise splashed gold across the horizon, he dashed to the stable, thankful he'd not drunk enough the night before to give himself a sore head. He threw on the barding, which he had finally had time to have made in his white and red colors.

Chapter 17

At the foot of the promontory was the usual chaos as three thousand knights and men-at-arms formed into a column, as it spread out more than a mile long. Half were sworn to Pembroke, the rest to Lincoln and the Baron of Clifford. Thomas wended his way to the front of the first squadron, forming up four abreast through men mounting, snorting horses, and impatient shouts of the serjeants. He took his place next to the glowering Sir John Vaux. Thomas glowered back and then shrugged. He had no quarrel with the man. Geoffrey and Hugh found spots in immediately in front of him, this squadron made up of knights and men-at-arms answering to the Pembroke and Lincoln. The second was Clifford's.

After two hours of ordered confusion, the leaders took their places at the head of the column with their banners and that of England and dozens of smaller pennants flopping in the spring breeze off the Clyde. The sun peeked through thin, wispy clouds that raced across the sky.

The outriders peeled off to scout ahead and their flanks. The serjeants rode by shouting that no one was to depart the column without the express command of the earls. The trumpets blew, and with the clop of hooves and rattle of harness and weapons, they rode past fields where men and women raised their heads to watch them leave. The priest at the village church made the sign of the cross over them. A dog ran alongside them barking. In front of the tavern, Florie and three other whores waved. She blew him a kiss. He chuckled to himself. Mayhap it was to him.

They splashed across a ford in the Clyde. With his helm off, the breeze ruffled his hair like Florie's fingers. The day grew grayer as they rode through the pine forest where masses of bluebells like thick carpets that filled the air with their sweet fresh scent. The scent did not stop the horse flies. He slapped one on his neck and scratched the bite with a sigh.

That night they made camp on some nameless braeside. As the sun went down, Thomas put up his tent as a hundred sprouted around him down to the edge of a narrow burn that ran nearby. Pembroke had set the sentries, but Thomas could not settle. He tossed in his tent and at last, rose. A sneak attack on a force this large was unlikely. He was sure his uncle did not have enough men. But his uncle had thought that at Methven. Sir John had thought that at Glen Trool. He walked through the night past campfires lit with pine branches that sent up thin ribbons of smoke and horse lines that stank of shit. At the top of the hill, he turned to look in every direction. There was nothing but a soft breeze that rustled pine branches and the banners.

He drew in a deep breath. The night air was fragrant with the scent of heather. The purple sky strewn with stars. Shaking his head, he went back to his tent.

Chapter 18

NEAR LOUDON HILL, SCOTLAND

May 10, 1307

Groggy, feeling as though he had only shut his eyes,
Thomas sat up, not sure what had awakened him. Shouts
from the sentries broke the dawn's quiet. He was on his
feet, scrambling for his sword belt before the sound ended.
His belt in his hand, he ducked out of his tent. Wisps of
fog drifted in the faint light. Two scouts were dismounting
in front of Pembroke's pavilion. The camp roused like a
beehive kicked over. Pembroke rushed out, his hair matted
from his bed and his squire behind him holding his
cuirass.

One of the scouts sketched a half bow. "My Lord, we
found them."

"Where? How far?"

"Only half a day's ride." He pointed to the south.
"There is a huge..." The man looked puzzled. "It is a hill
shaped more like a giant rock, and it towers hundreds of
feet above the moorland. They are camped there near its
foot. I managed to sneak close past their sentries in the
dark. It is King Hob. I give you my oath on it."

"Blow the assembly," Pembroke ordered and ducked back into his pavilion.

The trumpets began to call out, blaring a cry. *To horse. To horse.* As Thomas dashed back to his tent, shouts, the clatter of lances, the neigh of horses filled the camp. In his hurry, cursing his lack of a squire, he fumbled his way into his mail hauberk and coif, pixane, chausses, and gauntlets. It was as good as the armorer at Carlisle could provide for him at a day's notice but not a bit of it plate, as so many knights had begun wearing. He envied them but shook off the thought as he lowered the great helm onto his head. His dirk hung by his belt in the front and over that he belted his sword. Lastly, he picked up his shield.

When he stepped outside, men and horses hastened through the early morning chill. The heather sparkled with dew. Grooms were buckling barding on the horses; camp-fires were being kicked out. The trumpets shrilled again.

He grabbed a lance from the pile and hurried to the horse line. His gray palfrey was armored almost as heavily as Thomas. It did not have the speed of a courser but was reliable and well-trained as it had proven at Glen Trool. Once more, he gave a silent thanks to Lord Gordon for the gift. How many times had that man saved his life, he wondered? Someday, he would repay the debts though he could not imagine what repayment would be enough.

He wheeled his horse and cantered to where the columns were forming, the front under the banners of Pembroke and Lincoln. The sun peeking into the sky was a molten ball of gold that spilled across the horizon. How many would find this to be their last sunrise? Would he be one of them? His mouth was so dry that his tongue felt like leather.

Beside him, John de Vaux was grumbling angrily under his breath. Pembroke signaled, and the serjeants called to move out, the two squadrons arrayed beneath fluttering pennants. Ahead of him on a handsome charger sat a lanky knight in a surcoat with the armorial of Stewart of Bonkyl. Behind, the grooms were striking the hundreds of tents. As the sun burnt off the tendrils of fog, Pembroke and Lincoln led them off.

The column turned its path to the west, whipped by a cold wind. Purple heather grew to the horses' knees across heath dotted with gorse, and dark green bushes sprinkled with tiny white roses. The animals had fled before their coming, but overhead a hen harrier performed a sky dance on the wind.

After an hour, the top of Loudoun Hill peeked above the horizon. Once more, scouts thundered back to report. They pulled up and gesticulated wildly as Pembroke, Lincoln, and Clifford listened. A buzz of speculation swept through the front of the column and worked its way back. "They're drawn up in battle array," a knight to Thomas's left said, repeating what he had just heard from the next man down. Messengers galloped back and forth along the column. The trumpets brayed at a long and low pitch.

Sweat trickled down Thomas's face and the back of his neck. He stood in his stirrups, trying to see ahead to what they were facing, but all he could make out was the towering column-like mass of Loudoun Hill. Thomas shifted his grip on his lance, his heart thundering. *Would his uncle finally stand and fight?* The rush of his racing blood echoed in his ears.

The column inched forward once more. Orders were repeated across the squadron to spread into battle forma-tion. Thomas shook out his reins and nudged his horse into the space between Hugh and Geoffrey as John de Vaux moved to the other side. Soon they were in a line of seventy horses across, and there was only one line of horses in front of him. Behind, the rest of the squadron was forming into a broad formation, with numerous curses and demands to give way. Thomas slowed his pace for a moment to gain more room for when he had to couch his lance.

He worked spit into his mouth. It would be better once the battle began, but the waiting made every nerve twitch.

He again stood in his stirrups and caught a glimpse in the distance of banners, the royal lion rampant banner, the blue with white stars of Douglas, black and yellow of Campbell, the mail fist of Clann Domhnaill. The sun glinted off their spears. He squinted, trying to make out how many, but they were formed in a schiltrom. Impossible to tell the number, though it could not possibly be many. His eyes narrowed at a familiar acrid stink. He cast his gaze all around. Black peat water stood around clumps of bracken surrounding the narrow path to the Scottish army and beyond.

There was a shout, and they picked up their pace to a fast walk.

"Why don't we flank them?" Geoffrey demanded.

"Look at that water." Thomas tilted his head to the side. "A peat bog. You may be sure Pembroke recognizes it. Might as well try to charge through the ocean."

"Oh, well. We'll ride them down." Geoffrey snorted derisively. "Spears against mounted knights and men-at-arms have no chance."

The trumpets blared. "Charge!" Pembroke bellowed. "Charge!"

Thomas let his lance drop onto the rest and lowered his head, bringing his shield to his chest. All around was a clatter as a thousand men did the same. Their hoofbeats grew to a rumble. He spurred his horse to a full gallop.

On one side, a horse squealed as metal crashed. There

were shouts. No time to look. Thomas galloped on. On his right, a horse went down, thrashing into a bog pit. "'Ware!" he shouted. "Close up! Pits to the side!"

Geoffrey crowded him, his horse's bouncing barding bumping against Thomas. "Move over." But there was no room to move. Ahead of Thomas, a rider blundered into another. The two horses reared and plunged. One stumbled, throwing the knight. Thomas bent forward, pommel pressing into his belly and prayed his horse could jump while burdened with rider and armor. Its feet tangled, and it went down on its haunches, beside a rider who shouting curses. But it was past the tangle of fallen horsemen, and his mount scrambled and heaved itself to its feet.

Suddenly, thatch disappeared under the hooves of the horses ahead of him. The front line crashed into a trap, a deep trench. Clattering armor, smashing lances, thrashing, heaving horses formed a tempest. The screams of men and horses were deafening.

"Pull up!" Thomas shouted. "Pull up! Pull up!"

Thomas's palfrey heaved itself to a halt two feet from the ditch that had caused utter disaster, eight feet wide and at least that deep, studded with wooden spikes. He tried to wheel, but the riders behind him coming at a gallop formed an impenetrable hedge as they tried to pull up. The way back was blocked by the onrushing horses. One rider barreled into Hugh. Both knights crashed into the ditch on top of another horse that was kicking in its death agony. The bodies of horses and men piled up in the trench. Some horses and men struggling to halt their headlong rush reared to a stop but more hurtled into the death trap.

He gave a desperate look at Geoffrey and kicked his horse to go onward. The sound of his heartbeat hammered in his ears. The palfrey snorted and neighed as he forced it down on top of a dead mount. It scrambled onto another body. He threw aside his lance and used his reins to whip it, raking it with his spurs. He clenched his jaws, stomach clenching. Don't look at what is under its hooves, he told himself.

The horse used its powerful haunches to surge out on the other side. Geoffrey, beside him, shouted, "On them!"

Thomas kicked his sweating mount, its sides heaving, to a canter only to realize there was another trench covered with thatch and branches in front of them. He went cold and jerked his horse's head to turn to the side, going too fast already to wheel. Geoffrey barely missed crashing into him. "Trap!" Thomas screamed at him. "Another trap!"

An unwary knight galloped onto the thatch and disappeared inside the trap with a crash.

On the other side of the ditch, a hedge of spears gleamed catching the sun, three men deep.

Gasping for breath, Thomas slowed his mount and turned its head in every direction. What to do? Dear Jesu Lord.

John de Vaux, his courser pawing and snorting and covered to the hocks in blood, had made it over the body-crammed ditch along with a dozen or more other knights. The only way forward was across another spike-studded ditch.

Behind was chaos as some tried to force their way forward and others fought their mounts to turn to flee. Shouts of anger, fear, and dismay combined into a rumble like the crash of the ocean. From the rear came the blare of Lord Clifford's trumps and bellows of "Retire! Retire!"

He leaned his head back. Thin clouds sailing over a clear blue sky and below piles of bodies lay in the trap his uncle had laid for them. Geoffrey looked at him, showing the whites of his eyes through the slit in his helm. Thomas tried to call out to him to flee, but his throat cramped closed. He motioned to go back. Flushed with fury, he forced his mount over the bodies back the way he had come.

As they retreated, shouts, whistles, and jeers echoed over the battlefield from behind them.

* * *

PEMBROKE HAD his banner planted on a hill only an hour's ride from the battle. Armor clattering, Thomas threw himself from his mount and dashed his shield to the ground. He jerked off his helm and threw it down. All the remnants of the charge were riding in, silent and grim.

Hugh dismounted slowly, pulled off his helm, and looked at Thomas, white-faced. "Hugh…" He shook his head as he sank to crouch, forehead resting on his palm.

Pembroke stood beside a different horse than he had ridden out on, his surcoat dirt and blood-streaked. His thin face forbidding, his jaw working as though he were grinding his teeth. Lincoln stood, filthy, silently grinding his teeth, jaw muscles bulging.

Clifford strode up to Pembroke, his face stiff with anger. "Why did our scouts not find those trenches?"

Pembroke pulled his brows together as he looked grimly about the battered men.

John de Vaux stormed over to thrust his face into Clifford's. "Why did you call a retreat?" His spittle flew from his mouth in his fury. "We would have defeated them if you had come to our aid."

Clifford had an ugly twist to his mouth. "How dare you speak so to me?"

"I dare because we would have won except for your cowardice!" De Vaux's face twisted in rage, and he launched himself at the baron.

Thomas straightened, his muscles jerking tight and dropping his hand onto his hilt. Geoffrey raised his head, wide-eyed.

Clifford sidestepped and hit de Vaux in the face so hard there was a solid crunch as the bridge of the knight's nose met Clifford's mailed fist. Blood ran down De Vaux's face as he grabbed for his sword. He had it half out of the scabbard when Pembroke lunged between them.

Pembroke shoved de Vaux back with both hands. "Enough!" Tight-lipped, Pembroke scowled into de Vaux's face and then from him to Clifford. "I am governor here. And I say, enough."

Clifford spun on his heel and stalked away, back straight and stiff as a spear.

Pembroke turned his gaze once more onto de Vaux's face, but his expression eased. "Save your fighting for the enemy."

Vaux held his hand over his nose, blood dripping between his fingers. He gave a stiff nod.

Running his hand over his face, Thomas crouched down beside Geoffrey with no idea what to say. Although Hugh had been the elder, the two had been squires together, so they'd told him.

Geoffrey tried to summon one of his broad smiles. "He died as a knight with honor. He..." He swallowed. "He would have liked that. And he made his confession before we left, not that he ever did anything to confess. The silly priesty-face." He blinked hard.

"Aye." Thomas blew out a long breath. "We could pay to have prayers said for his soul."

Geoffrey nodded. "He would have liked that too. The daft..." He coughed and shook his head.

The grooms were riding up with the sumpter horses.

Pembroke summoned his scouts and walked some

distance away to where he could give orders without being overheard. Clifford had joined him.

Nothing would help Geoffrey's grief, so for something to say, Thomas tilted his head toward their leaders. "What do you think they will do?"

"I do not know." His voice was hoarse. "Are we in any condition for another battle?"

Thomas gave a weary sigh, not sure that a dozen nights' sleep would restore him. "We still outnumber them. But no, I do not think we are ready for another fight, if you could call that a fight." He hammered his fist against his thigh. "How do you fight against traps and low trickery? They are fighting like nothing more than brigands and scoundrels."

A few minutes later, a dozen scouts and several messengers galloped away, and the trumpeters, acting as heralds, went through the camp calling out to make camp.

The next morning trumpets blew assembly, and they turned east. Rumor spread that the Bruce had somehow disappeared and that Pembroke planned to join forces with the Earl of Gloucester and his strong force of infantry near Ayr Castle. Messengers the next day brought word that in a sneak attack during the night, his uncle defeated Gloucester and driven him to retreat to the safety of the castle. Thomas's stomped to the edge of the camp and glared across the moorland. Over and over, he replayed the battle in his mind, trying to understand how it could have gone so wrong.

All the way back to Bothwell, Thomas focused on how to defeat his uncle's traps. Geoffrey had no japes to lighten his dark mood, so they rode in silence. At least he found Florie still in Bothwell. When she called him her brave knight and welcomed him with murmurs of pleasure at night in his tent, he almost believed her and even found he could smile.

He would have liked to have been in the room when Bishop Langton arrived to meet with Pembroke. If he brought money for the campaign, Thomas suspected he also brought commands from the king to find Robert de Bruce forthwith. For the next week, he was busy with Pembroke's orders to the army to see that they repaired their armor and weapons.

When Philip de Mowbray galloped with the tattered remains of his force, ambushed by the Black Douglas, cursing, Pembroke dashed a cup of wine against the wall. Then he ordered the patrols redoubled. So Thomas spent much of his time in the next weeks leading scouting parties on the lookout for signs of either the Bruce or the Douglas.

Chapter 19

Two weeks after the defeat at the Battle of Loudon Hill, Thomas, the banner of the Earl of Lincoln fluttering on his lance, led ten men-at-arms in a scouting party, Geoffrey riding alongside him carrying the banner of Saint George on his lance.

"Look." Geoffrey pointed.

Thomas halted his mount and shaded his eyes to peer across the low hills toward the fringe of Paisley Forest. A flock of birds had taken off in a mass from the thinly-spaced pines. "Something disturbed them."

He urged his horse forward with seat and heels and motioned for them to follow. As he trotted forward over the crest of the brae, ten horsemen appeared at the base riding in the opposite direction. Light reflected on the leader's armor.

"There they are," Thomas shouted.

A knight was indeed leading a small group of mounted men-at-arms in leather brigandines. And above them fluttered a pennant with a blue chief above a white field.

"That's the Black Douglas!" Thomas spurred his horse

and hammered down the slope, lowering his lance as he went.

Douglas shouted, "Ride!" but riding downhill and already at a gallop, Thomas was gaining fast. He glanced over his shoulder, drew his sword, and wheeled his horse about. As Thomas hurtled towards him, he slowed to a trot.

Thomas glared into Douglas's unhelmeted face, and then like that day in Scone so many months before, he fixed his eyes on the shield with its device of three white stars on the blue chief. There. He must hit it there. Just below the center star.

At the last second with inches between, Douglas turned his shield at an angle, so Thomas's lance made a tearing whack, splinter flying, sliding along it instead of with Thomas's full force. Douglas rose in his stirrups and swung as Thomas hurtled past.

Once past, Thomas used his legs, heels, and reins to circle. He accelerated back towards Douglas who wheeled his horse. Thomas's lance hit his shield square on before he could maneuver. The impact threw Douglas back over the cantle of his saddle as his horse cantered away. Thomas let out a yell of triumph. He tossed aside his lance. He would meet the Black Douglas on even terms and prove who was the better man.

Douglas hit the ground, cursing. He surged to his feet, grabbing his sword where he had dropped it.

Clashing metal behind him told Thomas that the others were fighting, but he had no time to even glance as he cantered towards his opponent.

"Jamie!" someone shouted.

As he neared the Douglas, he received a blow like a battering ram in the middle of his back. Totally caught off-guard, it made him lose a stirrup and threw him forward half-way out of his saddle. To try to save himself, he let go of his sword and grabbed his pommel. The horse dragged him a bouncing, painful step. He released his hold on the pommel and fell flat on his stomach in a haze, stars exploding before his eyes. A horse galloped past, missing his head by inches.

An approaching voice shouted. There were thundering hoofbeats.

Thomas's stomach roiled. He lay in the heather, looking at a purple clump of flowers. He lifted his head off the ground. Gingerly, he tried moving. His stomach roiled. He moved his arms and legs. Rolled over with a sigh of relief that everything still worked.

Geoffrey knelt beside him and gave him a hand, and Thomas winced his way onto his feet. "I thought you were dead for sure. I…" His face went vacant for a moment, but then he shook his head. "That was a brute of a blow."

"Not quite dead." He wrapped his arms around his body as though hugging would lessen the pain in his back. But it would pass. It always did.

"I killed the man who hit you in the back. He was using a cudgel of all things. But the Douglas had already re-mounted, and they galloped off."

"Thanks. Where are the men?"

"Our men took off after them into the forest. I wager they will split up and slip away."

"God damn that hurts." He put his hand on the bruise where he'd been hit. "But not as much as losing the Black Douglas." His well-trained mount walked back to him, and he grasped the pommel for support. "How many dead?"

"Two and one wounded besides you. We killed three of them before they ran."

He stayed still, grateful he was only sore. Their men clattered up. Thomas ordered them to make camp for the night. Slowly, he limped to the injured man and squatted beside him, asking how he fared.

"Nasty slash on his leg." His face was pale and sweaty. "Wrapped it up, but the blood is..."

Thomas could see that blood was already seeping through. He patted the man's shoulder. "Stay still and rest."

Night had closed in, so Thomas consulted with Geoffrey about moving the men. The Black Douglas might return with more men since he knew where they were. But the injured man who might bleed out if they moved. Thomas put out sentries and commanded they make camp.

Once the campfire was built and horses tethered, Thomas dozed off, head resting on his knees. When he awoke, the campfire sent up sparks in the dark. Some of the men snorted and snored in their sleep, but stars silhouetted the dark shape of the sentries.

Geoffrey came and sat beside him. "At least we gave as good as we were given this time."

Thomas nodded. Considering the disaster of Loudoun Hill, Pembroke could hardly reproach them. The sick feeling in his stomach had passed. When he twisted back and forth, the muscles shouted in protest. But it was nothing worse than bruises he'd had many times. He thought about mounting and riding in the morning and groaned.

Late in June, it was a relief when Pembroke finally announced that they would march the next day for Carlisle. That last day, Thomas and Geoffrey walked down the twisting road to Bothwell town toward the alehouse, and Thomas hummed a tune. There was still one night to enjoy Florie's company, but something else made Thomas smile. "With the entire army of England..." He waved his hand as though it stretched out before him. "It will be enough to put an end to the perfidy. No tricks or traps will suffice."

Geoffrey nodded. He'd had no japes to tell since the battle at Loudoun Hill, but now he laughed if a bit, grimly. "I look forward to collecting a debt from King Hob."

* * *

WHEN THOMAS, along with a dozen of the Earl of Lincoln's retinue, followed the earl into the hall in the royal residence of Carlisle Castle, the chamber was full of a low murmur of talk. At one end of the great apartment were long tables covered with fine white linen, groaning with platters piled with food: stuffed piglet, enormous savory pies, stewed pigeon, onion salad, and bowls of apple moyle, and sweetmeats. Busy pages and squires were serving a well-dressed company of men and a few women.

At the head of the room, King Edward sat in a throne-like chair by Bishop Langton and Humphrey de Bohun, Earl of Hereford and Guy de Beauchamp, Earl of Warwick. Thomas raised an eyebrow at how pale the King had grown, his cheeks sunken.

In spite of a trio of minstrels playing in the gallery, the company, taking its cue from the King, was in solemn spirits. Considering, Thomas had to admire the earl's equanimity as he walked heavily to the edge of the dais and bowed.

Thomas glanced at Geoffrey and strolled casually to the top of the long table and took a cup of wine from a page. He picked up a sweetmeat and edged a little closer to the dais as the King shook a finger, baring his teeth and glaring. The earl climbed the steps to the dais and spoke quietly to him.

Try as he might, Thomas could not make out what was being said. Thomas sipped his wine and wondered if he could slip a little nearer, but when de Bohun, his heavy, dark brows drawn into a scowl, looked his way, Thomas turned away.

Instead, he went looking for something to eat. After days in the saddle, the piece of bread and cheese he had eaten before changing his clothes to attend the king's gathering had left his stomach empty and growling. He bypassed the piglet with a shudder. They were too associated with Satan for his taste and instead settled for a large chunk of mutton pie seasoned with onions, pepper, and rosemary. The savory scent made his mouth water.

Geoffrey, a slice of pigeon on his knife, said, "At least the food is good even if everyone looks as though they just bit into a sour apple." He lowered his voice to a whisper. "Do you think the King looks... well?"

Thomas shook his head.

The door opened, and Pembroke entered, followed by a dozen or so knights of his retinue in tunics of every color of the rainbow. He paused until the King returned his gaze before he went to make a deep bow.

King Edward's face contorted, and his nostrils flared. He repeatedly jabbed a forefinger finger at Pembroke, his pale cheeks flushing with color. Pembroke spread his hands as though explaining himself, shaking his head. The King grasped the arms of his chair and pushed himself to his feet. His voice was strong as ever, however ill he might appear, when he shouted, "Useless the lot of you! Afraid to lose a few men in order to do your duty!" He was swaying. Bishop Langton reached out a hand to him, but the King brushed it furiously away. "You... you force me to defeat the traitor myself. And I shall!"

The king's legs gave way, but before he could collapse

to the floor, de Bohun grabbed him under one arm. Warwick wrapped an arm around him from the other side. The two of them supported Edward, who was murmuring something and shaking his head. But his feet dragged the floor as they bore him through a door at the rear of the dais.

Thomas ran his fingers over his lips as he gazed around. Everyone stared silently after the departed king. Geoffrey was wide-eyed. Pembroke crossed his arms, his face pensive. Lincoln looked grim. The bishop scurried after the others out the door. After a moment, Thomas swirled his wine in his cup.

What sort of King would the prince make? A young and vigorous king might be a good thing.

BY MIDMORNING UNDER THE JUNE, sweat trickled down Thomas's neck and plastered his hair to his forehead. He had at least half-believed the rumors that the King was dead of a bloody flux, but now before the gates of Carlisle, they awaited his appearance to lead the levies toward Solway to cross into Scotland. Or so they were told. After an hour of waiting, the air stank of shit and horseflies buzzed around them in torturous swarms. He waved the swarm away from his face. He was lucky to be in the Earl of Lincoln's following, which at least was at the front of the army, which stretched for miles. At the tail end of the force, the stink of horse shit and the flies would be a hundred times worse.

Hundreds of banners hung lank in the still summer air above the shimmering armor of thousands of knights, more thousands of mounted men-at-arms, and countless infantry bristling with spears, Welsh archers by the thousand, and wagons piled with provisions out of sight at the rear. This was an army large enough to crush the rebellion and put an end to the fighting—if it ever moved.

Next to him, an older knight in his thirties wearing a surcoat with the blue and white checky of the Stewarts grumbled, "At this rate, we should reach Scotland by... never."

Thomas snorted a chuckle through his nose. "Sooner than that, I hope."

The man tilted his head to look Thomas up and down. "I've heard of you. Thomas Randolph, aye? I am Alexander Stewart of Bonkyl."

Thomas gave the fellow Scot, a thirtyish looking man with sparse sandy hair, a half bow from the saddle.

From behind them, Geoffrey said, "Very little sooner, but we shall be too old to do our wives any good if ever we have them." He clicked his tongue. "Pay me no heed, how can we find wives when we spend the next twenty years waiting to start for Scotland."

Thomas and Alexander snorted with laughter. But then, a flurry of activity erupted near the gates of Carlisle. Geoffrey said, "Huzzah. At last."

Thomas stood in his stirrups and twisted. He craned to see if it was at last King Edward. In a few minutes, steel armor engraved with gold flashed in the sun. King Edward rode through the army astride a ponderous black destrier, followed by the earls. A sparkling gemmed gold circlet banded his gray head.

Thomas twisted his reins around his fingers. The shimmering armor did not hide how cadaverous the King appeared, his cheeks and eyes sunken, his skin ashen. For a moment, the King paused and bent forward in the saddle. He straightened, and proceeding at a steady pace, reached the head of the arm. Trumpet calls resounded. Sighing with relief, Thomas shook out his reins and urged his horse to a walk.

They inched away from Carlisle, dust gusting up at each hoof fall. He looped his reins around his pommel and uncorked his flask, took a mouthful of wine, and swished it around before he swallowed to wash the dust and then offered it to Stewart.

Stewart took a swig and handed it back. He nodded toward the King through the two rows of knights ahead of them. "At least the rumors were wrong."

"Mmmm…" He wasn't going to mention that he doubted the rumors would be wrong for much longer. But perhaps the King only looked ill and was recovering. A man so ancient would not regain his strength quickly. After all, King Edward neared his sixty-ninth year, unimaginable to be so old.

They rode past sheep being sheared; women bent weeding the fields. Men with scythes harvested the hay. Wayns moved off the road to let them pass.

The sun was beginning its downward path in the afternoon when there was a cry of alarm that sounded like Pembroke, then shouts.

"Can you see what's the to-do?" Stewart asked.

Thomas leaned to the side, trying to see past those in front of him. The king's destrier no longer had a rider.

"Halt!" Lincoln shouted. "Halt!"

Since they were barely moving at a walk, Thomas pulled up at once. Serjeants echoed the command time after time down the long column.

"We cannot have gone more than a couple of miles." Stewart grimaced. "This does nae bode well."

A few minutes later, they were given the command to camp for the night.

Chapter 20

BURGH BY SANDS, ENGLAND

June 7, 1307

The land stretched out flat, and half an hour's ride away lay a wretched hamlet of a dozen thatch-roofed cottages and a tall square stone church tower. Beyond it, Thomas could make out the blue of the Solway Firth and the broad reach its white sands. Across the firth lay Scotland.

Surrounded by a dozen guards and leading the way, a canopied litter curtained in red and gold hung between a pair of bay rouncies. The swaying vehicle crept along, two monks riding jennets close beside it. The Earl of Lincoln was riding behind the litter along with Pembroke, Bishop Langton, Humphrey de Bohun in particularly ornate armor, and Guy de Beauchamp, followed by the miles-long column of men.

One of the monks tilted his head as though listening and then leaned toward the litter. He pushed back the curtain and stuck his head in. Pulling back, he turned in his saddle and called out, "We must stop!" He dropped his reins and sat wringing his hands.

He trotted up to the monk, stuck his head into the litter, pulled it out, and pointed ahead to the hamlet. The monk shook his head, but Lincoln cut him off with a slash of his hand.

Thomas chewed his lip as Lincoln rode to the other earls, and they conferred. "This is not good at all. Not at all. How long can it go on like this?" He watched the plodding pace of the litter and its guards. "They are taking him to the church."

As the litter proceeded, Pembroke shouted, "Halt!" The shout was repeated back through the miles of the column.

Alexander Stewart groaned. "Within sight of the Firth, and we stop yet again."

"They should have had the King turn back days ago." Thomas slid from the saddle and led his horse to the front of the column as they dismounted to stare after they litter of the ailing king. "If he has a bloody flux…" His gaze flitted around the thousands of men as they stared after the sick King. Young, strong men often succumbed to the dreaded sickness. And when Thomas had seen him at Carlisle, the King had not been strong, nor had he been young for many years.

Geoffrey led his horse to stand beside him, face drawn up into a worried frown. "Most of us do not remember when he was not our king."

Thomas twisted his reins around his hand and untwisted them as the litter continued its snail-like progress. He started when Lincoln said, "You. And you." Still mounted, the earl pointed down to Thomas and then Geoffrey. "You may serve as my attendants."

Thomas threw himself back onto his horse and followed the earl at a canter. They caught up to the litter as one of the monks, the younger of the two, pulled back the thick curtain. The other signaled for two guards to help him. He knelt and gently lifted the king's legs and helped him turn and sit up. There were brown stains down his legs. A fierce stink emanated from within. A look of distaste passed over Lincoln's face, quickly wiped away. Thomas swallowed.

The other monk, a gray-haired, round-faced man with a severe mien, said to the guards, "Put your arms beneath him and lift him. Gently, by the Blessed Mother."

The first monk stepped out of the way as the guards lifted King Edward who limply put his arms around their shoulders. Another guard rushed to open the wooden church door as they carried the King up the steps. The older monk took a bag from his jennet and signaled the other to follow him as he hurried into the dark doorway of the church.

Lincoln glowered at the remaining guards who stood looking bereft. "Why are you standing there? Find the priest of this bedamned place. Bring his best bed for the king! Cushions! Blankets!"

Somewhere in the baggage train was furniture for the king, but it would take time to have it found and brought.

As the guards scurried away, the earl scrubbed his lower face with his hand. He frowned at Thomas. "You shall not whisper even a word of this. Do you understand me?" He included Geoffrey in his glower. "Say one word, and I shall have you both in a dungeon. Now stand guard outside the doors." He stomped inside and slammed the door.

Thomas raised his eyebrows, but his belly felt hollow. He went to stand on one side of the door. It would be a long afternoon. The guards and the local priest lugged in a feather mattress and piles of bedding, but they never emerged again. Eventually, grooms came and led away their horses. The afternoon shadows lengthened, and sunset dyed the western sky red. He threw a glance at Geoffrey. "Do you suppose they remember that we have not eaten?"

Geoffrey snorted. "Probably not."

At last, the sun sank below the horizon, and the sky turned a midnight blue. Footsteps crunched on the dry ground, and a shape approached.

"Here."

Thomas fumbled the hunk of bread Alexander Stewart tossed him but managed to save it. "Thanks."

Alexander threw a chunk to Geoffrey and leaned a shoulder on the wall. "What's going on?"

Thomas clicked his tongue on the roof of his mouth. "Not knowing could keep you out of Lord Lincoln's dungeon."

"That bad, then?"

Geoffrey grunted. "Bad enough. I would not suggest sticking your head inside that litter before it has been cleaned."

"Och. That's the way of it, then."

Thomas tore a bite of bread off with his teeth and chewed. When Alexander handed him an uncorked flask, he took a swig of the sour wine to wash it down. "Wonder if we will be here all night."

"I think we are the least of what Lord Lincoln is thinking on," Geoffrey said.

The three men shared the wine as the night grew darker. When the flask was empty, Alexander gave a raspy scratch of his chin and said he'd be off for some sleep.

"There were many nights like this, I stood guard with…" He trailed off and shrugged.

There was no response Thomas could think of to what Geoffrey was thinking. After a minute, he said, "Sit down and sleep for a bit. I'll keep watch and warn you if anyone is coming. There is no threat here, and the king's own guards are within. Then you can watch for me for a time." He shook his head hard and stomped a few times to be sure he was awake.

A few hours later, he wakened Geoffrey and sat slumped against the wall. His eyes closed. It seemed only a moment later when he leapt to his feet, hand on his hilt.

"Did you..." He cleared his throat. "Did you hit me with something?" He rubbed the sleep from his eyes and glared in the dim light at Geoffrey, who was chuckling.

"Threw a pebble at you. It's almost dawn. Lauds rang, and you did not even stir."

Groaning, Thomas flexed his stiff shoulders and gazed around. A thin line of golden orange rimmed the eastern sky. In the distance, the campfires of the army glowed, too far for Thomas to hear the snores of men and whickers of horses. His stomach rumbled. "How long do you think Lord Lincoln will leave us here? I am sure they have forgotten us."

The church door slammed open so hard that it bounced. A guard raced onto the steps. "God damn, where is my horse?"

"The grooms made a horse line beside the church," Geoffrey told him.

The man left at a run. Thomas watched after him, his mouth open and then closed it. Geoffrey raised his eyebrows. Thomas stepped to the open door and peered around the edge. Near the front of the church in the flickering light of lamps, the monks knelt, praying beside a bed where the figure of a man was beneath a coverlet. Looking down, motionless stood the Earl of Lincoln.

Thomas softly closed the door and crossed himself.

The morning had grown bright and warm when

Pembroke galloped up and threw himself off his horse. He frowned from Thomas to Geoffrey and turned to two of his own guards. "You, relieve those men." He turned back to Thomas and said, "And the two of you, keep your mouths shut. One word of anything that has happened here, and I will see that you in a dungeon." He stomped into the church, slamming the door.

Numb with exhaustion, Thomas walked around the corner to find his own mount, Geoffrey a step behind him. They threw on the saddles and tack and mounted. As they rode towards the awakening camp, two of the king's couriers thundered past at a gallop.

* * *

MARCHING the army back to Carlisle had taken only one day, unlike the four days it had taken to reach Burgh-on-Sands, with only a hundred men left behind as guards, Geoffrey amongst them. Thomas gave him a sympathetic clout on the shoulder at being left behind before he joined Alexander and the thousands of others on their way.

They set up the camp up outside the walls of Carlisle. Tents sprouted like mushrooms, horse lines set up, and latrines dug, which would not keep the place from stinking of piss as soon as the bored soldiers got drunk and could not be bothered to stagger to use them. Pembroke had the camp patrolled to break up the constant fights and to drag to the dungeon of Carlisle Castle, anyone who dared mention the absence of the King. Thomas was envious as Alexander saw his men setting up their tents, anxious for the day that he would raise his own men, impossible while he was in Lincoln's retinue.

The next morning Thomas suggested that they slip away as soon as the gates of the city opened. If they were early, they might be ahead of the hundreds of other knights seeking shelter that did not involve baking in the summer's heat in a tent. Guesthouses at the monasteries were already filled with nobles.

Thomas bypassed the first several houses with ale poles looking for a place off the beaten path. With the hatred between the English soldiers, the Welsh archers, and Scots knights and men-at-arms, any place crowded would be more a battleground than a tavern. Down a shadowy close, they found an inn that catered to laborers but was clean and smelled of ale and mutton pottage. It was empty so early in the day, only one aged gaffer bent over a cup of ale. At the sight of Thomas's silver from his rents, the smiling tavern keeper showed them a large loft that took up the upper story. He said for two half-pennies more, he could supply straw-bags for sleeping. They lodged their horses in a paddock at the back.

Soon they sat in the summer sunshine on a bench outside the tavern enjoying the peace after the constant cacophony of thousands of soldiers arguing, snoring, and lying about their skill in a fight.

"How long do you think we will be here?" Thomas asked.

Alexander took a good look around to be sure no one could overhear them. "It depends on where the Prince is. Or was. And how long it took a message to reach him."

Thomas lifted his cup and took a drink. "London, I heard. But who kens if that is true?"

"Five days each way, at the least, if that is true." He grimaced. "More delays. I hoped to pass near Bonkyl on our way north to see how my family and my lands fare."

"My father left our lands in the hands of a good steward. And Lord Gordon has overseen them." He ran a hand through his hair. "I need to spend time there, but dinnae

149

ken when that will be." He chose not to bring up that he had no family left except for his uncles with whom he was at war, though no doubt Alexander knew that.

"It fashes me that my mother and sister Isabel are alone, with only my brother, although our keep is strong enough. I left a strong force of guards, but—" He spread his hands and drew down his brows.

Thomas chewed his lip. He could not imagine how worrying that would be. If James Douglas treated the people at Alexander's estate of Bonkyl as he had at Douglas Castle... The idea tied Thomas's stomach into a knot. No words seemed as though they would give ease to Alexander's worry.

Alexander sighed. "The walls are strong, and there have been nae attacks yon. But I want to see for myself."

Stretching out his legs luxuriously to loosening the kinks from tedious days in the saddle going nowhere, Thomas finished his ale. He stood and through the doorway signaled the tavern keeper for another jug, while they waited for some food. After the man went back inside, he said, "His body will have to be taken to London for the funeral, aye?"

Alexander nodded his head. "Do you think the prince will accompany it? There cannae be a funeral without the prince there. And there is the proclamation..." He leaned to the side to be sure the tavern keeper or his one customer were not near. "He must be proclaimed king and crowned. I dinnae ken how that will be done."

"Could they not proclaim it here?" Thomas waved a hand, deciding he would not take a chance on joining those who were being dragged to the dungeon by being too specific about what they would proclaim.

"Mayhap." Alexander scratched the sandy stubble on

his cheek. "I am nae to clear on these English customs. But I suppose I had best become so."

"Have you heard about Piers Gaveston?"

Thomas raised his eyebrows. "What about him? The King exiled him to Ponthieu. For life."

"That was the old King. I heard a rumor that the prince—" He said the word with careful emphasis. "—will recall Gaveston."

"Do you think it's true?" Thomas lowered his voice to a whisper. "His father is barely cold and nae even in his grave."

Alexander grunted. "I wonder what Lancaster and Warwick and Bishop Bek will say about that if it's true."

The tavern keeper brought them trenchers filled with large mutton shanks in rosemary-scented gravy and boiled parsnips and onions. These kept them occupied for several minutes. Perhaps a long wait for the prince to arrive was not such a bad thing.

Shaking off the numerous concerns, they finished the food, polished off the ale, and then walked to a weaver on the street of merchants. Here Thomas ordered a gold-colored pennant with three red cushions within a double red border.

The weaver looked somewhat askance at an order from a Scot until Thomas showed him his coins and paid a deposit. He then was effusive about what a beautiful pennant it was as he sketched out what it would look like and promised it would be ready in a sennight.

Alexander wrinkled his brow. "What do those pillows mean?"

"My grandfather telt me they stood for wealth, but we aren't. Wealthy, I mean. My father said they meant his father and grandfather were lazy sods. But that was my father's jest. I think they hoped one day we would be." He laughed. "I mean wealthy, nae lazy sods."

* * *

JULY 20, 1307

A boy dashed inside the door of the tavern. "There's a procession on the way to the castle! There's horses and more horses and men in all kinds of colors! And trumpets and drums! Come see!"

Thomas and Stewart exchanged glances. They both rose and walked toward the door.

The tavern keeper, hovering to look outside, said, "I'd wager it is the prince."

By the time they reached the castle gate with half the city, the outriders had already passed and the twenty trumpeters. Thomas elbowed his way through the press of onlookers, not caring who cursed at him, with Alexander right after until they were within sight of the city gate. The entire garrison of the castle formed lines along the street, pikes held upright.

The trumpeters raised their instruments and gave another deafening blast. Over the noise, Thomas could hear from further up the street cheers and shouts of, "It's the prince!"

Prince Edward paused to toss a handful of pennies to the crowd. He was followed by a cavalcade, silks shimmering in the afternoon sun, gems glinting in rings and pins, horses draped in colored leather worked with ornate embroidery. The people of Carlisle, drawn by the fanfares, cheered and commented, barking dogs and grubby urchins ran alongside frantic with excitement.

"There's Pembroke. When did he go to meet the

prince, I wonder," Thomas said. "And Lincoln too and Bishop Langton."

Alexander, who had been in England longer than Thomas, was able to point some others out for him.

"There is Gilbert de Clare." The richly dressed boy could not be more than sixteen. "And there are the Earl of Richmond and the Earl of Lancaster. Here comes Warwick." The trumpeters were blowing another fanfare when Prince Edward drew abreast of where they stood, and they bowed.

"What bishop is that?" Thomas asked, pointing to a heavy-jowled, frowning churchman, his thick body encased in black velvet and a gold chain about his neck from which suspended a jeweled cross. He gave a wry chuckle. That velvet must be sweltering in the summer's heat.

"That is Bishop Bek."

Thomas raised his eyebrows. All his life, he had heard of Bishop Bek, more a warrior than a bishop and a close friend of the late king. "Do you ken? Is it true he actually fought at the Battle of Falkirk?"

Such a thing was almost unheard of for a bishop.

Alexander rolled his eyes. "I've heard the same story, but I'm nae old enough to have been there." He pointed. "That next to him is Bishop Halton, Bishop of Carlisle."

The cavalcade clattered south on Castle Street away from the castle. The prince again scattered coins that urchins scrambled to scoop up out of the dust.

"Wait, where are they going? The cathedral?"

"That must be it," Alexander said. He shoved his way through the crush to keep the prince within sight.

Someone gave Thomas a hard shove in the middle of his back. He answered by bringing his elbow back into the man's belly. There was an Oof! He gave Alexander a nudge to keep going. They wriggled and pushed their way through the growing throng until they were before the cathedral with its slender pinnacles, soaring towers, and rosetta window.

Guards formed up around the steps to keep back the shouting, excited crowd as the cavalcade spread across the grass, and Prince Edward and Bishop Bek rode their horses up the stone path and stopped before the high arched doorway.

Bishop Bek held up a hand and, his ponderous gaze sweeping the crowd. He waited for silence. After a tense minute, he intoned. "Our great King and dread lord, Edward the first of that name, has died at Burgh-upon-Sands valiantly leading his army. I declare by descent of heritage that Edward of Caernarfon is now our King."

The silence was profound.

The Bishop stood in his stirrups and bellowed, "The King is dead! Long live the King!"

The new King had a look of intense satisfaction on his face as the bells of the cathedral began to toll. Gilbert de Clare and the Earl of Pembroke took up the cry. Thomas shouted, "The King is dead! Long live the King!" Soon the entire city echoed with it.

Thomas grinned wide. Having a young, strong King had to be better. Now they would march to Scotland and restore peace. He clapped Alexander on the shoulder. "You shall see. We will be glad of this day."

Chapter 21

CARLISLE, ENGLAND

Seven days after leaving to escort his father's cortege towards London, the new King returned, having turned that duty over to Bishop Bek. The talk all over Carlisle Castle was that he would send for Piers Gaveston. Thomas could not resist listening to the gossip about the young man the late King had hated so much. Most of it was what he had heard before that Gaveston swaggered and made fun of men above his station. But much of it seemed to Thomas to be jealousy for how well he did at jousting for he had defeated every noble he jousted against.

Having served so long in the retinue of Lord Lincoln, he would have a higher place at the table than before, so when the king had it announced that there would be a feast before the army marched the next day, Thomas brushed his best tunic so he would not embarrass himself.

The great hall was brightly lit with lanterns, and the tables swathed in snow-white linen set with pewter trenchers when Thomas followed the stream of silk-clad men in. They dipped their hands in rose-scented bowls of water as heralds took them to their appropriate place. The table where the herald was placing the Scots was on the far side near the wall, but the herald's disinterest meant that they could choose where to sit, so Thomas joined Lord Gordon, his son William, and Alexander Stewart came to sit with them halfway up the table's length.

"Thomas, I have heard good things of your part in the battles despite the poor outcomes," Lord Gordon said.

"I'm glad of that, My Lord." He introduced them to Alexander, and they made themselves comfortable on the bench as it filled.

In the minstrel gallery, a dozen minstrels began to play loud enough to carry through the chatter as two hundred knights and lesser nobles took their places.

"Have you heard what route we will take?" Alexander asked. "If we travel near enough my lands to check on how they fair, it will be a relief to me."

"To all of us if we can do that. But if we can put an end to this rebellion…" Gordon cleared his throat. "Mayhap that is best to save for after the feast."

Thomas shrugged, willing to change the subject. "Do you know this Piers Gaveston at all?"

"I've seen him joust, and he won against more experienced knights. That I can tell you, but know him? Nae, I've never spoken to the man."

Thomas lowered his voice. "I was there when the old King hit the prince because of offering the Gascon land. I admit I am passing curious. What about the man enraged him?"

The music stopped, and trumpets played a flourish. The herald called out, "Be upstanding for His Grace, King Edward." Thomas jumped to his feet, craning his neck to see them enter.

King Edward and Piers Gaveston, tall and broad-shouldered, strolled into the hall chatting, heads close. A young woman went before them dancing and doing flips. Edward wore a slender golden crown circling his brow, looking much the young king, his red tunic embroidered with eagles of pearl and gold. Compared to the king's fairness, the Gascon was dark of hair and of skin, but his clothing was as rich as the king's, satin embroidered with a leaping stag.

When the King sat in the throne-like chair on the dais, Gaveston sitting next to him, he gave a negligent wave, and in the gallery, the minstrels once more began to play. The nobles paraded in Pembroke, Lincoln, young Gilbert de Clare, the Earl of Richmond, the Earl of Lancaster, and Bishop Halton.

Next, servers carried in an enormous subtlety and placed on the same table, a castle three feet high with inner keep and curtain walls of sugar and a moat filled with spun sugar.

A herald called out, "Your Grace, I bring you the feast." Fifty servants in the royal livery paraded in carrying platters of food, swans dressed in their feathers, whole pike with capers and ginger, several whole boars roasted with honey and pepper, miniature pastries filled with beef marrow, sweetmeats and bowls of frumenty. The delicious scents of roast meat and spices filled the air. A server filled their cups with claret.

Thomas had not eaten earlier, knowing there would be dozens of dishes, and his stomach growled. Alexander grinned at him, and he shrugged. He cleared his trencher of the pike and pastries, and then the server loaded it with swan and frumenty. The entire hall was full of noise and chatter and laughter, the guests taking their cues from the King and Gaveston.

The King clapped his hands, and four dwarfs ran in, followed by a bear. They leapt and tumbled and made a four-man tower while the bear shambled around them in a clumsy dance. It all seemed to delight Piers Gaveston, who began to pelt the dwarfs with sweetmeats. One snatched a sweetmeat out of the air and tossed it back in Gaveston's direction. The knight threw back his head and roared with laughter.

The dwarf's act over, the King stood, causing everyone to rise to their feet. He lifted a silver wine cup. "To the return of my brother Perrot!"

Thomas emptied his cup. The server refilled it the instant he sat. In the minstrel's gallery, a female singer joined the musicians. No sooner were the first dishes cleared away than they set the next remove before them. Thomas's head began to swirl with all the wine that he drank to wash down the enormous amounts of food.

* * *

"AT LAST." Alexander climbed into his saddle.

Thomas sighed. "Hopefully, this time, the march north will go better. And faster." He mounted and sat, tapping his finger on his pommel.

Bright waves of orange spread out from the sun as it broke over the eastern horizon. The trumpets blew in a shrill call to ready the march. Saddles were being cinched. Loaded wagons were clattering into long lines. Knight after knight mounted their chargers, shouting and cheering to be off at last. Several staggered. The rising sun was already wilting the grass that would soon be trampled under their hooves.

The foot soldiers fell in behind the rows of knights in rank upon rank, sunlight catching on spear and sword. In the glow of dawn, the army of England spread like a crashing flood, large enough to crush anything in its path.

Even from afar, mounted on a massive destrier at the front of his army, the new King was magnificent. His heavy plate armor was gold inlaid in elaborate scrolls, and his gold crown blazed with jewels. Even his red cloak shimmered with a leopard formed from gems. He shone like a second sun.

But the royal banner drooped in the still air. Behind the king, wilted Lincoln's purple lion banner, the blue and white stripes with red martels of Pembroke, Warwick's red banner with its gold band and crosslets, and on and on out of sight, more than Thomas could count.

The King set his horse in motion. Horns wailed through the sun's morning glow *move out move out*. Serjeants shouted commands. Armor and weapons clanked. Row by row, the army moved out. It would take hours for the last rank to begin their long march to Dumfries, where King Edward would take oaths of fealty from his Scottish subjects.

Over the creak of saddle leather and thud of hooves, Geoffrey said, "If this is nae enough to defeat the Bruce's ragtail following, you may roast me and serve me as supper."

A bead of sweat trickled down Thomas's face, tickling like a flea. He snorted. "In this heat, we may roast in our armor before we even reach Dumfries."

Alexander grunted. "Wait until the noonday sun is cooking us before you complain."

Though now they were moving at a decent pace, it would be long days in the summer heat to reach Dumfries. And how much longer to find the Bruce, only the good God could know.

Chapter 22

DUMFRIES, SCOTLAND

August 6, 1307

Thomas stopped by the doorway of the great hall of Dumfries Castle. At the head of the hall, King Edward sprawled in a chair looking bored and restless, a table with a wine flagon and cups at his elbow. Piers Gaveston, the Earl of Lincoln, and his governor of Scotland, the Earl of Pembroke, and the Earl of Lancaster shared the dais. High above, halfway to the vaulted ceiling in a minstrel's gallery, a minstrel played a lute. Up the right side of the chamber stood a long table served by busy squires and pages at which lounged a drunk and cheerful company of English nobles, laughing and talking. They largely ignored the Scots gathering at the entry of the room, including him.

Just above the steps to the dais was a table at which clerks sat placed to the side of the King at a lower level. A herald called out, "Patrick de Dunbar, Earl of March."

Dunbar, withered and gray-haired, shuffled up the steps to kneel before King Edward. Without bothering to straighten, the King held out his hands. Dunbar thrust his between them and swore fealty to by the grace of God

Edward, King of England, Lord of Ireland and Scotland and Duke of Guyenne. He bowed, stepped awkwardly back and hobbled off the side of the platform. At the side table, he accepted a cup of wine from a page.

Thomas gazed at the table of viands and wondered how long this whole business would take. *His fealty was to the English King whoever that was. Repeating it means nothing. And I would call many much more illustrious nobles on before him.*

The herald intoned, "Domhnall, Earl of Mar." A well-dressed sprig of fourteen rubbed his hands up and down his thighs before he quickly climbed the steps and knelt to take his oath.

Alexander grumbled, "They could have let us pour a cup of wine before we stand in a herd for an hour.

Lord Gordon, standing in front of them in the queue, said quietly, "Be glad they are letting us to the table. It was a courtesy we were not given in Berwick."

Thomas gave a wry smile. *Signing the Ragman Roll... Older men always brought up ancient history.*

It happened while Alexander was gazing longingly at the wine flagons, and Lord Gordon and Thomas were standing side by side watching Mar gabble his oath. The newcomer came striding toward the front of the hall and stopped facing Lord Gordon and Thomas

A tall man with red hair fading to gray. Neat features marred with a scar on his cheek, smoothly shaven, trim figure inside a gray tunic of the best silk. A man of about fifty, a man who radiated command, a man looking at Thomas with open loathing.

John Comyn, Earl of Buchan.

"Randolph," he said with his voice thick with hatred. "If you weren't under Lincoln's protection, you'd be a dead man."

Thomas blinked. "I had nothing to do with Badenoch's murder."

"You're a Bruce. You're filth by birth, and one day I shall be glad to see your head on a pike."

Alexander looked nervous. Without a doubt, Buchan was the most important noble in Scotland and a man with immense influence. He controlled much of the north of Scotland with his strong castles and close clan ties. And his unyielding vengefulness was clearly perceptible.

Thomas felt Lord Gordon stiffen beside him, about to spring to his defense, and gave a slight shake of his head. He said calmly and distinctly, "I am sworn to King Edward, and if I learn you have questioned my loyalty to him, I'll meet you on the field."

Buchan glared. "You'll prove a traitor just like your murdering uncle. Blood tells."

The herald called out, "John Comyn, Earl of Buchan."

He turned on his heel and walked onto the dais without another word. Eyes narrowed, Thomas watched Buchan give his oath of fealty.

"He is a powerful man," Gordon said slowly, "and it would be wise to make sure you have good friends at court."

"Mmm," Thomas said dryly. "It would be indeed."

Eventually, it was Thomas's turn. He dropped to his knees and repeated the oath he had so given to King Edward's father. He bowed and strolled to the table where he took a cup of claret from one of the servers. Finding Lord Gordon, he said, "Do you ken why we are to bide until all the oath-giving is done? Is that a usual thing?"

"Nae. It is not usual, and I dinnae ken the why. Mayhap there is something more than we ken of this to-do."

"Thomas!" Geoffrey of Abingdon exclaimed. "It is too long since I've seen your ugly Scottish face, man."

Thomas chuckled at his friend. "It has seemed of late that wherever I am, you are elsewhere."

As the Scots continued their oath-giving and joined the throng at the table, the gathering grew ever more raucous until Thomas had to wonder if the King could even hear the oaths.

Geoffrey's face split in a grin. "I heard a good jest the other day that I am sure you don't know."

Laughing, Thomas said, "Not here, you loon. This is important company."

"They don't look as though they'd object to a jest. Though I heard something that was no jest."

Thomas raised his eyebrows.

"The Black Douglas made a night raid on Morton Castle. They drove him off, but he got away with much loot."

Alexander joined them, and Thomas asked if he had heard Geoffrey's news, and he nodded.

"Everyone is talking about him and looking over their shoulder for his sneak attacks," Geoffrey said.

Gordon stroked his chin. "Something needs to be done to put a stop to that."

"Aye," Thomas agreed as he picked up a piece of ginger cake. They munched on tarts filled with veal and the cakes as the rest of the Scots lined up to renew their oaths.

After the last of the oaths, the King shook his head as though throwing off his boredom and sprang to his feet. "My good sirs—we are here not only to receive our rightful homage from our Scottish nobles. Today we raise to a new honor our dearest brother, Piers Gaveston. All here today shall bear witness that as of this day, Piers de Gaveston is Earl of Cornwall."

The Earl of Lancaster, sputtered, staring at the king. "That title was meant for your true brother, not some… some… some upstart." He turned to Gaveston, eyes narrow and gaze searing. "It is a royal title, and you cannot give it to him."

Gaveston stood with his arms crossed. His mouth twitched into a sneering smile at the earl.

"How dare you question me!" Edward roared.

The sound of the lute faltered and ceased. Thomas paused, tart halfway to his mouth as across the room, everyone fell silent, gazing in alarm up at the three men.

"Lancaster! Think about what you are saying." Lincoln stepped past his son-in-law. "Your Grace, he spoke in haste without thinking. He meant no disrespect. Please forgive his words." He spread his hands and continued in a soothing tone, "Lancaster, our late King indeed intended that earldom for his youngest son, but it has in the past been held by those not of royal blood. Giving it to his dear friend is within His Grace's rights. And we can find other titles and lands for the King's young brother."

Gaveston laughed, looking straight at Lancaster. In spite of his years in England, his speech still had a touch of the singing accent of his native Gascony when he said, "Sire, pay no heed to the Fiddler. It is no matter what he thinks as long as I continue in your affection. You have my most humble thanks for such an honor as you have done me today."

The King nodded to Gaveston before he turned back the onlookers. "I signed the charter of the granting the gift. Now eat and drink. This is a day of celebration that my Scottish subjects have shown their loyalty and that I have rewarded Perrot." He glared up at the gallery. "Why have you stopped? Play!"

Gaveston whispered something to the King and slipped away.

Thomas let out a breath he had not realized he had been holding. He finished the tart he still held in his hand and emptied his wine cup. "I think I have had enough of some of this noble company. Let us find an alehouse."

Gordon shook a finger at his son. "Dinnae drink too much."

William cast an uneasy glance toward the king. "Do you think we'll be noticed leaving early?"

Thomas bit his lip and considered Edward, who had turned his back as he talked to Lord Lincoln, ignoring Lancaster standing nearby. Odd Gaveston leaving, but Thomas could easily understand if he also had enough of the company. "In the crowd, if we are subtle about it, we should be able to make our way out." He eased his way into the crowd toward the door, nodding and smiling to the men he passed, careful not to look back to see if the others were following. Soon he slipped out the door of the keep and held it open for the other three when they joined him.

"Do any of you ken where there is an alehouse?" he asked. "I did not see one when we rode in."

Geoffrey winked. "And you were looking, if I know you."

"Och, there is one not so far." William strode out.

Chapter 23

Thomas motioned to the others, and they followed him where Geoffrey pointed down the street along the River Nith. They turned onto a narrow wynd. A spreading elm sheltered the front of a broad thatched house where an ale pole hung in the front.

It's brown daub finish and painted timbers gave a cheerful appearance. A few tradesmen and apprentices stood at the window counter, waiting for their dinner and mugs of ale or cider. Others sat cross-legged in the welcome shade of the elm, taking advantage of the breeze. Thomas pushed the door open and walked into a long, narrow, low-ceilinged room. On one end was a large stone fireplace where a small fire gave off the sharp scent of peat. The wooden floor was being swept by a young boy. On the other side of the room was a low wooden barrier behind which stood two kegs and an alewife with broad shoulders and a round, cheerful face. Ahead and to the left were several long trestle tables. Men-at-arms tucking into bowls of pottage filled two of them

The windows were all open to let in a breeze and the

summer sunlight. Thomas headed for a table near a window. William, Alexander, and Geoffrey slid into the benches around it. A thin, ginger-haired man came over and asked them their pleasure.

"Does one of those kegs have cider?" Thomas asked.

"Aye. My wife makes a braw cider as well as her ale." He smiled enthusiastically.

"Bring me a mug. No. Bring a jug of cider." He cocked his head. "Make it two jugs. And cups for all of us."

William laughed. "You dinnae change ever, Thomas. As bossy as ever, just like when you helped me with my sword work."

Thomas grinned. "Very well then, if you dinnae want any, I shall drink your share."

"Nae, you will not!"

The man returned with cups and two jugs and held out his hand for the coins that Thomas dropped into it.

Thomas took a deep drink and gave a loud sigh of satisfaction. The cider was thick and tart, and Thomas licked a drop from his lips. Just how he liked it.

A stir at the door and a hushed murmur across the room made all four turn their heads.

In the doorway stood Piers Gaveston. His dark eyes swept the room and took in the measure of Thomas and his three companions, his eyes gleaming as though he was looking for a jest.

With the man looking right at them, there was nothing to do but stand. Thomas made a half-bow. "My Lord earl, we are sharing some good cider. Would you join us?"

The corner of Gaveston's mouth curled up. "It makes a change from the best wine."

Thomas waved to the tavern-keeper who was wringing his hands. The man gave off to scuttle over with a cup he wiped out as he came. They sat, scooting to leave the king's favorite a large part of the room on the bench.

The alewife hurried with a new jug of cider. She bowed and begged if there was anything else they could bring, but Gaveston waved them away once the man had poured out a cup of the cider.

Gaveston took a drink and rested his elbows on the table. He was a well-built man; the strong hands, each decorated with two heavy gold rings, grasped the cup of cider. He looked around the room with a wry smile. "Edward would like this place."

"Would he?" Geoffrey said, sounding in doubt.

"Oh, aye. He loves low taverns and talking to minstrels and almost anyone except the nobles of the court. And you can be sure that his nobles disapprove of his taste in liking inappropriate company, me most of all. And be sure to tell him of it."

"But he's the king," Thomas took a long drink of his cider.

Gaveston snorted. "Did that silence Lancaster today? Though I admit that old Burst-Belly stood up for him."

Thomas laughed and choked on a mouthful of ale, coughing. He spluttered. "Burst-Belly?" He wiped his mouth with his sleeve, trying to contain his laughter as the others sniggered, either at his spitting cider or the name, Thomas was not sure which.

"What other nickname fits?" Gaveston smirked. "One of these days that fat belly will burst and twins will spring out."

Wiping tears from his eyes, Thomas said, "I should nae laugh at him. He's been all that is kind to me. But by the saints, he has the fattest belly of any knight I ever saw."

Geoffrey nodded solemnly. "I worry for his poor steed.

Every time the earl mounts, I am sure the beast will become swaybacked from the weight."

They all burst out laughing, Gaveston joining in the loudest of all. They returned to their cider, laughter fading to smiles. Gaveston said, "You are good company. The King and I need more people around us who know how to laugh and jest, especially in this dour Scotland."

"Wait," Geoffrey said. "I almost forgot. I told you I heard a jest that I'm sure you do not know."

"Let us hear it then," Gaveston said.

Thomas leaned his elbow on the table and squeezed the bridge of his nose. He chuckled helplessly.

"No, Thomas. Listen. This is good. I heard that Bishop Langton had lost some of his teeth and complained of the rest being so loose that he was afraid they would soon fall out. 'Never fear,' said one of his friends, 'they won't fall.' 'And why not?' asked the Langton. His friend replied, 'Because my testicles have been hanging loose for the last forty years as if they were going to fall off, and yet, there they are still.'"

Now it was Gaveston who sputtered into his cup, his eyes bright with mischievous humor.

Thomas's shoulders shook with laughter with his forehead resting in his hand as William and Alexander were bent over with laughter. Then he drew down his brow. Odd to miss the disapproving look Hugh would have given.

Gaveston said, "Edward cannot stand that man. I shall be sure to repeat your jape to him. But if I know him, and I do, Langston will lose more than his teeth."

Shaking off the grim thought, Thomas said, "You must not encourage Geoffrey, Lord Cornwall. I fear his mother must have had too close an acquaintance with a jester, and we want to hide it from his father."

"Hoi!" Geoffrey punched him on the arm. "No insults

of my mother. I learn my jests with no help from any jester, she…" He frowned. "She never…" He scowled at Thomas with a glint of laughter in his eyes. "Just do not do that."

Thomas held up his hands. "I apologize to the good lady for blaming your jests on her."

Geoffrey started laughing and waved for another jar of cider.

Gaveston refilled his cup. "The King would enjoy your company. When we return from our sweeps of this dour land for the rebels, I plan a feast for him and will make sure I invite you."

Thomas raised his eyebrows. "Sweeps?"

"Aye. A column will go east, west, and north. One of them should find King Hob."

"When do we leave?" Thomas asked.

"Soon."

Alexander's eyes lit up. "If I may join the sweep to the east, mayhap I can take a day to visit my own lands. I am eager to check on my mother and sister to be sure they are well."

"That can be arranged." Gaveston's mouth twitched in a playful smile.

Chapter 24

BONKYL CASTLE, SCOTLAND

As they rode down the dirt road through the edge of the forest followed by Alexander's force of a score of men-at-arms, the valley before them opened into planted runrigs beside cottages. There were a few people on the road and more men harvesting in the fields with scythes and women tying up bundles of grain. The children stared at the small column. The workers stopped and watched. Then they began shouting and running towards them.

"They have recognized you," Thomas said.

The church bell began to ring. By the time they reached Bonkyl Castle on its mound, the gates stood open for them, and a crowd of shouting people and a couple of barking dogs followed. Past the drawbridge within the stone curtain wall, an acre of ground held the large four-story stone tower house and the profusion of sheds for cookhouse, bakery, brewery, armory, chapel, stables, and barracks. As the men-at-arms dismounted, families rushed to greet them with excited cries.

A lady of sixty with chestnut still mixed in her graying hair and a lass of about eighteen with pink lips and eyebrows like wings awaited them on the entrance to the keep. The lass took his breath away. She was about eighteen; her face was narrow, high nosed, with eyes as blue as any he had ever seen. Her hair, golden brown like dark honey, hung to her slender waist. Thomas tried not to stare.

A cluster of servants came out of the cookhouse, and several grooms hurried out of the stables to take the horses' bridles. Alexander slid off his mount and bent to kiss his mother. Tall and buxom, she was pure Gaelic. She kissed his cheek, beaming a smile of delight at the unexpected arrival of her eldest son. He turned to embrace his sister, even taller than her mother, and she threw her arms around his neck.

Alexander said, "Mother, Isabel, this is my good friend Sir Thomas Randolph. Thomas, Lady Bonkyl."

Thomas bowed over Lady Bonkyl's hand before he turned to Isabel, took her soft fingers in his rough hand, and bent over them. When he straightened, he held them for a moment, before releasing them.

The second floor where they entered was taken up by the great hall where servants scurried around with trays of food and drink. The men-at-arms, joined by a number of women and children, sat at the long trestle tables to be served as Lady Bonkyl, Isabel, Alexander, and Thomas sat at the high tables on the carpeted dais.

"John is off towards the river, supervising the harvest. He must nae have heard the bells."

"My brother," Alexander said.

Platters of saffron custard tarts, roast capon stuffed with apple, and spiced venison with onions were set before them, and the ladies encouraged them to eat enough to feed an army. The bottler poured out cups of hippocras. They pressed Alexander for news, making sure to include

Thomas, wanting to know all the gossip of the English court, what the new King was like, and Isabel asking questions about the ladies' fashions.

Thomas tried his fumbling best to describe the gleaming blue silk of kirtle Queen Margaret had worn but gave up when Isabel put her hand to her mouth to hide a giggle, her eyes dancing with amusement. He smiled at her. When she returned it, his heart sped up. "I fear I am nae help, My Lady."

She tilted her head. "Nae, I find I like the idea of a gown the color of sapphires." She gave him a quick half-smile. Thomas's face grew warm. He took a long sip of the wine to hide it.

Her mother tutted. "Nonsense, Isabel. Now, Alexander, have you found any appropriate lady whom you are interested in marrying?"

"I have hardly seen any ladies, which makes it hard to meet one to marry." He turned to Thomas. "My sire had marriage plans for me, but after his death, those——" He shrugged. "——they didnae work out."

"If you are ever to have an heir, you need to find a wife." She gave him a stern look, but it was as much fond.

"I intend to once I have time. And it is nae as though I dinnae have a brother should it come to that. Though with God's mercy, it will nae."

Margaret Bonkyl put another piece of roast capon on both of their pewter trenchers and gave them a look that said that they had better eat it. "Och, then once this fighting is done, I expect you to come home and find yourself a lady wife. And a husband for your sister."

Alexander nodded, his mouth full of venison and tart. When he had swallowed and had a sip of the spiced wine, he said that he was giving serious consideration to a good match for his sister.

Isabel smiled into her wine cup. "I am nae in a hurry. I want a good husband, and that might be harder than merely any husband."

"Certes, I would only find you a good husband," Alexander said, sounding offended.

The chatter went on until even Alexander's mother had exhausted the subject of marriage, Isabel asked no more questions Thomas could not answer about fashion, and Alexander had quizzed out every detail of what had happened in his absence. Stomach so full, he felt his eyes droop, Thomas excused himself to walk off the meal by exploring the castle and Alexander said he would go find his brother.

Thomas climbed the ramparts. Below, the land lay untouched so far by the renewed war, a quilt of ripe golden fields set in the purple of heather. How long would it be before the same could be said for the rest of Scotland? He rubbed his face and went to explore the rest of the castle. The stables and armory were full and well maintained. He poked his head into the chapel and wandered around the corner to the herb garden, where the scent of herbs was so mixed it was hard to pick out just one. There were lavender and the sweet scent of creamy pink roses. In a corner, a bush of rosemary and nearby sage added their tang to the melody of smells. It was so well-tended that it must be much prized by Lady Bonkyl.

"You found my favorite place," a soft voice said behind him.

When he turned, Isabel, basket in her hand, had entered the garden through a door into the keep. "It is…" He smiled, breathing in the scent. "It is soothing. Much work must have gone into it."

"Mother planted it, but the now she allows me to tend it." She went to one of the rose bushes and took scissors out of the basket to snip off a wilted bloom. "Even with nae fighting nearby, I am confined to the castle. I miss hawking most of all." She turned to face him. "Do you think there will be battles here? Armies fighting?"

"It may be so. But if we can capture de Bruce and the Black Douglas first, then it will all end. I hope we do. Then you can cease worrying about being attacked."

"Mayhap. We cannae risk going out to hawk or even take a ride on a nice day. Tending the herbs is at least outdoors. But I miss the way it was before."

Thomas bent and snapped off a sprig of lavender and twirled it in his fingers. "As do I." He ducked his head, his heart speeding up. "We can take a ride before we leave." He cleared his throat. His face was hot, and he hoped he was not blushing like a lass. "I mean, with Alexander and your mother and our guards."

She snipped another wilted flower, smiling. "How long can you stay?"

"Only two days. We must rejoin the main party as it searches toward Edinburgh. But tomorrow, there will be time. And it should be safe with your brother and me and our guards."

Isabel turned and smiled into his eyes. "I would like that." She turned, touched his arm before she flitted in the door.

* * *

THE NEXT MORNING, THE LADIES' security being of the utmost importance, Thomas agreed that they should saddle themselves not only with their own score of guards but with an additional half-dozen from the castle garrison. However, John said that he had to attend the harvest. In the bailey, Thomas knelt beside Isabel's bay rouncy and formed a cup with his hands to help her mount. Once in the saddle, she arranged the long skirts of her mint green kirtle modestly over her legs and settled her reins in her hands.

To his pleasure, Lady Bonkyl made no objection to riding beside her son so that he could ride beside Isabel. It was a short distance to the outlier of the woods on the high ground above the banks of the Blackadder River. Isabel smiled and pointed out the birds and plants, obviously enjoying herself. She guided them to her favorite places to ride and the best spots for hawking.

She chatted about her falcon when Thomas asked. "I have Earrach. He's bonnie, a sparrowhawk. And he sits on my fist and studies me as if to say let us see how this goes." Her brow puckered in a frown. "He looks so sad to not be able to fly for prey as he used to."

The name Spring for her falcon was perfect for her as well, with her cascade of chestnut hair down her back from beneath her barbet and her sparkling eyes as blue as the spring sky. Thomas realized that she was waiting for him to respond, so he pulled himself from his silent admiration. "I am sure that soon you will fly him again."

The river ran like a ribbon below them. Overhead, calling its name, *bi glic, bi glic* and showing his white belly and wings, a bird soared. It dove into the river grass to dig for its dinner. Isabel gave an excited shout. "See if you can keep up!" She grinned, shook out her reins, and bent over her horse's withers as it took off in a fast canter.

Alexander yelled, "Isabel, no!"

Thomas took off after her. A roe-deer skittered away before him out of some brush. For a moment, he lost sight of Isabel, though he could hear her laughing. He tightened his legs and signaled his horse to go faster. When he caught up, she had dismounted, her mount chomping on grass. She stood near the water, a purple primrose in her hand.

He slid from the saddle, grinning. "When your brother does find you a husband, you will lead him a merry chase, will you nae, lass?"

She caught his gaze and held it briefly, then looked away. "And if I do, Sir Thomas?"

He reached for her hand. "I expect he will enjoy it." He glanced over his shoulder to be sure her brother was not yet within sight, but he had only a moment. He tugged her hand to make her step closer and kissed her forehead. "If he is the right husband."

"There they are," Alexander called from a distance.

Thomas shared a private smile with her and knelt to give her a step up into the saddle again. The next day when he left with Alexander and their tail of men-at-arms to rejoin the Earl of Lincoln's column, Thomas smiled back over his shoulder at the castle. He must return soon.

Chapter 25

DUMFRIES, SCOTLAND

Thomas drew his mouth in a tight line as they rode into Dumfries. Three weeks of riding for nothing. Led by Lord Lincoln, with two thousand men that included fifty other knights, the column had swept all the way to Stirling and had found no sign of Robert or the Black Douglas. Not even a whisper of where they might be. If any of the people of the villages had knowledge of them, they had denied it. Thomas had no doubt that they'd withdrawn into the fastness of the Highlands, where finding even a much larger force might be impossible.

Now under a clear, late-summer sky, they clomped along the dusty road to where they had started, but dark clouds on the western horizon hinted at coming rain. The fields were full of men and women frantically working on finishing the harvest ahead of the coming change in the weather. A few lifted their heads to watch the column pass, but most continued swinging their sickles and tying the stalks into bundles, they would then haul into barns.

Alexander scowled. "Mayhap smaller groups would do

better finding the Black Douglas. It wouldnae be so easy to ken where we are to hide from us."

"You might be right. I think Lord Gordon would be amenable to such an idea. This has done nae but waste our time."

"Would the King be amenable, though?"

"The only way to find out is to ask. We could bring it up to Piers Gaveston first. If he likes the idea, I think the King will allow it." Thomas bit his lower lip. "First, we must learn what the King's plans are."

"They have nae had the funeral for the late king yet. He will have to return to London for that soon. It cannae be put off forever. And the coronation as well."

Geoffrey nodded. "Lincoln is sure to return to London for that as well and require we in his retinue go with him."

The camp of the rest of the king's army, who had already returned from their sweeps to the west and north, stretched by the River Nith. Lincoln ordered his serjeants to see to his men setting up camp beside the rest and turned to ride to the castle.

Thomas snorted. "I was afeart that every bed in the town might be claimed, so before we left, I paid that tavern-keeper to hold a corner in his loft for us. And my stomach thinks my throat has been cut." It did not matter in the least if the hay-filled palliasse had fleas or was lumpy. He just wanted ale, hot food, and a night's sleep without the snoring of a thousand other knights and men-at-arms in his ears.

Thomas had stripped off his armor and donned a tunic and chausses when a servant in the livery of Piers Gaveston climbed into the loft.

"Sir Thomas," the man said. "I had to search the town for you. Lord Cornwall desires that you attend him along with your companions. I am to show you the way."

"Ummm... Certes." Thomas blinked. "Whatever the earl desires." He shrugged at his friends. They went to the paddock for their horses and followed him to the river and some distance along it away from the burgh through thick stands of elms.

Past a break in the trees, a skiff was tied at a short wooden pier. A dozen guards in royal livery stood at ease on the shore. King Edward, hands akimbo, dressed in a red silk tunic embroidered with a leopard on the chest, looked down at the small boat as Piers Gaveston threw back his head and laughed at something he said.

The two men must have heard the thud of their horses. They turned. The guards came erect, hands on their swords, but Gaveston said, "They are expected."

Thomas slid from the saddle, led his horse to the pier, and a guard took the reins as the others joined him. Blinking, he bowed to the king, speechless at the oddness of the scene.

"Here. These are my new friends," Gaveston said with a crooked smile. "Thomas, Alexander, and Geoffrey. But your friend William is not with you?"

"William is attending his father."

Gaveston shrugged and turned to the King. "They're good company, I tell you. Just what we need after a day spent with Warwick and the Fiddler."

"Mmmm..." Thomas coughed. "Thank you, My Lord."

"If my Perrot likes you, that is good enough." With a lithe step, Gaveston holding the bow, the King entered the boat. It rocked as he settled himself and picked up the oars. "Come on. Do not keep us waiting."

"You heard him." Gaveston stepped carefully into the skiff and sat in the pointed prow next to a basket.

Thomas followed. The skiff rocked as the others

climbed in, and Thomas held his breath. Perhaps he should mention that he did not know how to swim. The water lapped around them and he shuddered.

The King dipped the oars into the river and began to row, grinning. "They hate it when I do this, or anything else that I enjoy. All of them. They'd chain me to the throne if they could. But Perrot knows better."

The splash of the oars and gentle rock was not so bad, Thomas thought, still hoping that today was not the day he had to learn not to drown.

Gaveston chuckled. "Thomas looks a bit white. Not fond of boats, are you?"

Thomas forced a laugh. "I... ummm... do not know how to swim."

The king's eyes widened. "I love to swim." He grinned.

"One of his jesters followed him into the water and almost drowned, but he pulled him out. Even gave the man a goodly sum of coin for endangering him—even though it was the man's own fault." Gaveston pulled a wineskin out of the basket and uncorked it. "You see. If he tips us over, His Grace will save you." He took a deep swallow and handed the wineskin to Thomas.

Edward sputtered in amused indignation. "I never tip a boat over..." He shrugged. "Well, almost never."

Thomas took a good long drink of the claret. He needed it. Then he handed the wineskin to Geoffrey sitting beside him on a board near the square end of the boat.

"You should learn, Thomas," Alexander said from behind him. "It is not so very hard."

Thomas studied the water, but there was no way to tell how deep it was. He gulped. "I suppose."

"Or I could tip us into the water and give you a swimming lesson this very day," Edward said.

Holding his hands up and managing a smile, Thomas said, "I am willing to wait, Your Grace. Truly."

Gaveston smirked. "Do not worry. He does not want to give you a lesson badly enough to ruin those clothes." He retrieved the wineskin and took another drink. "Geoffrey, I told the King that you're as good with a jape as his jesters. So I want you to prove that I was not lying. Tell him your best one."

The King continued his rhythmic rowing, his shoulders working beneath the silk, but he tilted his head, eyes fixed on Geoffrey.

Thomas could not help his grin since the royal attention was no longer fixed upon him. Geoffrey's mouth worked a few times, nothing coming out, and his face turned red. "I... I..."

The King raised his eyebrows.

Looking desperate, Geoffrey scratched the back of his neck. "It is not that good, but I did hear about a bookseller in Cambridge named Alfred, an exceedingly jealous man who thought himself quite the scholar. He racked his brains for a way of finding out, without a shadow of a doubt, whether his wife had fucked any other man. By a deeply matured contrivance, well worthy of an educated mind, he lapped off his cock with his own hands. 'Now,' he thought, "if my wife becomes pregnant, she will not be able to deny her adultery.'"

Gaveston guffawed.

The King's mouth worked as he seemed to think over the jest before he gave a loud laugh. He pulled the oars in to rest and held out his hand for the wineskin. "That is not a bad one. Not bad at all. And we have known some priestly scholars who would be fit for having their cocks removed."

Thomas clutched the edge of the skiff and prayed that

their laughter did not shake the boat so much that it tipped over.

"There is nothing like the smell of river water and working up a sweat using your own muscles." Edward gave a satisfied smile.

Gaveston pulled a large pie out of the basket and used his knife to hack off a hunk, which he handed to the King before he cut one for himself. Then he passed it around. Thomas bit into his slice and hummed at the taste of the sweet cheese filling.

"I am giving that feast for the King on the morrow. His Grace commands that you must attend."

Edward winked. "He gives it for me and not to celebrate his new title. And I shall announce his betrothal as well." He shoved the last bit of pie in his mouth. "From the looks of those clouds, we had better start back." The King began rowing back the way they had come.

Thomas swallowed and moistened his lips. He would never have a chance like this again. "Your Grace, I had a thought when we were returning to Dumfries."

"What was that?"

"That a small force of Scots hunting for the Black Douglas might have more success. We know the country and would be less likely to give him an alarm, so he goes into hiding." He glanced around the river's edge, not looking at the King. "It would be a great blow to the Bruce to lose that man if we could catch him."

"What do you think, Perrot?"

Gaveston rubbed his chin. "What Scots did you have in mind?"

"Lord Gordon and his men for one. And Alexander. Gordon may have an idea of who else might join us, but I think we should keep the force small."

"I see no harm in giving that a try. Give him permission, sire."

The King nodded slowly. "Very well. I shall tell Lincoln that you are to remain in Scotland."

Thomas blew out a breath, and Alexander gave him a pat on the back.

Edward continued rowing. When the pier came into view, he said, "If Lincoln and all the rest have their way, I shall never do this again."

"They will not have their way. I intend to see to it," Gaveston said.

* * *

THE NEXT AFTERNOON, Thomas brushed and shook out the tunic and chausses he had brought for the oath-giving. Nothing he could do would remove the wrinkles from being stored in his bag. That could not be helped. The landlord brought up a pitcher of water, so he and Alexander could lave off their sweat and dirt before they donned their clothes.

"Lord Gordon is certain to be there. And mayhap we can manage a word with Gaveston," Thomas said.

Geoffrey joined them as they walked through the street to the castle. "The King is returning to London for his sire's funeral, and…" His face tightened as he took a deep breath. "Thomas, I count on you to collect that debt from King Hob for me."

Thomas grimaced. "I hope that I can, but for the now, I am part of Lincoln's retinue. But if I find a way to remain, I shall remember that debt."

When they walked through the castle gate, they joined a river of silk, brocade, and satin in every imaginable color flowing toward the great hall. Some of the guests were entering to find their places, but more were milling in the bailey, enjoying the unseasonably cool breeze beneath the cloudy sky. Thomas swept his gaze across the crowd, searching for Lord Gordon.

He bowed to Lancaster, whose mouth was pursed up as though he'd bitten into a sour apple. He turned; Geoffrey was offering sympathy to the glum Aymer de Valence for the death of his mother.

"You seem to have made powerful friends," the Earl of Lincoln said when he lumbered up to them in a red velvet tunic, looking older and grayer than when Thomas had first seen him, the lines in his face deeper. "First, making sure that Alexander was allowed to visit his family and now to remain in Scotland when we leave."

"I was grateful for the permission," Alexander said.

"There is nothing wrong with having powerful friends. Some might even say I have a mite of power." Lincoln pursed his lips. "I am not pleased to say that we shall be leaving for London in three days, but the late king's funeral and our new king's coronation cannot be delayed longer. And he must go to France for his bride. We will raise a new army and return next year."

Alexander nodded his understanding.

Lincoln continued, "And of course, my retinue will go with me, but mayhap you would like to accompany us after all, Stewart. Someone mentioned you are looking for a wife, and I can think of several ladies who would suit. Such a tie with England could increase your standing at court."

"You are too kind, My Lord, but I have a duty to see to my family and my lands with rebels still at large."

Lincoln frowned. "Oh. Forgive me. I did not think your family would be in danger so far from the fighting. It seemed peaceful when we rode near there."

"For the sake of his mother and sister, I pray to the

Blessed Mother it stays so. My Lord, I need to say——"
Thomas coughed, coloring. "——I can never repay you the
debt I owe. For your trust and for convincing the King to
take me into his peace."

Lincoln almost smiled. "You have given me no reason
to regret it, Randolph. But I want to avoid unpleasantness
with Gaveston, so I must take my place. He will have
arranged at least fifty dishes most of which will give me
indigestion." He nodded to Thomas and trudged into
the hall.

Thomas sighed. "I should not have laughed at him
when Gaveston made him a jape."

"It was a jest. It did him no harm." Geoffrey shook his
head. "Sometimes, you're almost as much of a priesty-face
as poor Hugh was."

"That reminds me. Before you go, I must give you
some coin. When you reach London, have prayers said for
his soul, as we discussed."

Geoffrey's face lengthened, his mouth downturned.
"Aye. I will."

They joined the stream of men flowing into the great
hall. Although the afternoon was only half spent, the great
hall was ablaze with lanterns on every column and
beeswax candles on every linen-draped table. Thomas held
his hands over a basin by the door as a server poured rose-
scented water over them, and another held out a towel. He
joined the crowd awaiting his name to be called by a
herald to be shown to his place. A page in Gaveston's livery
escorted them down the broad central aisle. The gallery
above was packed with musicians playing flutes, sackbuts, a
bombard, lutes, harps, fiddles, tambourines, and drums.

People's eyes followed him as they were being taken so
high in the chamber, past tables down both sides of the
hall. He was not related to the English King to be seated

on the dais. He swallowed and chewed the inside of his lip. Let them look, he was going to sit there if that was the King's will.

He caught Gordon's eye and nodded, but with so many eyes on him, this was no time to talk.

At least the place they were given was at the end of the high table, the furthest from the King, thus offending the fewest higher-ranked nobles possible. He supposed that Gaveston and the King did not care whether they were offended or not.

Thomas de Kirkcudbright, Bishop of Galloway, stood and gave a brief blessing. By the time he took his seat, servers at every place were pouring claret into the cups and platters carried in filled with slices of capon in a thin cinnamon sauce, beef marrow fritters, eels in a peppery sauce, roast loin of venison, and marzipan cakes. A woman in a silky kirtle twirled in and danced to wild applause.

By the time they reached the sixth remove, Thomas had long since lost count of the dishes that had been placed before him. He hid a yawn and barely nibbled on a candied plum because if he ate much more, it would not only be Lincoln who would be a 'burst belly.' The entertainers were now a dozen midgets tumbling and forming towers.

When the act tumbled their way out, the King held up his hands for silence. The music from the gallery died away. Still seated, he announced that when they returned to England that his dear brother Perrot would be wed to his niece, Margaret de Clare, sister of the Earl of Gloucester.

There were a few low gasps and total silence. Thomas raised an eyebrow at Geoffrey, who pursed his lips and gave a slight shake of his head.

The Earl of Pembroke rose and lifted his wine cup. "To

the Earl of Cornwall and his noble bride. May their marriage bring them great joy."

Thomas joined the rest of the company in rising and lifting their cups and cheering, while Lancaster, Warenne, Hereford, and Lincoln looked as though a dose of nasty medicine was being forced down their throats.

Edward rose. He clapped Pembroke on the shoulder as the company rose to their feet. The servitors hurried in to offer trays of spiced wine and bowls of candied ginger and cardamom to aid digestion as they ended the feast.

Geoffrey mumbled, "That will have set the cat amongst the pigeons, if making him an earl did not." He took a bit of ginger to munch.

"Much as they do not like it, there is nothing they can do." Thomas tilted his head toward Lord Gordon. "I must speak to him." He eased his way through knots of men muttering in undertones about the news.

Gordon nodded and edged into a corner. "I have news that will interest you," he said quietly. He motioned for Alexander to join them.

Thomas raised his eyebrows.

"The Black Douglas once more captured Douglas Castle. He killed its captain and put it to the fire again."

"Did he kill the whole garrison?"

Gordon scratched his cheek. "This time, he let them go. Even gave them a few coins to reach home."

That made Thomas rub his head. Not what he would have expected. "When did it happen?"

"Three days ago. I only received word of it a few hours since."

"He wouldnae lurk nearby though."

"He is said to be yon in Ettrick Forest, seeking easy prey to attack."

Thomas rubbed his lips with his forefinger. "The forest

is wide. We cannae search all the way from Ayr to Selkirk. We should start at Douglas Castle where he was last kent to be and go from there. He'll obviously nae longer be there, but we may pick up his trail."

"After being away so long, I only have ten men with me. But it would be a long delay to return to Inverkip to raise more."

Alexander said, "I have a score of men, and with yours, we should match the Douglas's numbers. And we could search eastward through the forest and then go to my lands to raise a levy if need be. That wouldnae be out of our way."

Thomas squelched a smile. At Alexander's lands, he would have a chance to see a certain bonnie lassie. "So it is agreed that we ride for Castle Douglas." Thomas waited for their nods. "We'll leave as soon as the King and his army depart for London."

Chapter 26

DOUGLAS, SCOTLAND

The streams were swollen by early autumn rains, so they had to search for fords to cross. Under slate skies, rain dripped through the pines, and the horses' hooves squelched in the muddy road. They kept scouts ahead and flanks watching not only for attackers but for any signs of groups of men having passed. But there was no sign, although a scout brought down a deer that fed all the men well.

The rainy day was followed by a bright, cool one when they crossed the Douglas Water. The ruins of the castle gaped before them, a blackened shell.

Thomas dismounted and blew out a long breath. He led his horse to what had been a wall but was now a pile of rubble. He pointed to a hole half-filled with rainwater. "They undermined it to bring it down. After it was burnt, I suppose."

"He means no one to hold it," Gordon said.

William looked down into the long, rubble-littered trench. "Must have been a big job."

"Aye." Alexander crossed his arms as he scowled

toward the gatehouse, which still stood with the gate only a few blackened boards on the ground. "The question is which direction would he have gone from here?"

The thatched roofs of the little town that serviced peaked beyond a curving road. Thomas said, "Let us see what the people of Douglas town have to say."

"If I were them, I wouldnae say a word," Alexander said.

"Most likely, they willnae, but we might still learn something if we talk to them."

Men were doing the autumn plowing of the rigs. Many looked up and then away as Thomas and the others rode passed. Children played in the muddy street. Beside the houses, chickens clucked and scratched for worms. A woman sat on a bench in front of a cot using a spindle.

Thomas dismounted and said to the spinster, "Is there an alehouse in town, goodwife?" He patted his scrip that gave a clink of coins.

The woman pointed down the street to the largest house in the town with a sour look. "Mhairi sells her ale. Ale and other things."

Thomas nodded his thanks, handed her a quarter penny, and led the way down the street, where he knocked on the wooden door.

The front door was open to a narrow central corridor, and he could see through the cottage and out the back door to the yard where a boy stirred a cauldron. Thomas tethered his mount by the door. A woman wiping her hands on her kirtle came to the door. "Is there something you need, My Lord?" She was a decade older than Thomas and missing several teeth but must have once been handsome. A reedy girl of about ten peered around her, looking curious.

"If you are Mhairi, I'm telt you would sell us some mugs of ale. Our men and we thirst, and I have coin."

She crossed her arms and regarded him warily. "My lass can carry them a jar and cups in the yard if Your Lordships want to bide inside." She motioned for the four men to enter. "Jonet, fetch their lordships cups of ale and then take a jug to their men. No dallying now."

She turned back to Thomas as he sat at one of the two tables near a central hearth where a peat fire glowed. The room was comfortably warm after the autumn chill. "What business do such fine lords have in our little village?"

"Accompanying Lord Gordon to Inverkip."

Jonet came with three wooden tankards. "Just tapped today," she said. Mhairi's glare drove her back to the barrel to draw ale for the men in the yard.

Thomas took a sip. The ale was indeed fresh with a pleasant bread-like taste. "It is braw."

Mhairi's lips curved in a thin smile. "Dinnae have many complaints, sir."

He swirled his ale while the other two men drank. Her coldness told him as much as words would. "I see that Castle Douglas is burnt, so no custom from there. That cannae be good for business."

She shrugged, her eyes darting to the side. "Castles are lords' business, nae mine. They fight and burn things. I keep myself to myself." Her eyes snapped back to him. "Och, My Lord, do you want aught else? I need to tend to the brewing and dinnae have time to stand havering."

"Would you have any food? Pottage?"

"I have fresh bread and a good cheese if it please you."

With a disgruntled look, she went out the door to the cookhouse in back. Obviously, she wanted them to leave, but he just sat there, sipping the ale.

When Jonet came back in, Thomas raised his mug. "We'll have another, lass." She took their tankards to refill them and returned with them, lingering, eyes wide with childish curiosity. "The castle burning must have made a big fire," he said, encouragingly.

"Aye, the smoke from it filled the whole sky. There was shouting and yelling and all. And Lord Jamie's men came for ale. We were run ragged with the two-score of them."

"Jonet!" her mother yelled. "You take yourself out to help your brother stir the cauldron. Castles are nae business of ours." The woman thumped the bread and cheese down on a platter, glaring at her daughter.

Thomas dropped a handful of half-pennies onto the table. Mhairi and the other villagers knew much more than they were saying, but there was no way to convince them to say more than they'd learned from the lass.

As soon as the bread and cheese were finished, they upended their tankards to get the dregs, ordered their men mounted, and rode away from Douglas town. "It is nae far to Lanark," Thomas said.

"Aye," said Gordon, "and it has a busy fair that brings in people. If we can find any rumors of where they are, that would be more likely than here. Whether they are loyal to the Douglas or frightened, I dinnae ken, but they'll nae talk."

Thomas snorted. "Of course, they are frightened. Who wouldnae be? I ken well-armed knights who look over their shoulder when his name is mentioned."

Past the burnt Castle Douglas on the ride to Lanark, there was no sign of the war being fought. Fields were being plowed for winter planting, in barns they winnowed the grain to be milled. Laborers paused to give them wary looks as they rode by. They passed farmers' wains carrying tied grain. Everyone looked over their shoulders and eyed them uneasily.

When they reached the west gate of Lanark, only one merchant's wayn waited to enter so late in the afternoon. The guards waved it through with a nod. When Thomas reached the gate, the serjeant called "Halt." A pair of guards in iron-studded brigandines held up their spears to bar the way. "What is your business?"

Thomas glanced at Alexander and raised an eyebrow. They were traveling the wrong way now to be on their way to Inverkip.

"Seeking shelter for the night on my way to my home at Bonkyl," Alexander said.

The guard eyed Alexander's shield. "Blue and white checky. A Stewart, right enough."

"Is there an inn or a monastery where we might find rooms?"

"Aye." The serjeant scratched his stubbled chin. "There is a Greyfriars Monastery that has a guesthouse. And the inn rents straw paillasses in the loft." He gestured to the guards. "Let them pass, lads. They're sworn to King Edward."

The gate opened onto a cobbled street. Lanark was built around its castle. West of the town, it rose high on the east bank of the River Clyde, its square keep and high walls visible from every part of the burgh. They wended their way through the crowded street, people warily stepping out of the way of the armored men.

The inn was easy to find, a wide two-story building with a slate roof. They dismounted and pushed their way inside. Lord Gordon asked the innkeeper for beds and meals for his men. The innkeeper agreed that he had suffi-cient straw palliasses in the loft for them. Gordon and Alexander ordered the men not to draw attention to themselves and asked directions to the monastery where the accommodations would be more comfortable.

"We could demand shelter at the castle," Alexander pointed out.

"Nae," Thomas said. "There will be merchants at the monastery who may well have news. They're more likely to have heard rumors than the guards."

It felt good to stretch his legs as they walked through the fair. Farmers hawked their cabbages, onions, apples, and sacks of wheat and oats crowded the market square. Merchants stood under striped canopies with stacks of pottery and fur. Horse tack hung from racks; jewelry glittered on tables. Women examined piles of linen and wool plaids while bakers' boys cried out that their pies and buns were fresh and cheap.

The gray-robed porter at the monastery gate said there was room in their guesthouse for four more. He summoned a groom to take their horses and a young brother who escorted them past the church and the cloister to a stone building at the rear of the grounds. The long corridor was whitewashed, and a wooden crucifix hung at the end, with doors opening along one side. The friar opened the last door at the end. "The other chambers are full, so you will have to share the bed, but it is commodious enough. You are most welcome to join us in the refectory for supper when the bell rings." He gave a courteous bob of the head and left.

Thomas plopped onto the wide, wool-filled mattress. He patted it. "A bed. I call that braw as long as you dinnae kick in the night." It was an improvement on the prickly straw-filled paillasse he'd slept on at the inn or the cold ground for that matter.

Lord Gordon snorted. "Crowded for four. William can take the blanket and make himself a pallet on the floor."

William gave a resigned sigh.

Thomas slapped Williams' arm. "Be glad that is it dry. And that you're nae my squire set to cleaning my armor." He poked at a bit of dirt on his armor, opened his bag, and changed into a tunic and chausses. He would think about the chore of cleaning his armor later.

By the time they had all changed, the bell for supper was ringing, so they trooped out into the hall and followed two finely-dressed merchants in the autumn dusk through the garden to the refectory.

Thomas ran his hand across his face. "Let us split up so that we can talk to as many people as possible. Dinnae ask questions, or else news is sure to reach the Douglas. If we tell them about being with the King, they are sure to respond with news of their own." Gordon gave him an amused look that made his face color, but he shrugged. "William might nae think of it."

The large center table had grey friars in their grey habits all around it, but a side table was set for guests. A dozen guests sat around it, all merchants in well-cut wool tunics and cloaks. There was a bowl by the door for hand washing. Once he dried his hands, Thomas scanned for a likely looking place to sit. There was room on the bench between a big, portly man, not fifty, clean-shaven, and an urban looking man with iron-gray hair and brows. When the prayer was finished, Thomas crossed himself and nodded to them.

A server placed bowls of a fish pottage and baskets of fragrant brown bread on the table. Thomas took out his spoon. He dished up a generous serving and said, "Och, aye, there is nothing like good Scottish fish. English is nae half as good." It was good. The fish so fresh it must have been just caught, well-seasoned, and with plenty of onions and parsnips.

He dipped up a bite and waited for a reaction. "Have you been in England then?" asked the younger man.

"Serving with King Edward." He nodded. "The new one, that is."

The man chewed his mouthful of food thoughtfully. "What do you think of him?"

Thomas glanced around, making it clear this was not for everyone's ears. "Much like his father in looks. But he named his boon-companion Piers Gaveston as the new Earl of Cornwall, and that set his nobles on their ears."

"He has already taken his army back to England, aye?" asked the older man.

"Aye, that he has. Forgive my discourtesy, friends. I am Thomas Randolph of Nithsdale." He offered his hand.

"Johne Duncanson," the older man said, shaking his hand.

Richerd Wrycht introduced himself and said, "That explains what is happening in Galloway. I'd nae suggest going that way."

Duncanson raised an eyebrow. "What is happening yon?"

Thomas hid a satisfied smile behind his cup as he took a sip of ale.

"Everyone in Glasgow says the Bruce is burning all the Macdowall lands there because they turned his brothers in to the English. Nae a house, crop, or barn left standing that belongs to that Ilk they say. He waited until the southrons were busy elsewhere."

"If the Bruce is harrying those lands, he must have raised a large force. But that is a good way away." Thomas took a bite of the pottage. "I heard that Castle Douglas was burnt."

Wrycht leaned forward, elbows on the table. "The

Douglas is said to be somewhere in Ettrick Forest. My guard telt me that he was seen near Peebles."

"I heard that, but he has nae attacked any merchants or burgesses. He goes after the English patrols. Wherever he bides, I shall make sure he has nae reason to do me ill."

Thomas nodded. "Wise. The market here is busy. Fear of the Black Douglas has nae harmed it. But the Douglas might make anyone nervous."

"I am leaving to return to Perth. Neither the Bruce nor the Douglas is likely to make it past its good walls."

"Aye. Glasgow is safe enough to my mind as well though it has nae walls."

Thomas sighed and finished his fish and a large slice of bread and some frumenty. The two men did not seem to know more than they'd said. It was disturbing news that his uncle had a large enough force to harry the lands of the Macdowalls. He and the others would continue to focus on catching the Black Douglas with his small force. That would do considerable harm to his uncle if they could find the damned scoundrel.

On their way back to their chamber, Thomas told the other men that the Douglas was said to be near Peebles.

"That's better than I did," Alexander said. "Even though Jonet said he only had two-score men, I think we should go as we said to Bonkyl, and I'll take bring some of my guards. My brother can recruit men for the castle from our people to make up the force."

"Peebles is on our way, and we should search yon though I agree that raising more men is a good plan."

Alexander laughed. "More men or seeing my sister?"

Thomas grinned. "Mayhap both. But the Douglas matches our numbers, so we should do that.

William bumped Thomas's shoulder with his own. "Found yourself a lady, aye?"

Lord Gordon shook his head at them, though he gave them an indulgent look. "Let us rest and leave on the morrow. We can keep a watch for indications of him on the way. We'll pass through Peebles and see what we find there."

Chapter 27

PEEBLES, SCOTLAND

Rain dripped from Thomas's nose and dribbled down the back of his neck from his wet hair. He shivered. His horse splashed through puddles, and the rain bounced when it hit the ground. There would have been several hours of sunlight left if they had seen the sun even once in the day.

Lord Gordon pointed past the fringe of the pine forest. "Peebles."

Thomas studied the sprawling village, where some of the cots were large enough to be two or three rooms.

"Yon is a malting." Alexander pointed. "It is large enough for all of us. And I want out of this rain. It is God damned stoating down."

Thomas led their sloshing way onto the road to the long stone building and slid off his horse. Sloshing, they tied their horses near the door so that they could munch on the sodden grass. Thomas unsaddled his mount and hoisted the saddle and his bag.

He opened the door and stepped inside and breathed in the scent of toasting malt. It was more than roomy enough for their party of thirty men. The circular kiln at one end with a fire lit in the fire hole sent warm air and smoke through the flue and through the bed of grain spread on a lattice of sticks, warming the whole place. He stuck his head out the door. "Everyone inside. We can dry off and rest for the night."

Lord Gordon and Alexander trooped inside, shaking off the rain from their cloaks, and rubbing their hands, followed by their men. Thomas sent one to guard the front, two to watch the road into the village, and one the horses with a promise they would be relieved later.

They all threw their saddles and bags into the corners.

One of their men had brought down three capercaillies while they rode. The man started to pluck the large birds. "Hope the taste of these does nae find its way into their malt, but we need something warm in our bellies."

Thomas stripped his hauberk. Even his linen gambeson was so damp and clammy he was tempted to take that off too.

William said, "I saw a well. I shall bring back some water."

Thomas shivered again and slicked back the blond strands of hair out of his eyes. "The last thing I want is more water."

"None of it went inside, you loon." The younger man plunged out the door as though he could dodge the raindrops.

Alexander held his hands out to the fire in the kiln. "We should be dry by morning. But Jesu God, I hope the rain stops by then."

Thomas sat, leaning back against the wall. He took out a small flask of oil and a cloth to tend to his armor. He sighed. "When I was a lad, I thought being a knight would be an adventure."

Lord Gordon snorted. "All squires think that."

The man plucking the fat capercaillies said, "Almost ready to go over the fire."

Gordon walked over and frowned into the kiln. "They cannae go directly onto the fire. What can we prop the spit up with?"

The door opened, and William bounced in with a grin. "Look what I found."

A ginger-haired wifey in a hodden-grey kirtle and a lad of about ten carrying a basket followed him in. "I am nae 'what.'" She scowled at him. "I could take this basket back home with me."

"He means nae harm, but he is a gormless lad at times," Gordon said. "And whatever you have there, we shall be grateful and pay you well."

"I saw him at the well looking foolish enough." She pulled away a cloth to show a large jug of ale and a stack of oat bannocks. "The ale is my neighbor's brewing, fresh tapped only two days ago." She pointed at the birds. "And I'll take these and cook them for you, so you dinnae ruin them."

"We would be grateful, goodwife. And if you would sell us some food to go with it, that would be braw." He gave her several half-pennies in exchange for what was in the basket, and the woman and boy carried the large plucked fowls away.

"Not water!" Thomas grinned as he snagged the ale. "Anything but water to drink. There is enough on the outside of me." After he had a glug, they passed it around, and Thomas patiently rubbed oil on his hauberk to stave off rust.

A few hours later, the wifey brought back their roasted birds, large enough that they all could have a slice along with the apples, cheese, and bannocks, and then Lord Gordon changed the guard. The ale was long since shared.

Thomas yawned so wide his jaw cracked. "Before we leave on the morrow, I want to make a sweep around Peebles."

"It seems Douglas must ken every spot for an ambush." Gordon frowned. "We'll have to proceed carefully."

"Aye," he said around another yawn. He re-donned his hauberk and went out to check the horses. The rain had stopped, but the dark and dreich day had turned into a moonless night with no sign of a break in the clouds. He hurried back inside and wrapped himself in his cloak, too weary to care that the floor was hard and the armor uncomfortable. With a seeking hand, he felt for his sword to make sure it was by his side. There. Somewhere an owl gave a forlorn hoot. He bent his arm for a pillow and closed his eyes...

* * *

A CRASH OF WOOD... Thomas sat straight up, heart thudding. "What the devil?" Black shapes filled the doorway. They rushed in. He scooped up his sword and was on his feet, shouting, "Awake! We're attacked!"

The attackers thundered in spreading across the room. One of Gordon's men yelped, "I am nae armed." Another's dirk clattered onto the floor.

A man pressed a dirk at Gordon's throat. Thomas kicked him in the face as Gordon grabbed his sword and leapt to his feet. "Flee!" Thomas threw himself in front of Gordon. A sword bit through his mail into his own arm.

Lord Gordon shoved William toward the door, then Thomas had no more time. He spun and lashed out a swipe at his attacker. When their swords rang, he recognized the Black Douglas and cursed.

"Randolph," the Douglas backed off a step. "Yield!"

Thomas gritted his teeth from the pain. "Brigand." He went at Douglas hard. Steel rang on steel. He drove the Douglas back, but the damned man met every blow, teeth gleaming as he smiled.

Changing the direction of his blows, Thomas swung at his stomach and nicked Douglas's armor. He followed with a slash. Douglas caught the slash and pushed back. In the dim light of the fire, Douglas smirked. Gordon's men, hands raised, had swords at their throats.

His eyes intent on Thomas's face, Douglas circled like a dog searching for an opening. Thomas hacked low at his leg.

Douglas leapt back, hopping over a saddle. He cursed and swung. Thomas parried his cut though it hammered his injured arm and launched a counterattack. He drove Douglas back against the wall and reversed his hold to slam his hilt into Douglas's sneering mouth, staved off with Douglas's forearm. But blood dribbled from down his chin.

Their swords locked, and Douglas shoved him back. Low, high, backslash swinging so hard that the swords sparked when they met, step, slide…

Douglas knocked a blow aside and danced back for another try. "Mayhap you grew over-fond of the English king." He came at Thomas, grunting as he hammered at his head and shoulders.

One of the Douglas's men dodged out of their way.

He blocked the blows, but his torn arm screamed with each strike. He felt the burn of slashed skin. Blood ran down his arm, dripping onto the floor. Steel rang on steel, but his blows were slower and weaker. He had to win now. He took half a step back, raised his sword high, and slammed down in a strike that would have split Douglas's head like a melon.

Douglas's sword leapt up to parry. He returned with a

blow that raked across the slash on Thomas's arm. Blood sprayed. Douglas came at him. Each parry splattered blood. His arm was going numb. He dodged a blow at his head. Staggered. Tripped over a bag. Went down on one knee, struggling to raise a sword gone too heavy to lift.

Douglas knocked the sword from his hand. A kick in the chest slammed Thomas flat on his back. Douglas lifted his sword over his head for a final blow.

Dazed, Thomas waited. It took a long time hovering above him.

"James. No!" Someone grabbed Douglas's arm. "No! Not the King's kin!"

There was a pause. "You're right, Robbie." Douglas lowered his sword and spit out a mouthful of blood. "Tie the traitor. And stop the bleeding. He mustn't die before we reach the King."

Thomas shoved himself up with his elbow, his other arm hanging limp. "Aye. A brigand will drag me to a brigand."

Douglas sheathed his sword and pointed down at him. "Shut your mouth or you'll be gagged."

He would save his words for his uncle then. The room wavered, and he wondered how much blood he was losing. His elbow slipped from under him. He felt boneless. Floating.

Robert Boyd said, "Let me see that arm before you bleed out." The man knelt beside him and poked at the wound. "It's nae deep, but he's bleeding like a stuck pig."

"How did you let two of them escape?" Douglas turned in a circle, narrowing his eyes at his men. "But what have we here?" He raised an eyebrow. "Cousin, you've taken to keeping bad company."

Alexander shook his head. "Jamie Douglas. I was hoping we'd see you coming."

Douglas smirked. "Nae one passes through this forest that I dinnae ken it. I'd word days ago you were searching for me. These are your men and Lord Gordon's men, I take it."

"Aye."

"We'll tie them up. Most likely, someone will release them in the morning, assuming the people are feeling generous. But you two shall come with me."

Thomas winced at the pain when Boyd poured wine into the slash and jerked the bandage tight around his arm.

"We'd better give him time for the bleeding to stop," Boyd said. "We can sleep out of the rain and leave in the morning."

The same wifey opened the door for the boy who staggered in under the weight of a big basket of cheese, bannocks, and ale. "Lord Douglas, I saved most of the food for you and your men."

Douglas tugged his forelock. "My thanks, Mariam. And for sending us word that they were here."

Thomas closed his eyes and ground his teeth. He should have known they were not to be trusted.

Chapter 28
LOCH TULLA, SCOTLAND

Robert Boyd had washed the slash in his arm with wine and bandaged it tight, but it still throbbed with fever. The slash burnt, but the fever was worse, making his stomach roil. Sweat plastered his hair.

A sentry's horn blew long and plaintive as they rode through the fringe of the Scotch pine. Their horses' hooves thumped in the padding of pine needles. Below, campfires sent up hundreds of tendrils of smoke in a curve around the edge of Loch Tulla. Beyond, Ben Crauchan rose like a dark colossus.

"It's the Douglas and Robbie Boyd. They bring prisoners," a guard shouted. "Tell the King."

He straightened his back and squared his shoulders as they rode down the slope past the wood fires and horse lines. He was a prisoner, but no craven.

The liquid sound of a Gaelic song floated from one of the fires. It made Thomas's heart hurt. It had been so long since he had heard his mother's language. Men squatted around venison sputtering over cookfires, but the scent turned Thomas's stomach. At another, raised voices drowned out laughter. Pikes were stacked in pyramids and a wayn piled with swords.

Two men strode toward them, Robert de Bruce in the lead followed by his brother. "Jamie Douglas! I didnae expect you." He was thinner than before, with new lines etched around his eyes. He wore a simple gold circlet for a crown and battered mail for armor.

"Your Grace——" Douglas paused. "——We took two prisoners. One especial I had to bring to you myself."

One guard grabbed Thomas's arm and unresisting he let himself be pulled from the saddle. He staggered and then spread his legs to steady himself. He raised his chin and looked his uncle straight in his eyes.

The Bruce's lips thinned. "Nephew…"

Douglas grabbed his arm, but Thomas jerked to free himself. When the man gave him a vicious kick to the back of his leg, it knocked him to one knee with a painful thud. He narrowed his eyes at Douglas before he raised his eyes to his uncle.

"Och, lad, so you return to me. I am glad to see that they spared you Alex's fate. And Nigel's. And Thomas's. All of my brothers except Edward. But your head is still gey firmly attached." The Bruce slowly shook his head. "You have played the traitor, Thomas. But all you need do is ask, and I shall forgive you."

"Forgive me? I am alive nae thanks to you or the oaths you swore when you were crowned." His voice shook with fury, so he took a deep breath to steady it. "I owe my life to Lord Gordon and Pembroke. And King Edward, who forgave me for following you and for being a fool."

His uncle gave a bark of bitter laughter. "I give you we were fools. At Methven, I was a fool to trust in English honor."

Thomas struggled to his feet, dashing a quick glare at the Black Douglas. "How can you speak of honor? You? You ran from the battlefield at Methven. Fled the gey kingdom you swore to protect. And returned like a brigand in the night, sneaking, hiding. Attacking with stones and boulders and hidden pits." He glowered at Douglas. "Desecrating bodies thrown down a well." Looking back to his uncle, he narrowed his eyes. "Honor is the last thing you have. I am ashamed we are kin."

A grim smile twisted the Bruce's face. "You swore me fealty. You have broken your oath. But I offer you mercy."

"You?" Thomas braced, his legs apart, prepared for a blow, eyes narrowed, lips pressed to a tight line. "Reproach me for breaking my oath? You who broke your own oath to King Edward! I beg no mercy from your dishonorable hands."

The tendons of the Bruce's neck stood out rigid, like whipcords. "Is it honorable that King Edward has my sister Mary caged outside like an animal? That he hanged knights for following their liege lord? A pretty notion of honor you have."

Thomas bared his teeth in a snarl. "King Hob—"

"Silence!" his uncle roared. "I shall nae bandy words with you further. You have drawn your sword against your sworn king, and your words are lèse-majesté. The penalty for those crimes is death. You should meet with that punishment, but for your mother's sake, I still my hand. You shall be held in close ward until you come to your senses, nephew. In Sir Robert Boyd's charge, you shall remain. Until you remember who I am. And remember your duty to your sworn king."

Thomas tilted his chin up. His whole body was shaking with fever and fury.

Boyd grabbed his arm and jerked. "You need a good kicking, but I shall nae give it to you. Go."

Limp with the fever, he feared he would stumble but stiffened his back to keep upright. Boyd shoved him toward a campfire. Behind, Douglas said, "And a cousin of mine, I brought you as well, Sire."

Thomas sank onto the ground, resting his back against a tree trunk. He propped his bound hands on his bent knees and leaned his head back, closing his eyes as a shiver ran through him. His anger faded, and his eyes drooped.

"You. Dinnae move."

Thomas snorted. If he could, he would escape, but not today. Not when walking across the camp was beyond his strength. He drifted into blank darkness and yelped awake when someone jerked the bandage loose and glared at a gray-haired, round-faced man, tonsured in a gray friar's robe who bent over him.

"Is it bad, Brother Fillan? Does he have wound fever?" Boyd asked.

The friar pushed harder on the wound and wrinkled his nose when pus oozed out. Thomas sucked in a breath and tugged his arm free.

"Nae. He will heal once I clean out the corruption and put on a good poultice. Another day and he might have lost the use of it." The monk nodded to himself. "Yarrow, groundsel, pennywort, nettle, and garlic boiled in wine." He rose, knees creaking. "Give him some strong wine to drink, Sir Robert. This will be painful. And unbind his hands."

Thomas twitched a wry smile at Boyd. "That's you telt."

"Aye. I'll leave them unbound if you give me your oath nae to escape."

210

Thomas tensed. "I am giving nae oath. I have one given to King Edward, and that is enough."

"Thrawn dolt," Boyd muttered as he cut the binding. He shoved a cup of wine into Thomas's left hand. "You had better drink that."

Thomas took a mouthful and made a face at the sour taste. It was not quite vinegar but close, so he gulped it down as fast as he could.

When the friar returned, he had Thomas lie back on the ground. Boyd straddled his body and took firm hold of his arm. Thomas clamped his teeth shut, sweating, when Brother Fillan squeezed out the pus, sewed it closed, and then smeared the hot poultice onto the slash. If Boyd had not been holding him down, he'd have hit the damned friar.

"I shall grind some birch bark and leaves for a tea."

Thomas groaned. "Sounds tasty." He closed his eyes. If Boyd wanted to bind his hands, he was welcome to do it. Even the pain in his arm would not keep him awake.

He awoke, his stomach hollow with hunger and his bladder crying to be emptied. He pushed himself up with hands still untied.

Boyd stood across a low burning fire where bannocks cooked on a griddle. "I'll nae keep you tied, but if you try to escape, you'll regret it."

Boyd pointed him toward the latrine pits where a sullen guard followed him. When he returned, a bannock sat on a stone beside the fire. "Is that mine as well?"

"Aye. Did you think we would starve you?" He pointed at a cup. "And Brother Fillan said for you to drink that, so do it."

Thomas grimaced and picked up the cup. But the slightly bitter taste was not as bad as he expected. Then he broke off a piece of the warm, oaten flatbread to shove in his mouth. The camp was busy. Thomas scooted back to lean against a tree, calculating that there were at least seven or eight hundred men sharpening swords and pikes, repairing bows and tack, cooking over campfires, and a few just lazing about. His uncle was hunkered down deep in a quiet conversation with his brother, Edward, with Maol Choluim, Earl of Lennox, and Niall Campbell of Strathbogie.

"I had heard you were fighting the Macdowalls," Thomas said to Boyd.

Boyd sat on a stump and took a whetstone out of his scrip. "Och, we taught them who is King right enough. They shall be some time licking their wounds. We've other business the now."

The familiar, quiet *whis whis* of the whetstone on steel almost soothed as he wondered what business took them so far north, near the John Comyn's lands.

Alexander strode up and hunkered beside him and said, "You look a mite better."

He grunted. "That friar's poking and poultices seem to have done me good." He gave his friend a long look. "I didnae ken you were a cousin to the Douglas."

"Aye. His mother was my aunt." He shrugged. "I cannae say I know him well. His father sent him to France for safety."

Thomas lowered his voice. "Have you heard what their plans are?"

"Jamie left to return to Ettrick Forest. But as for the King, the Earl of Ross and John of Lorn have signed truces with him, so he is safe from attack from those quarters."

Thomas raised his eyebrows. "Truly?"

"Aye. And I have the impression that the Bruce is

expected somewhere. Has some meeting planned. We ride north on the morrow, though no one has said for where."

Thomas stared past the mass of Ben Crauchan. "The Earl of Buchan's lands are in the north." All the north of Scotland was under the control of the Comyns, sworn blood enemies of the Bruces since that day his uncle had killed John Comyn at Greyfriars Kirk. But where might he attack such a formidable foe?

Chapter 29
INVERNESS, SCOTLAND

Thomas scraped up the last of the bean pottage from his bowl. Along with fifty or so of the Bruce's men who had slipped into the burgh of Inverness, he sat around a refectory table at Inverness's Blackfriars Monastery. The black-robed friars had served them with warm pottage, cheese, and fragrant loaves of bread. He took the heel of the bread and a bit of cheese and shrugged at Alexander, who glanced from the corner of his eye at the far table.

There Robert de Bruce leaned forward, elbows on the table, talking with his brother Edward, Gilbert de Hay, and Boyd. The portly, well-dressed Provost of the Burgh of Inverness and half a dozen men dressed hodden-gray wool tunics, and chausses sat with them. They leaned forward as Robert murmured.

At last, one by one, the men nodded. Robert rose, which caused everyone in the room to leap to their feet. Thomas stood more slowly.

When the strangers bowed, Robert reached out his hand and clasped each man's and slapped them on the shoulder, one by one. He motioned for everyone to follow him into the courtyard where two wayns stood half filled with hay.

Flurries drifted on the air, and a light coating of snow squelched underfoot.

Robert said, "Remember, the first must go through the gate stop and the second halt below the portcullis, so they cannae lower it."

"Aye, we ken what you have in mind. And my cudgel will be ready below my seat," the burliest of the men said in a gruff voice. "Who will you have under the hay?"

The Bruce looked around at the men. "This will be the dangerous part. We can wait no closer than the base of the castle mound without raising the alarm, so it will take a minute for us to reach the gate. You must kill the guards and hold out until we reach you. For this, I need my best." After listening for a moment as each man demanded the King choose him, he pointed one by one to four men, all muscular and in good iron-studded brigandines. "You ken what you must do. When we reach the gate, it must be open."

Two of the soldiers climbed into each wayn, and the drivers covered them with hay. Two drivers took their places on the bench, shook out their reins, and the wagons clattered into the cobbled street. Thomas glowered as the soldiers broke up into twos and threes and hurried after them.

Half an hour later, there they were, Alexander and Thomas—and four guards, of course—standing in the gloom of a sloping street within sight of the gate of Inverness Castle on its high mound, the Saint George banner of England hanging limply above the keep. His breath was a series of white puffs in the chill air that carried a scent of more snow. The wayns sat at the base of the castle mound.

The soldiers, including his uncle, crouched behind the buildings nearest to the castle.

He chewed his lip. He could try to shout a warning to the guards on the walls but doubted they would pay note to a shout from so far away. One of the guards beside him had his dirk in his hand. Was it worth the risk? He ran his hand through his hair, mind racing.

A bell tolled in the nearby Blackfriars Monastery. In the distance, a dog barked. The drivers cried out to their horses and climbed the incline. As they neared the gate, Thomas opened his mouth, but a dirk pricked his throat. "Dinnae even think on it," a gruff voice said.

Heat burnt his face. He closed his mouth.

The last wayn stopped beneath the iron portcullis. A guard shouted at the driver, and the Bruce's men leaped to their feet. They raced up the hill shouting, "A Bruce! A Bruce!"

Thomas waited for the gate to crash down as shouts filtered down on the breeze. A body lay bleeding on the cobbles, but whose? An archer on the rampart turned, raising his bow, and was thrown, screaming to the ground below. A body lay bleeding, but whose? His uncle's men flooded through the gate. More shouts, but they were too far to tell whose, to determine what was happening.

Thomas chewed his fingernail, throat tight.

Then someone tore down the banner and raised the Bruce's Lion Rampant. The guards gave a shout of triumph.

He and Alexander tromped between their guards through drifting snow flurries and gathering darkness up the incline. A body lay in a puddle of blood in the gate. Thomas scrubbed a hand over his face.

In the middle of the bailey yard, English men-at-arms

were handing over their weapons and one by one walking out the gate.

"Where is Boyd? We are to deliver these back to him," one of the guards said to a passing soldier.

"In the keep."

Inside it was chaos. The Bruce, his brother, and Boyd stood in the middle of the vaulted chamber as men carried down armor, swords, pikes, and bows to stack on the long tables. Others carted down furniture and hangings.

"I'll be back at first light with the rest of our men." Edward shouldered Thomas out of the way as he left.

Thomas crossed his arms and cast his gaze across the busy chamber, anywhere but at his uncle.

The guard with the dirk tilted his head at Thomas and told Boyd, "This one would have given us trouble, but I dissuaded him. The other was quiet enough."

Boyd nodded and dismissed them.

Alexander turned in a circle looking astonished at the chaos. "Do you think you can hold the castle? Why are you removing everything?"

"Hold it?" The Bruce laughed. "I have nae intention of holding it. I'll destroy it and keep it out of the hands of our enemies. First, we will remove any valuables. What we cannae use, the people of the burgh can."

Thomas blinked.

"The English cannae hold the kingdom if there are nae castles for them to hide in. That is why Jamie destroyed Castle Douglas. Why I'll destroy every castle that I take. And I mean to take every castle in Scotland. Starting here in the north."

Alexander's eyebrows went up. "Take them by stealth, you mean. As you did here. What about the Comyn of Buchan?"

"That is what I mean. I have nae time nor men nor

siege machines to take them by siege. But by stealth, we are taking them. One by one. As for Buchan, I mean to deal with him." He clasped his hands behind his back and smiled. "Rethink your fealty, Stewart. Join me in this, and we shall drive the English out of our land."

"Alexander…" Thomas said, his chest heavy. "You cannae." A realization washed over him that this had been his uncle's plan all along. He brought them with him to see the castle taken and show them how he planned to win. He grimaced. More sneak attacks.

"We've seen what he can do, Thomas. He is beginning to win." Alexander's eyes gleamed. "Has started winning."

"One castle. Taken by trickery." He threw his hands in the air. "One castle is nae taking back Scotland."

"This castle. And Castle Douglas. And he won at Glen Trool. And at Loudoun Hill. And harried the Macdowells. Frightened Ross and John of Lorn into making a truce." Alexander looked at the Bruce for a long moment. "Aye, this is a new way to fight them. It can work. I see that, but…"

The Bruce smiled encouragingly. "But…?"

"My family is in Bonkyl; my mother, sister, and brother. You ken that the English will seize it if I hold with you. And Jesu God, you must ken what might happen to them then. Agree to allow Boyd and his men to accompany me there. With their help, I'll slight the castle myself and bring my family here to safety. Provide a house for them here." He glanced at Thomas out of the corner of his eye. "Let Thomas go with us since he is in Boyd's ward. I have a two-score of good men there holding my lands. If I give you my fealty, they are yours."

Thomas opened his mouth and stared at Alexander. He needed to tell him how wrong he was, but the words wouldn't come.

"Boyd, what say you?" the Bruce asked.

Boyd frowned. "A long trip, at least a week each way. Mayhap more returning with women, but Bonkyl is a strong castle. Slighting it and gaining the men, there would be a victory without even a sword raised. Why would you not? And the Stewarts are good Scots. If Alexander joins us, it may encourage the High Stewart to come over as well."

The Bruce held out his hands. "Sir Alexander, I receive you into my peace. You are a free man."

Alexander sank down on his knees and placed his hands between the Bruce's.

Thomas's chest squeezed so tight he could not breathe. He turned his head away, his lips in a tight line. How could Alexander do this? How could he? The words of the oath were drowned out by the buzz in his ears.

Chapter 30

RANNOCH MOOR, SCOTLAND

Thomas watched snow-covered ground under his horse's hooves as they rode across the savage landscape of Rannoch Moor. The black peat bogs all around gave up a sour stench that added to the desolation. Behind them trailed two score men-at-arms occasionally grumbling about the cold or exchanging tales of their deeds in the recent fighting. Beside him, Boyd broke the silence to ask Alexander about Bonkyl, so Alexander told him about the castle and his eagerness to reach home.

"Time to make camp," Boyd said. "This is nae country to ride after dark."

Surprised to see that the sunset had cast a red curtain across the mountains of the Blackmount, Thomas blew a weary puff and unsaddled his horse. Boyd had chosen a dry hillock for camp amidst the peat hags, clumps of dead moor grass, standing water, and in the distance a single skeletal tree.

With his horse tied alongside the others, he turned in a slow circle. Around them was a rock-ribbed, waterlogged sullen emptiness thrust into relief by the beauty of the surrounding blue mountains as night engulfed them. If any place in Scotland could make a man realize his smallness, it was Rannock Moor.

In fours and fives, the men were building small fires and preparing for the night. From the supplies carried on their two sumpter horses, Boyd ordered bread and cheese handed out. He used his steel and flint to set light to a hunk of dry peat. Dark was closing in fast; it was growing colder just as fast. Thomas held out his hands to the frail heat.

"So, are you going to refuse to speak to me forever, Thomas?" Alexander asked.

He sighed. "I am nae refusing, just dinnae see anything to say."

"I value your friendship, man. Can you nae see why I did what I did?"

Thomas gazed up at the vast dome of the blackening sky as stars winked into sight. Within this vastness of sky and land, he felt the merest irrelevance. What difference did it make if he understood or not?

"You did what you thought you must."

"I did what I thought was right." The light of the fire reflected on Alexander's frown. "Can you tell me you dinnae want our kingdom back, our own laws back and nae one executed for resisting English might? Nae having the English robbing us with their taxes, and our own King if we can somehow win? I dinnae believe that, Thomas. And the Bruce has found a way. If he faltered at the start…" He spread his hands. "Och, so he did, but that is in the past. We have a way forward."

Thomas swallowed a thickness in his throat. "I ken that you believe that. But I cannae so forget that he fled the battlefield and the kingdom. That men who trusted his oath died for it. You weren't at Methven. You didn't see your friends dying around you or dragged off to be hanged. See their heads upon spikes."

"Hell mend you, man," Boyd growled. "Have you paid nae attention this whole time? The King never fled the kingdom. We never left. They hunted us like the veriest vermin. We took refuge in the isles and later in the north in Christina Macruarie's lands. But we never left!"

Alexander shook his head. "Boyd, there is nae point in shouting at him."

"Very well. He hid like vermin." Thomas ran his fingers through his hair. "While after the battle, his own goodbrother and dozens of others were hanged like felons. Had Lord Gordon nae lied to save me, I would have joined them. Should my loyalty be to the man who abandoned us to die or the men who saved me? You tell me that, Boyd."

"Damn you, think about what Alexander is telling you. Give your loyalty to our kingdom, whether you are grateful to the King or nae." He tensed his eyebrows, squinted, and shot Thomas an intense gaze. He took a fierce bit of bread, chewing as though he was at war with it.

Thomas pulled his cloak tight around himself. A heavy silence wrapped around them. At last, he tried to smile across the fire at his friend. "You could have picked a warmer season to go home."

"At least it will be warmer when we reach there. And plenty of fires. A pity we cannae stay until Yuletide."

"Aye, but we should have your family settled in Inverness by then," Boyd said in a more moderate tone. "On the morrow, we head toward Tummel and should find it warmer as we move south."

Engulfed again by the vastness of Rannoch, Thomas sighed. A guard moved, outlined against the fading sunset. "Boyd..." He picked up his bread and turned it in his hands. "I... I'll think about it."

Chapter 31

BONKYL, SCOTLAND

When they rode past the fringe of the forest, the valley before them lay under a dusting of snow. The road was empty, but thin ribbons of smoke rose above the thatch roofs of the cottages. As before, the church bell tolled as they approached. Doors opened and faced peeked out. Thomas supposed the people were less eager to rush into the cold to greet their lord than leave their summer labors.

They rode on and clattered over the drawbridge over the moat. Grooms rushed out to take the horses. Lady Bonkyl and Isabel hurried out the door bundled in cloaks.

"Alexander! We have been fashed half to death! Your men returned without you."

John Stewart came out of the armory with a puzzled, worried look but gave bows all around.

Boyd pointed to the gate. "Wat, Cailin, on guard at the gate." He gave Thomas a pointed look.

Thomas smiled to himself. For the moment, he was just happy to see Isabel again.

"Come within. Come within," Alexander said. "You

may greet me in warmth." He turned to the men. "Inside all of you."

The rush of heat from the blazing fireplace was heaven after the winter chill. Alexander kissed his mother's cheek. When Isabel threw her arms around his neck, Thomas took a step toward them but stopped himself. He licked his bottom lip, drinking her in with his eyes.

She turned to him, smiling, and held out her hands. "Sir Thomas. Welcome."

He kissed her hand, holding both as long as he decently could before he turned to her mother. "Lady Bonkyl. I am glad to see you looking well."

"Sir Robert Boyd of Kilmarnock. My mother, Lady Bonkyl, my brother John and sister Isabel."

Boyd gave Lady Bonkyl a deep bow, but her raised eyebrows had to mean she knew he was a follower of the Bruce. She exchanged speaking looks with Isabel and John.

Alexander told the men to take their ease in the great hall and scratched the back of his neck. He paused as though not sure where to start. "Let us go to the bower where we can be privy, and I shall give you my news."

Lady Bonkyl turned to a half dozen servants waiting to greet their lord near a side doorway. "Have wine brought to the bower and ale and warm food for Sir Robert's men."

Thomas gave Isabel a reassuring look, but from her expression, it had only increased her alarm. She followed her mother up the stairs, Thomas and the others trailing behind. In the bower, Lady Bonkyl settled on a padded stool. Isabel scooted a stool close and reached for her mother's hand. Alexander closed the door behind him.

After taking a deep breath, Alexander said, "I have sworn fealty to King Robert."

Lady Bonkyl covered her mouth with her hand and went pale.

"How could you?" John demanded.

"Much has happened that you dinnae ken, John. I have reason to believe that the Bruce is gaining the upper hand. But for the now it puts Bonkyl in danger. And anyone here. So I am taking you all to Inverness for safety."

"Inverness?" Isabel said the word as though it was on the other side of the world. And he supposed that for them it was.

"Aye. You will be safer there. I promise you. But before we leave, I must slight Bonkyl Castle."

"Alexander. No!" John said. His mother was shaking her head.

"It is our home. How…" Isabel bit her lip. "Why?"

"Because if I dinnae, the English will take it and use it against us. I have made my decision. The only one that I could make."

"Sir Thomas." Isabel gave him a wide-eyed appealing look. "Do you agree with this?"

He squeezed his eyebrows together. "I have nae given the Bruce my fealty. But he is right that since he has, you are in danger here. The English will take the castle. Or would if it were nae slighted."

She stood, wrapping her arms around herself. "Forgive me… I must… I must go." She hurried out the door, closing it softly. Thomas felt an ache in his throat. He could not blame her for taking it hard. They would destroy her only home and all that she knew.

Lady Bonkyl's forehead was furled in a deep frown. "Alexander, where are we to bide after that? Where will be safe?"

"The King has taken Inverness and slighted the castle. He has gifted me a house he took from one of the Southron knights when he drove them out. I ken that it is nae your home, but it willnae be forever. We can build a manor house once we have peace." He picked up her hand from her lap. "I swear I shall make it up to you and to Isabel."

Boyd cleared his throat. "We dinnae have much time. We must reach Inverness before the worst of the winter weather. You must prepare any belongings you are to take. And then the curtain wall must be mined to bring it down, and the keep fired."

Alexander crossed his arms, frowning. "What we cannae take, furniture and such can be carried off and used by our people. Our men must be prepared to march with us." He sighed. "I must tell them all this news myself."

"What about our servants?" Lady Bonkyl asked. "Our seneschal, constable, marshal? The farmers and weavers have homes. The grooms can go to their families, but those have only the castle for home."

"They can go with us and serve you or join me in the fighting."

Thomas twitched a wry smile at Boyd's heavy sigh. It would be a much larger party returning north, but at least with additional guards in case they were attacked.

"John," Alexander asked, "how many men-at-arms do we have? I telt the King two-score, so I hope I didnae lie to him."

"Almost two-score who are fit to fight with those of yours who returned. A few are too aged, but I have kept on for pity's sake."

"How many sumpter horses? We must carry as much food as we can and all mother's and Isabel's clothing, jewelry, plate, and such coin as we have. We brought only two."

"Nae many, only six. We've had little use for them."

"Then, that must do."

"We must use wayns," Lady Bonkyl said. "We cannae leave behind our furniture, our mattresses, our linens. Think of the loss!"

Boyd shook his head. "Not possible. We must escape notice from the English and cross lands nae wayn could make it through, Rannoch Moor for one. I'm sorry, My Lady. I ken how great a loss that is, but your lives would be a much greater loss. Nae just to yourself but to your children."

Alexander gave a sharp nod. "John, gather the men-at-arms for me to speak to. That first. Then I must talk to our people, explain what is happening, and warn them what to expect. Though if they dinnae resist, they should come to nae harm."

"What about me?" John replied.

"Do you trust me? That I would only do this if I believed that the Bruce can win?"

John nodded if looking reluctant.

"Then stand with me."

John managed a smile. "I'll gather the men."

Lady Bonkyl stood, her back straight but her hand pressed to her heart as though it pained her. "And I must plan what we may take with us."

Thomas bowed and left them to their tasks, hoping that he might know where to find Isabel. In the bailey, John was calling out for all the men to assemble in the great hall. Thomas bypassed him to go around the corner into the herb garden.

Isabel stood in the middle of a garden with shrubs pruned and bare of leaves, ground dusted with snow. Tears welled in her eyes. "It will never grow green again."

He went to her and took her cold hands into his, chafing them. "You shall have another. I promise."

"But... it willnae be the same." She hiccupped a sob. "Nothing will be the same."

Slipping an arm around her shoulder, he pulled her against his chest and leaned his cheek on her head. He could think of no words that would comfort her, so he rubbed his hand in a small circle on her back and rocked her gently, just holding her.

She took a deep breath, pushed herself back, and wiped her eyes with the heels of her hands. "You must think me a goose. I must be strong." She sniffled. "I will be. It..." More tears trickled down her cheeks. She lifted her chin, wiped her tears again, and looked thoughtful. "We cannae take Earrach, can we?"

Thomas took her hand in his. "Nae."

"Then let us go to the mews. I must release him." She looked up into his face. "He will be all right if I release him?"

"He kens to hunt for food, the main thing any falcon must do."

The mews were small. Hers was the only falcon, although there was room for several more. Obviously, Lady Bonkyl did not go hawking. She put on her thick leather hawking glove that hung by the door and got it onto her fist while Thomas removed the jesses from its legs and the bell from its tail.

She stroked the sparrowhawk's blue-gray head as they walked through the bailey and over the drawbridge. One of Boyd's guards nodded to him as he passed through the gate.

"It will confuse him when I am nae here when he returns," Isabel said.

Thomas smiled. "Aye, probably. But then he will go find something to catch. I think that is what makes them happy."

The hawk stared intently into her face. She stroked its head one last time, held out her arm, and flung him into the air.

When she gulped as the bird soared, he took her hand. He held it as they hurried back into the castle. "It was for the best."

They stopped at the doorway. "It was hard. I do wish I could be braver. I ken that my mother needs me to be strong for her."

"I think you are a braw lass who has a right to be sad on losing your home. Losing what you love. But you'll build another home… and…" He cleared his throat. This was no time to show his mind when she was distraught.

He opened the door for her as she gave him a puzzled look. "And?"

He put his hand on the small of her back as she went in. "Mayhap we can talk about it later."

* * *

THE WAY NORTH seemed to be taking forever.

Thomas had thought the way south was hard, but it was nothing compared to going north into the winter with two women and a train of sumpter horses.

They left Bonkyl amidst grumbling of men at early rising, the clank of tack and snorting of horses. At the foot of the castle mount, they halted. The front curtain wall was a line of rubble, but the keep itself still stood. They waited.

At last, a coil of smoke rose, and Alexander rode down at a canter. He pulled up, grim-faced. "It is done." They watched as flames curled out of the arrow slits. Crackles and snaps exploded. Children watched open-mouthed, their parents looking solemn.

Isabel hid her face within her hood, and Thomas could not tell if she wept. He wished he had some way to comfort her.

Their party was now fourscore with the men from Bonkyl added to their original guards. Most of the servants had gone to family, but Lady Bonkyl brought the castle seneschal, a thin, dignified man by the name of Herbert.

They carried the banner of Stewart of Bonkyl, but there was still much danger in lands controlled by the English. Had news of Alexander's change in allegiance yet spread? Would anyone recognize Boyd? They argued and debated whether it was safe to stop in towns or monasteries for shelter. Boyd said the risk was too great as he had insisted on the way south. Thomas argued that for the women, they should take shelter where they could. Alexander agreed.

At first in the lowlands south of the Forth, the land was rolling moorland that stretched away as far as the eye could see. Stone bridges spanned the many rivers and farms ringed stone tower houses. The road was well trafficked. For the sake of the women, Thomas swore he would not betray them, and Boyd gave in to his argument to find shelter, so they bided in monastery guesthouses the first two nights.

They followed the waters of the Tummel to the edge of Rannoch Moor. Time after time, they topped one of the basalt ridges for only more barrenness to lie ahead. It grew colder and quieter. The wind blew from the southwest, and plumes of snow like banners blew from the peaks of the Mamlorn, and they drew their heavy fur-lined cloaks close around them.

Within the moor held no farms or tower houses or monasteries for shelter. The next day was not so bad, but by the end of the fourth day, the women were white-faced and slumped in their saddles from exhaustion. They stopped to make camp before the early dark. Thomas wrapped a thick plaid over their cloaks and told them to rest. They would only be in the way as the men built fires, erected the small tents, and tended the horses. Isabel protested that she could help, but he said to keep her mother warm. They needed them both rested and strong enough to ride on the morrow.

He walked the perimeter of the camp, making sure the pickets were in place and alert. He cursed when he stepped into the edge of a peat hag and fell onto his hands and knees. Thankfully the others weren't there to laugh at him. He wiped off the sticky muck. Wet and cold, when he turned back, the camp was a welcome sight. The tents were up. The horses staked and chomping tufts of dried moor grass. Boyd sat skinning a brace of hares they had snared the night before. One of the men was tending a stewpot and another stirring oats with water and a lump of fat to cook on a flat piece of iron for bannocks.

Boyd looked up. "Next time, a peat bog will swallow you."

"Not a fate I'd relish," Thomas said, laughing. The damned man had eyes as sharp as an eagle. Isabel shot a puzzled look at the two of them. He smiled into her eyes. She returned it, and in the firelight, she blushed.

The hares gave the bean stew some flavor, warming them from the inside. They shared around the last of the ale they had bought at the monastery where they'd last slept. He followed Isabel with his eyes when she drifted to the tent she shared with her mother. One by one, the others crawled into their shelter to sleep for yet another weary day's ride.

Thomas was the last awake. His face drew into a frown beneath the night sky, black as the pit. He longed for Geoffrey to be in the camp, telling one of his quips. To make the night less dark and dour.

Chapter 32

INVERNESS, SCOTLAND

After leaving their men to camp outside the burgh, the sun was half-hidden behind a bank of clouds when they reached Inverness's south gate. They passed under the arch into a nearly empty street. The castle mount seemed misshapen with only the rubble of the castle atop it. Otherwise, the burgh was unchanged. A brisk, wet wind swirled around them as they rode through the street, and most people seemed to be sensibly within doors. Wisps of smoke drifted above the rooftops. Only a handful of farmers hawked their stored onions and apples and bags of oats in the market square though the shops fronting the houses were open selling leather goods, cloth, and clothing.

"What do we do now?" Isabel asked.

"Go to the guesthouse at Blackfriars. Then I shall make sure the house we have for you is prepared," Alexander said.

Isabel wrinkled her brow, her eyes narrowing.

Boyd grunted. "We must find news of the King as well."

Past the Kirk of Saint Mary, they turned onto Friar

Street. When Thomas rang the bell at the monastery, the porter opened the gate. In the courtyard, he hopped from the saddle and held her reins as Isabel dismounted. Grooms took their horses. The white-haired, distinguished-looking abbot hurried out to welcome them.

"Och, we understand." Boyd frowned. "Could your grooms feed the poor horses and let them rest without their tack? They've had a hard trip. If the ladies and our men can rest and warm themselves in the refectory, we would be grateful. We dinnae mean to bide here. But we need news."

Isabel slammed her hands on her hips. "You didnae drag me all the way across Scotland in the cold to wait here. I want to see where I am to bide."

"Isabel—"

"She is right," Lady Bonkyl cut Alexander off. "If it is nae adequate or there is work needed, then I must see. And Isabel and Herbert as well. We shall go with you. How far is it to this house?"

Thomas hid his smile behind a cough into his hand.

Alexander threw up his hands. "Very well. It is nae far on Friar's Lane on the opposite side from the kirk." He turned to the abbot. "Forgive us, Abbot Ciarach. I have a family matter to attend, but if our men and mounts could rest here for a short time...?"

"Of course, my son. Food and warmth are theirs."

Alexander looked to Boyd and Thomas. "I'll return as soon as I can."

John frowned. "I am going as well. I want to see for myself they're properly cared for."

Thomas clicked his tongue against his teeth. "I shall go with you. In case you need my aid."

Isabel ducked her head and gave him a smile from under her lashes.

He offered Isabel his arm, and they began walking behind Alexander and his mother, followed by John and Herbert. "Boyd is right that we must find word of the King and where he is. We will try the provost, I suppose. He should have news." Thomas made a noncommittal noise.

They stopped at a tall, narrow house, the first on the right side of the lane. Beyond it was a second smaller house and an apothecary shop on the next corner. Opposite was the mount on which stood the kirk.

Herbert cocked his head, examining the building. "It is large for only three, but we will need servants. At least, the roof looks sound."

Standing back, they studied the slate shingles of the sloping roof.

"Good solid door." Thomas rapped his knuckles on the blackened oak door studded with iron nails and a large iron lock. "No one could enter without permission." He walked to the single window and rattled the closed shutters that were solid to the touch. Nothing else broke the stone frontage.

Alexander took out the large iron key from his scrip and turned it in the lock with a squeak. He led the way into a narrow entry hall with only a bench and a row of wooden pegs on the wall and a dusty smell.

Isabel was biting her lip, so Thomas squeezed her hand. Reluctantly, he released it and said, "Let us see what the rest of it is like."

He pushed open the door on the left. They went into a high, spacious room, with stairs at the far end that went up to a solar loft.

"That roof is at least twenty feet high," said Herbert, craning his neck to look up at the cobwebby beams that supported the slate tiles. A table was knocked over, one leg broken, hinting that the last owner had protested his eviction. The stools lay overturned hither and yon. Rucked, disturbed rushes covered the floor.

At the far end from the loft was a wide hearth with an arched stone mantle and iron fireplace dogs. A single high-backed chair stood before it, and a couple of faded tapestries hung on the walls. John gave one of the stools a scornful kick.

"It seems sound, though not fit for our ladies as it is," Herbert said.

Lady Bonkyl made a humming sound. "Aye, but given time and some work, it could be a fine house. With fresh rushes, a cupboard, a new larger table, better tapestries." She nodded, sounding pleased with the challenge. "I can see it."

"Let's have a look at the solar and the yard," said Alexander.

Thomas was surprised to see that a kist and bed and feather mattress were in place in the solar, which Herbert said must be aired and cleaned before the ladies went anywhere near it. In the yard, they found a well dug well away from the other structures, a wash house, a chicken coop, a small stable, a privy, the remains of a garden, and a kitchen shed.

"It will take a gey deal of work," Herbert said, looking tired.

"Nae so much," Isabel told him. "Why it is much nicer than I expected. We need lamps and candles. They will brighten it as will fire in on the hearth. And in the spring, I shall plant herbs, even some flowers."

Thomas reached out and softly touched her arm.

"You're sure? This will truly do?" John asked. His mother patted his arm.

"Aye," Alexander said. "It will nae seem so much once you are rested. And you may guest with the black friars in

the meantime. It is a short stroll, so you can easily super-
vise as it is being readied. Herbert, find a maidservant and
cook to help. The friars can advise you on who would be
trustworthy." He took his mother's arm. "Now, we should
return because Boyd is sure to be fashing himself to
find news."

They walked back to the monastery, Thomas's mind
half on returning to his uncle and half on Isabel, walking
ahead of him speaking intently to her brother, his head
bent close to her as she spoke. Alexander looked over his
shoulder at Thomas and then shook his head at her. She
grasped his arm, shook it, and whispered something.
Thomas smiled. What was she so emphatically telling her
brother?

Thomas's heart sped up. Someday...

The monastery's porter called a lay brother to show
Lady Bonkyl and Isabel to the guest house at the rear of
the monastery grounds. Thomas's eyes followed until
another friar walked them across to the main abbey buildings and to the imposing abbot's house on the west side of
the cloister. Inside they were led upstairs to the abbot's
parlor, a large comfortably furnished room with a fire
crackling in the fireplace and a glazed window that over-
looked the courtyard.

Boyd and the provost of Inverness were already seated,
Boyd's eyes narrowed with an annoyed look. Abbot
Ciarach, behind his plain table, waved them to chairs, his
mouth in a thin line.

"Do you ken where the King is then? What is it you
dinnae want to say?" Boyd demanded.

The provost drew down his eyebrows. "Nae secret from
you, but it will do nae good for rumors to run wild, so I
want our speech private. The King..." The provost sighed
and rubbed his hand over his face. "He has been desper-

ately ill, confined to bed, carried about in a litter. Some say he is dying."

"What?" Boyd jumped to his feet, tipping over his chair. Thomas reached out and grabbed it before it clattered to the floor.

The provost continued. "His brother took the army and the King to Strathbogie for a time. But I've news that for the now they are camped near Inverurie. What will happen if he doesnae recover..." His lips thinned into a grim line and he gave a despairing shake of his head. "And the Earl of Buchan is said to be at Fyvie Castle with de Brechin and de Mowbray."

"Wait," Thomas said, his heart thumping. "What is wrong with him? What kind of illness?" He was sure his uncle had never been ill a day in his life.

"That I dinnae ken. A friar is with them, a Brother Fillan who is said to be treating his illness."

Boyd strode about the room. He whirled and slammed his fist against the wall. "We must leave immediately."

"I disagree," Alexander said. "There is nae point in wandering around in the dark, and it is nightfall. We should ride at first light."

Boyd slammed his fist against the wall again, turned, and opened his mouth as though to argue. He paused and let out a loud breath. "Aye. Very well. We ride for Inverurie at dawn."

Chapter 33

INVERURIE, SCOTLAND

The wind rattled the branches of the pines and made the grasses bow along the River Don. Thomas tugged his fur cloak tighter against the fierce bite of the cold as he rode beside Alexander and Boyd. It was late afternoon just outside Inverurie when they sighted a small stone tower house next to a yew tree with his uncle's camp of about six hundred men surrounding it. The camp rang to the sounds of pikes being sharpened and armor repaired.

Boyd led the way through the camp up to the dilapidated tower, its stones dappled with moss. The column followed hard behind them. Thomas swung out of the saddle before the rough plank door, and Alexander, John, and Boyd dismounted as well.

Boyd pointed. "You men tend to your horses and then set up your tents near the others."

Brother Fillan stepped out of a tent and walked toward the door, a cup in his hand. Boyd caught his arm. "How bad is it? They said..." His voice choked. "I heard it is gey bad."

"It was the winter illness and bad enough. He could

barely breathe. He burnt with fever and had a pain in his side was so bad he couldnae walk. We had to move him here in a litter, and the Comyn's men saw us move him. It didnae help that in winter, herbs and honey to treat him were hard to find. But thanks be to the Holy Virgin, he is no longer coughing up thick slime, and his breathing has eased. But it will take time for him to regain his strength."

Thomas's scrubbed both hands over his face, remembering the emaciated King Edward dying of the flux. But he had been an old man, and his uncle was young and strong. The monk must be right that the Bruce would live.

Boyd blew out a breath. "Thanks be to God."

"I need to tell him I've returned. If he is strong enough," Alexander said.

"He is. But keep your visit short. He must rest to recover." The friar knocked on the door and opened it. "Visitors, Sire."

Thomas let Alexander and Boyd go ahead of him into the shabby room while John waited outside. There was only the narrow bed and a rickety table, the rafters hung with cobwebs. But at least it was warm with a good fire on the central hearth and clean rushes on the floor. His uncle's armor was carefully stacked in a corner. Thomas hung back next to the door. His breath caught at the Bruce's gaunt and pallid face where he lay covered in furs.

"First, let His Grace drink this. Tea of marshmallow plant and thyme. We found a little honey to sweeten it."

The Bruce made a sour face and muttered a complaint, but he took the concoction and drank it down in a gulp. He croaked, "It will do me nae good when you are starving me to death."

"That you feel well enough to hunger is a good sign. I shall return with a bowl of barley gruel. If that sits well, we shall try some beef jelly."

The Bruce glowered after the friar before he turned his attention to Alexander. "You've returned," he said in a querulous tone.

"Sire, as I promised, I brought nearly two-score of men from Bonkyl and my brother John to swear fealty when... uh... when you are ready."

Boyd had his arms crossed, frowning down at the Bruce. "I should have kent better than go off and leave you. Look at the state of you."

The Bruce snorted. "Aye, had you been here I'd nae dared fall sick. But I am better, Robbie. Dinnae fash yourself." He grimaced. "As bad as they taste, the friar's potions and teas seem to have helped."

"If barley gruel doesnae kill you, I suppose you are better. Where is Lennox? He should have seen you were cared for better than this."

"I sent him to raise men. And I have been cared for well enough. At least on the morrow, I willnae spend the Yuletide soaking my blankets with sweat from a fever." His uncle turned a scowl Thomas's way. "And you. You still have nothing to say for yourself?"

Thomas dropped his gaze and shook his head, his chest tightening.

"Then be off with you." He waved a hand, letting his head fall back and closing his eyes. "Off with all of you."

His uncle was still much too ill to annoy further, so Thomas he slipped out the door. Boyd closed it behind them; his face was drawn up in a worried frown. Brother Fillan shuffled up, a steaming bowl and a spoon in his hands.

"Brother Fillan. You're certain he will recover?" Thomas asked, and Boyd shot him a surprised glance.

"I believe that he will. Many would have died, but the King is a strong man. Rest—" The friar held up the bowl.

"—and food, herbs, and prayers a should see him well. Now let me go to him while this is still warm."

Thomas reached out and pressed his hand to the nearby yew, not even as tall as the building beside it, swallowing a tightness in his throat. Its limbs were bare, its trunk not oversized like his old friend the Giant. But perhaps someday it would be with God's mercy.

"I need to find out what has been to do while we were gone." Boyd nodded to Thomas more pleasantly than usual and strode toward the camp.

Alexander said, "And I must see to my men."

Thomas took up his reins and walked toward the horse lines, his mind racing. What if he did beg his uncle's forgiveness? Lord Gordon could no longer be held responsible. Thomas had paid the debt for his life being spared. Hadn't he? And had Robert truly been wrong to flee Methven? Would he not have done the same? Had what he had done when he fled at Glen Trool been so different?

He had been so confident that Robert was wrong. But was that merely the certainty of a knight with too little experience to understand the reality of war? Was it as Boyd said that he was too stubborn to admit he was wrong? That Robert had never fled Scotland? His head began to ache with the questions spinning through it.

Once he tended his horse and set up his tent, Thomas sat alone before it on a stone watching the shadows lengthen. Alexander was avoiding him, and no one else was eager to speak to him... Damn them. His eyes prickled as he tried not to recall Geoffrey's jests, laughing together with good, steady Hugh looking on. He tried not to think of Lord Gordon, begging Pembroke for his life. Clouds moved in to cover the sky like a shroud. The more he tried not to remember, the more he did. He raked his hands through his hair and jerked at it.

A cheer rang over the camp. Thomas raised his head to see his uncle standing in the doorway of the tower wrapped in a fur, leaning against the doorpost, too weak to stand without help. But he was standing. Thomas jumped to his feet, heart racing. His uncle was going to live.

Darkness slowly encompassed the camp; the men grew quiet. Icy grass crunched under Thomas's feet as he paced through the camp. As he passed a tent, someone muttered in his sleep. There was a grunting snore from another.

They'd grown lax, used to his being there. The sentries were watching for the Comyn, not for him. He could slip past them in the darkness. In the distance, one of the horses snorted. He would have to escape on foot, but he could reach the English-held castle of Fyvie within a day if he made good time. His heart pounded as though it would tear out of his chest.

Carefully, silently, Thomas slipped through the camp, head down so the gleam of his eyes would not show if anyone turned his way. He reached the last tent and hunkered down. On the ridge ahead, a sentry, not even a silhouette in the black night, stamped his feet and muttered a complaint of the cold.

Thomas's breath hitched. It would be so easy. He would not be missed until morning. That would give him ample time to escape.

He took a deep breath and slowly blew it out through his lips and closed his eyes. He could escape to the English, to distant friends, and to the peace that came with Scotland conquered. Or he could turn back...

Chapter 34

December 25, 1307

The next day at midmorning, Niall Campbell galloped through the camp toward the tower with his two-score men trailing behind, shouting, "To arms!" In front of the tower, he threw himself from the saddle. The camp reacted like an anthill given a kick, men running every which way but most running toward Sir Niall.

From his tent, Thomas dashed up the hill. By the time he reached the tower, King Robert stood in the doorway, though he grasped the jamb to remain upright. "What is to-do?" he demanded.

Boyd, Edward de Bruce, Gilbert de Hay, William de Irvine, the King's armor-bearer, Alexander Stewart, and a dozen other knights crowded around with hundreds of men standing further back.

"Our sentries on the other side of Inverurie. De Brechin attacked them, wiped them out. I found our dead and tracked his force to Oldmeldrum." Campbell took a deep breath. "Sire, we spotted the banner of Buchan and a large force. Two thousand at least preparing to march as I galloped this way."

"Buchan thinks to find me abed, too ill to fight." Using the jamb as a prop, he pushed himself erect and glowered all about him. "Where is my armor. Bring it to me. Now! The rest of you. Why are you standing there?"

"Sire!" Brother Fillan rushed up to the King. "You are nae yet recovered."

The Bruce's face was pale, but he clenched his jaw. "Their arrogance has made me strong. As God wills it, I shall destroy them or they me."

Thomas's heart galloped, and he sucked in a breath. "Robert. Your Grace." He walked to his uncle and dropped to his knees. "Will you take me into your peace? Forgive me my past words and my deeds? I wronged you. But allow me to fight for you."

The King paused, still grasping the door, and looked down at him, his expression softening. "You ask it of me, nephew?"

"Aye. I do."

"Then, you are in my peace."

He had said these words before, but he must never again after today. "By the Lord God and all the holy saints, I swear I am your man from this day forward of life and limb and truth. So help me God."

A smile slowly spread over the King's face. Thomas returned it as he rose. His spun and his chest seemed so light he was almost weightless.

There was a cheer, and Alexander shouted, "Well done!"

"I need a sword," Thomas replied, and Alexander nodded.

"Now, My Lords. Sound the assembly!" The Bruce turned to go inside but stumbled.

Thomas grabbed his arm. He helped the King to the bed where he sank down. "Are you sure you can do this?"

"I must. Now bring my horse."

"I'll stay by his side," William de Irvine said. "Hold him up if I must."

Thomas gave a grateful nod and ran to don his own armor and do as the King had commanded. The horns called an urgent *To arms! To arms!* The camp filled with shouts and curses, the whinny of horses, the clank of tack, and the clatter of spears. Beneath a gray sky, flurries of snow drifted in the breeze. Men dashed through the winter chill to kick out campfires and saddle horses.

The trumpets blared again: *To arms!* Boyd passed him, buckling his sword belt as he ran. Thomas dragged on his gambeson and wrestled into his hauberk and the rest of his harness. Alexander came cantering up, already armored and tossed him a sword and belt.

"Any more news about where Buchan is?" Thomas asked him.

"A scout just reported that they are on the road between Barra Hill and the marshes."

To arms! The trumpets shrilled, *To arms!* He shoved on his great helm. "If the King doesnae need me, I'll join your men." He buckled on his sword and picked up his shield. He saluted Alexander and sprinted, clanking, for the horse line. The sun gleamed through a break in the gray clouds. If they died, he hoped it the sun would shine on it. He wondered if there was something wrong with him that he always thought about dying before a battle.

He saddled the King's braw stallion and William de Irvine's courser. Edward de Bruce, surrounded by fifty knights and men-at-arms, shouted to form into battle array as he led the mounts to the tower house.

His uncle stood with his arm slung across Irvine's

shoulder. Bearing much of the King's weight, the man half-carried him to his courser. Thomas slid to the ground. When the King grasped the pommel of his saddle, Irvine knelt on one knee so the Bruce could step onto the other. Thomas grasped his arm, hand on his back, and boosted him. With a grunt, the King gained the saddle and straightened.

Once ahorse, the King was resplendent in his gold-inlaid armor, red cloak embroidered with the lion rampant, and gold coronet. William mounted, and Thomas handed him the royal banner.

Edward de Bruce's banner unfurled as his squire shook it out, a red saltire on a white field. Behind him flew the gold and black gyronny of Niall Campbell. Thomas scanned the field for Alexander Stewart and his men. He picked out the standard first, blue, and white checky with a black band with Alexander beneath it. Nearby sat Robert Boyd.

Riding on the other side of the King, he and Irvine paced to join Sir Edward a few steps ahead. Fewer than seven hundred men, only a hundred of them knights, spread before the King. The rest were rank on rank of foot soldiers with spear and sword and shield. The King raised one hand high overhead and signaled to move out. The trumpets blared at his command.

His uncle swayed in his saddle and grasped the high pommel with one hand, but he kept his back stiff. When Thomas reached out a hand, he brushed it away. Northwest, they splashed across the narrow, ice-rimed River Urie and into the bare, rolling, snow-dusted hills and icy ridges.

The Bruce inclined his head toward the village of Oldmeldrum, a huddle of houses, on the crest of a ridge. On the right, Barra Hill rose above the other peaks.

"Edward, take your men and circle west. I want you on

his flank and make sure his scouts see you. I am going to circle right around the other side of Barra Hill."

A scout cantered up. "Your Grace, there are Buchan lookouts on Barra."

The King nodded. "As I expected. Let them see that we advance." He gave a grim smile. "And that I lead my men."

"I had nae thought of this, Sire." Thomas's mouth twitched with a grim smile. "Today is Yuletide."

The King's jaw clenched. "Then let us give Buchan a fitting Yule welcome."

"After we defeat him, we'll light a Yule log."

The Bruce lifted his hand and signaled a turn to the right. Awkwardly the mass of the small army shifted. On they went, the ungainly bulk of Barra Hill to their left, sheep scattering at the sight of them. They circled behind the hill and marched eastward through bare, rolling knolls toward Oldmeldrum.

Boyd cantered up. "Sire." He took a deep breath. "We dinnae have the men to take the village. We would be in the gey teeth of Buchan's force just outside it."

The King clenched his jaw, muscles working. "You think I dinnae ken that, Robbie? Now return to your place."

Within easy sight of the village rooftops and the bulk of Barra blocking them off from the main Buchan force, the Bruce held up a hand to call a halt. "Sound the trumpets." The trumpets blared long and low.

Thomas stared at his uncle. Had his illness disturbed his mind? Now the Buchan's scouts would know where they were of a certainty.

The King gave a slow nod of satisfaction. "About," he shouted. "Turn about." He wheeled his mount and gave it a slap with his reins. It sprang to a canter. He lurched but caught his pommel again and hung on. He lashed his horse to a gallop through a gap in his men, reeling. With a gasp, Thomas pushed him upright.

Once more, everyone turned. They cantered and jogged toward the hill and up the slope.

When they reached the summit, Buchan's lookouts had scattered like rabbits and were scurrying, shouting a warning, down the brae.

"Jesu God," Thomas said. Their movements had been a ruse.

Chapter 35

Buchan's force of thousands stretched before them, facing in the opposite direction, toward the village where their horns had sounded.

"Trumpets, blow the charge!" the King shouted. "On them!"

The King's main force raced down at full speed, horse at a gallop, foot soldiers running and leaping, screaming as they went.

"Why are you sitting there?" the King demanded. "I ordered a charge."

Thomas twisted his reins around his hand and untwisted them. "You are too ill—"

"Go!"

"I have him." Irvine pointed to a large stone. "Sire, sit. Watch the battle from there."

Thomas drew his sword. The ground sloped down to the Oldmeldrum Road, where the Buchan's force was a tangle of men and horses turned hither and yon. Comyn's huge blue banner was surrounded by chaos. Commanders on armored warhorses stood in their stirrups, waving their swords overhead, doubtless shouting commands. What should have been the front ranks of the enemy, all knights, were behind the levies, a swarming mass of untrained pikemen and farmers armed with scythes and axes. And the King's army was rushing down on them, screaming, "A Bruce! A Bruce!"

He put his heels to his horse's flanks and used his spurs. The mount nearly jerked his arms out of their sockets when it sprang away. He urged it with legs and heels to a gallop. His heart pounded in his chest in time to the hoof-beats. A trumpet blew a long cry, brazen and defiant. Boyd waved his sword and shouted, "On them!" A thousand other voices shouted. Thomas raised his voice in the cacophony, "Scotland! Scotland!"

Alexander was whaling at a knight with a yellow shield sliced with red rays, oak chips flying. Boyd caught a pikeman full in the chest as the dolt ran at him, his sword shearing through leather and muscle and bone. Thomas glimpsed Edward de Bruce's red saltire banner, so they had struck on the flank.

And then he was amongst them, and his battle was only the man in front of him. A spearman thrust at his horse. Thomas danced it to the side. The man pulled back for another try, but Thomas swung, knocking the spear aside and laid the man's face open to the bone with his backslash. Leaving the man shrieking on his knees, Thomas rode on.

Another spear thunked into his shield and stuck there. Thomas wheeled, jerking it from the man's hands. The man scrabbled for his sword. Thomas hacked downward, but the man got his shield up in time. He raised his shield high, thrusting with his sword as though it were a short spear. Thomas snorted at the fool and circled him, raining down blows, chips flying from the shield. The spearman backed up, keeping his shield high and slipped onto his ass in a puddle of ice-rimmed blood. He was worth no more time, so Thomas rode over him and galloped after another spearman, cutting him down from behind with a sweeping side slash.

A knight in Buchan's livery rode past, slumped in the saddle, an ax lodged in his back. Thomas's blood raced, heart pounding. No time for thought. One of the Buchan's knights, unhorsed, missing his helm, and in blood-splattered armor, made a grab for the bridle. Thomas charged. Taking an idea from the spearman, he lowered his sword as though it were a lance. His target turned, open-mouthed, and brought up his sword. Thomas's sword stabbed into his stomach through mail and muscle so deep he had to raise a foot to kick the body free.

When he turned to find another opponent, Buchan's infantry was trying to flee and the knights using the flats of their swords to try to beat them back into the battle. Thomas charged one of them, a broad and stocky man, wearing a mail hauberk who'd lost his helm, his hair matted with blood. He aimed a swing at his quarry's chest, but the man blocked it.

"Die, traitor," the stocky knight snarled between clenched teeth, bringing a savage side-swing that would have removed his head had it landed. Thomas slammed the blow aside. Steel ran on steel. They hacked at each other, blows thudding on their shields, and Thomas realized that they were well matched.

The knight reversed his swing and gave a savage chop. Thomas caught it on his shield with a shock that numbed his arm. The swordsman shoved in close, grinning. He swung. The sword made a ghastly scraping sound when Thomas caught it on his. They shoved back and forth as Thomas struggled to free his blade. He slammed his shield into the swordsman's shoulder, knocking him back. Sword freed, he aimed a swipe at him, but the stocky knight dodged back. On his return swing, Thomas scraped his face, laying the cheek open to the bone. He screamed and dropped his guard.

Thomas slammed him in the face with his shield. He screamed again as he fell, his foot caught in his stirrup, his leg twisted at a grotesque angle.

"Yield," Thomas shouted.

The man moaned. "I yield," he said, voice thick with pain. He no longer had his sword to surrender, so he slumped flat on the ground.

Thomas looked around for another fight, but the battle had moved past him. No one remained except corpses that lay scattered across the road. Overhead, ravens already circled. Edward de Bruce led his knights as they raced after the army fleeing through the hills. The infantry followed behind, waving their swords and spears over their heads in triumph.

The blood rushed in Thomas's ears, and he flushed hot with victory. Keeping his voice even, he looked down at the man at his feet, "I do believe we have won."

The trumpets sounded on Barra Hill, calling the army back. The sun had sunk onto the horizon, casting a blood-red light over the crest of the hill where the King sat on a stone beneath the Lion Rampant as it whipped in the wind. Thomas rode up the hill toward him.

Historical Characters

In approximate order of appearance:

Thomas Randolph—Lord of Nithsdale, nephew of Robert de Bruce.

Adam de Gordon—Lord of Gordon, formerly a supporter of Sir William Wallace, sided with the English after Wallace's execution.

William de Gordon—Son of Adam Gordon.

Alexander de Bruce—Younger brother of Robert de Bruce, scholar, Dean of Glasgow, executed by the English.

Robert de Bruce—Earl of Carrack, Lord of Annandale, later King of Scots.

Nigel de Bruce—Younger brother of King Robert de Bruce, executed by the English.

Thomas de Bruce—Younger brother of King Robert de Bruce, executed by the English.

Edward de Bruce—Younger brother of King Robert de Bruce.

Robert Wishart—Bishop of Glasgow and a leading supporter of Sir William Wallace and King Robert de Bruce, captured and imprisoned by the English.

Roger Kirkpatrick of Cill Osbairn—A supporter of King Robert de Bruce, reputed to have given the killing blow to John Comyn of Badenoch.

Mary de Bruce—Younger sister of King Robert de Bruce and married to Sir Niall Campbell, one of King Robert's most faithful supporters, captured and imprisoned by the English.

Christina de Bruce—Younger sister of King Robert de Bruce, married to English knight Sir Christopher Seton, captured and imprisoned by the English.

Christopher Seton—An English supporter of King Robert de Bruce, married to King Robert's sister, Christina de Bruce, captured and executed by the English.

James Douglas, Lord of Douglas—Supporter of King Robert de Bruce.

William de Lamberton—Bishop of Saint Andrews and a leading supporter of Sir William Wallace and King Robert de Bruce, captured and imprisoned by the English.

Robert Boyd, Lord of Kilmarnock—Faithful supporter and companion of King Robert de Bruce.

Aymer de Valence, 2nd Earl of Pembroke—A wealthy and influential English nobleman, particularly so during the reign of England's King Edward II.

Henry de Lacy, 3rd Earl of Lincoln—An English nobleman and confidant of England's King Edward I.

King Edward I—King of England from November 1272 until his death in July 1307.

King Edward II—King of England from July 1307 until he was deposed in January 1327.

John Langton—Bishop of Chichester and Chancellor of England.

Sir Piers Gaveston, Duke of Cornwall—Gascon nobleman and confidante, possibly lover, of King Edward II.

Anthony Bek, Bishop of Durham—Famous for his wealth and extravagance, a close advisor to Edward I and took part in his campaigns in Scotland.

Robert de Clifford, Baron of Clifford—A prominent English soldier under both Edward I and Edward II in the war with Scotland.

Humphrey de Bohun—Earl of Hereford, active in both the Welsh and Scottish wars under Edward I.

Guy de Beauchamp— Earl of Warwick, eventually became one of the principal opponents of King Edward II and his favorite, Piers Gaveston.

Sir Philip de Mowbray—A Scottish knight who supported the English, nephew of John Comyn of Badenoch who was killed by Robert de Bruce in Greyfriars Kirk.

Thomas, Earl of Lancaster and Leicester—A cousin of King Edward II and one of the leaders of his opposition and son-in-law of Henry de Lacy, Earl of Lincoln.

Ralph de Monthermer—1st Baron Monthermer, jure uxoris Earl of Gloucester and Hertford until his wife's death in 1307, believed to have warned Robert de Bruce that King Edward I intended to arrest him for treason.

Gilbert de Clare, 8th Earl of Gloucester, 7th Earl of Hertford—Stepson of Ralph de Monthermer who held the earldoms during his minority, a strong supporter of King Edward II.

John Comyn, 3rd Earl of Buchan—A leading and powerful Scottish nobleman, cousin of John Comyn, Lord of Badenoch who was killed by Robert de Bruce and one of his main Scottish opponents.

Historical Notes

I very much enjoyed the research into Thomas Randolph's life, but it was also more than usually frustrating. For an extremely important man in the history of Scotland, there are a huge number of blanks in his history. Filling them in involved a certain amount of extrapolation.

Thomas Randolph was regularly referred to in contemporary documents as the nephew of King Robert the Bruce, so there is no question that he was. What we do not know for certain is exactly how he was King Robert's nephew. His father was another Thomas who served briefly as Chamberlain of Scotland and Sheriff of Roxburgh, so Randolph had to be a nephew through his mother. His mother had to have been one of King Robert's sisters but which is simply not known. By extrapolation of information, it seems likely that she was the daughter of Marjorie, Countess of Carrick, King Robert's mother, by her first husband, Adam of Kilconquhar. He died in 1271 while on crusade, so since that is the case, Randolph's mother was born several years before that date. That there is no record of such a daughter is not astonishing, since so many records are spotty. Nor is it known exactly when Randolph was born, which is relevant to his age when the events of this novel occurred. The author of Scots Peerage, one of the more valuable resources on Scottish nobility, speculated that he was born in 1278. However, he failed to take into consideration that Marjorie of Carrick was only born in about 1256, which makes that date of birth for Randolph highly unlikely. The probability that she had a grandson when she was twenty-two years old would require extraordinarily early childbearing by two generations of women to the extent that I dismiss it as a possibility.

What is known is that Thomas Randolph was listed specifically as a child witness of the coronation of King John Balliol in 1292. Between that date and the coronation of Robert the Bruce in 1306, there is no mention of him in any record. He apparently witnessed no charters or other documents, took part in no battles, and was not a signator of the Ragman's Roll. He was not knighted until King Robert did so at his coronation. When Randolph was taken prisoner after the Battle of Methven, he was referred to in documents as a 'young knight.' To make a very long story short, I came to the conclusion that the most likely date for his birth was circa 1288. He was therefore, too young to have done those things before 1306. While this is based on speculation, such as that his grandmother and mother gave birth at about the age of sixteen, which was the approximate normal age for noblewomen to begin childbearing, it is not contradicted by any known documents and fits with his absence from the normal activities of an adult nobleman.

That he was a squire to Adam de Gordon, Lord of Gordon, is also speculation but again a reasonable possibility considering that there are many indications of a particularly friendly relationship between Randolph and Gordon over a lengthy period. How he came to be saved from execution after the Battle of Methven is an interesting subject of speculation. Every one of Robert the Bruce's other family members who were taken prisoner were executed, some quite brutally. So were the other prisoners from that battle who were hanged. It had to be either the Earl of Pembroke or a Scot accompanying him who convinced the earl that young Randolph had no responsibility in the uprising. It is more likely that it was a Scot such as Gordon who had a close relationship with such a young man. Randolph was sent to Gordon's castle to be kept prisoner with a strongly worded command from the Earl of Pembroke that he was not to be granted parole but was to be held in ward.

After that point, the facts of Randolph's life are more easily documented. There is no doubt that after he was released from imprisonment that he fought on the side of the English, insulted his uncle to his face after he was taken prisoner by James Douglas, and was held prisoner for some time before he was taken back into his uncle's peace to fight faithfully for him. The exact point at which he made peace with his uncle was not recorded but putting it before the Battle Inverurie is not unlikely.

There is also considerable disagreement about when the Battle of Inverurie took place. John Barbour, who is remarkably accurate having had access to men who were at these battles, placed it on Yuletide of 1307. Fordun placed it in May the following year. Many historians believe that Fordun was correct, but I find Barron's argument for Barbour's date extremely convincing, so I used that date in the novel.

The documents and records I made use of in research are myriad. They include original sources such as *The Brus* by John Barbour, *John of Fordun's Chronicle of the Scottish Nation* by John of Fordun, *The Scotichronicon* by Walter Bower, and The *Chronicle of Lanercost* translated by Sir Herbert Maxwell. By modern historians, I depended largely on *The Scottish War of Independence* by Evan Macleod Barron, *Robert Bruce and the Community of the Realm of Scotland* by Geoffrey W. S. Barrow, and *Robert the Bruce, King of Scots* by Ronald McNair Scott as well as *The Scots Peerage* by Sir James Balfour Paul, Lord Lyon King of Arms.

The jokes are translations with changes to English names and locations from *Liber Facetiarum* by Poggio Bracciolini, completed about 1452 and are quite legitimate examples of medieval humor. The work has been much translated and is available in English.

Glossary

Afeart—(Scots) Afraid.

Anent—Regarding, about.

Arming tent—A tent set aside for jousting contestants to don their armor.

Anyroad—(Scots) Anyway.

Aye—Yes.

Bailey yard—The defended area around a castle keep within the outer curtain walls.

Bairn—(Scots) Baby.

Bannock—(Scots) An unleavened flatbread made with oats traditionally cooked on a griddle.

Barbican—Double tower above a castle gate or drawbridge.

Bide—Remain or stay somewhere.

Bonnie—(Scots) Attractive or beautiful - applied to both men and women.

Brae—(Scots) A hillside or sloping bank.

Braw—(Scots) Fine, excellent.

Brigandine—Medieval armor, typically one made of canvas or leather with protective iron plates attached.

Burgh—(Scots) An autonomous chartered town. Burghs had rights to representation in the Parliament of Scotland.

Burgher—A citizen of a town or city, typically a merchant of substance.

Cannae—(Scots) Cannot.

Canny—(Scottish) Careful, prudent.

Cateran—(Scots) A band of fighting men of a Highland clan.

Chausses—Medieval tight-fitting garment worn by men to cover the legs and feet; medieval armor covering the legs.

Chivalry—A group or troop of knights.

Curtain wall—A fortified wall around a medieval castle, typically one linking towers together.

Dagged—The lower edge of a piece of clothing with the edge cut in scallops or foliations.

Daft or Daftie—(Scots) A foolish person.

Courser—A swift, strong horse often used as a warhorse.

Destrier—The largest, heaviest variety of warhorse.

Dinnae—(Scots) Do not.

Enarmes—The straps by which a shield was held on the arm.

Fash—(Scots) To worry or annoy.

Forbye—Besides, in addition.

Gey—(Scots) Very.

Good weal—The public good, the good of society.

Greaves—Armor used to protect the shins.

Hauberk—Full-length coat of mail.

Hell mend (someone)—A curse expressing anger at someone, often for making bad decisions.

Hie—Go quickly; hasten.

Ken—(Scots) Know; Kent—Past tense of 'ken'.

Kist—(Scots) A large strongbox, typically made of wood that is used for storage or shipping; a chest.

Mail coif—A mail hood often worn with a hauberk.

Merlon—The solid part of an embattled parapet.

Nae—(Scots) No; not.

Och—(Scots) Expression of regret or surprise.

Palfrey—An ordinary riding horse.

Parapet—A low protective wall along the edge of a roof or tower top.

Pixane—A mail collar giving additional protection to the lower neck and shoulders.

Quintain—A post set up as a mark for practice in tilting with a lance, usually with a sandbag attached that would swing around and strike if a tilt missed.

Recet—An area set aside at medieval tournaments for resting men and horses.

Sassenach—(Scots) Derogatory term for an Englishman.

Scrip—A small bag or wallet.

Sheriff—The king's highest representative in a county, responsible for collecting local taxes and for maintaining law and order.

Siller—(Scots) Silver.

Strath—(Scots) A river valley.

Sumpter—A packhorse.

Tocher—(Scots) A wedding settlement or dowry.

Tolhouse—A medieval municipal building somewhat similar in purpose to a modern city hall or town hall in nature.

Undercroft—A vault or chamber under the ground.

Wattle-- Material for making fences, walls, etc., consisting of stakes woven with twigs or branches.

While—While.
Willnae—(Scots) Will not.
Yon—(Scots) That or those (objects or people).